AN ORKNEY MURDER

Leaving the grime of Victorian Edinburgh behind her, Rose McQuinn makes a long-anticipated journey to visit her sister Emily on Orkney. An archaeological team excavating a peat bog near Emily's home finds a body – could it be the thirteenth-century legendary Maid of Norway? It transpires that it is the corpse of a local woman, brutally murdered, and Rose realises that she probably knows the identity of the murderer. Reluctantly, Rose has to investigate, though she is all too aware that she will destroy for ever the happiness of those closest to her.

AN ORKNEY MURDER

AN ORKNEY MURDER

by

Alanna Knight

Magna Large Print Books
Long Preston, North Yorkshire,
BD23 4ND, England.

British Library Cataloguing in Publication Data.

Knight, Alanna
    An Orkney murder.

    A catalogue record of this book is
    available from the British Library

    ISBN   0-7505-2255-0

First published in Great Britain in 2003 by Constable,
an imprint of Constable & Robinson Ltd.

Copyright © 2003 Alanna Knight

Cover illustration © Anthony Monaghan

The right of Alanna Knight to be identified as the author of this
work has been asserted by her in accordance with the
Copyright, Designs and Patents Act, 1988

Published in Large Print 2004 by arrangement with
Alanna Knight

Magna Large Print is an imprint of Library Magna Books Ltd.

Printed and bound in Great Britain by
T.J. (International) Ltd., Cornwall, PL28 8RW

To ORKNEY,
and the many happy times
spent there with my family
and friends

Chapter One

Murder only happens in other families.

So we all pretend to believe. But domestic murder is more widespread than one might imagine.

According to James Payn, editor of *Cornhill*, 'one person in every five hundred is an undiscovered murderer. This', he adds, 'gives us all hope, almost a certainty, that we may reckon on one such person at least among our acquaintances.' When he expounded his theory to three members of his London club, they were able to name six persons of their various acquaintance who were, or had been suspected of being, successful murderers.

To read such sensational opinions in popular magazines is one matter, but as I was soon to discover for myself, the face of murder hides behind many benign masks.

The idea that the family of my father, Chief Inspector Jeremy Faro, lately retired from the Edinburgh City Police, might harbour an undetected murderer was as unlikely as his proud boast that his grandmother was a seal woman.

Having laid aside for the immediate future the mantle of Rose McQuinn née Faro, 'Lady Investigator, Discretion Guaranteed', I stepped off the steamer in Stromness that August day of 1896 with no thought of anything more violent than the certainty that I would have cheerfully killed for a cup of tea after a somewhat stormy crossing from Leith.

This was the prelude to a long-awaited visit to my younger sister Emily. We had been close as children and now I was looking forward to seeing her after a separation of more than a decade.

Emily had been content to remain in Orkney. After I left to become a school-teacher in Glasgow, she settled down and married Erland Yesnaby, a widower of ancient lineage, somewhat her senior. The intervening years since that event had been inexpertly bridged by a succession of vague communications, a weakness shared, I might add, with the majority of the Faro family. As I learned to my cost while I was in America, letter-writing is sadly not one of our finest achievements.

Happily anticipating a joyful family reunion, I made my way gratefully along a static quayside, on terra firma once more, first checking that my luggage was safely anchored on the back of my bicycle in a container artfully designed for that purpose by Jack Macmerry.

The machine had aroused some interest among my fellow passengers for such equipages were still regarded with cautious amusement despite the emergence of an occasional horseless carriage on the streets of Edinburgh: an event assuring those citizens of a lugubrious nature that this was a mere whim, a passing phase. There was no future in such outlandish, noisy, smelly means of travel, beyond a clear indication that the world was going to the dogs.

Bicycles? Yes, perhaps, but they were still deemed undignified, a little outré if not downright improper as a means of transport for ladies.

As I disdained to include myself in society's definition of a lady I cared little for such opinions. Years of pioneering life in the American West had set at naught the notion of behaving according to the conventions of middle-class Edinburgh.

To return to more practical matters. As Hopescarth lay some distance to the north-west of Stromness, I considered the advantages of a bicycle where only the fortunate

11

few owned carriages and most folk still travelled by cart, on foot or on horseback.

Prepared for the worst, I pictured a bleaker, remote and less populated area than Kirkwall, our home with grandmother Mary Faro after Mamma died in Edinburgh with a stillborn baby boy, leaving Pappa grief-stricken and at his wits' end about the future of two small daughters.

As for dear Emily, her worst fault over the years had been an irritating habit of ignoring what I regarded as urgent family matters. Her one-page replies to my letters contained little information beyond stressing that she was well (which was not always true as I was to discover) and ended as speedily as possible on a cheerful note in the hope that this also found me in good health and spirits (often a far from accurate assessment).

I tried to stir her interest from time to time by laying claim to a more dramatic existence in Arizona, mentioning occasional Indian raids, cattle lifted and property burnt. All of which failed to arouse any comment from Emily in her eventual replies.

After Danny's disappearance and the loss of our baby son, I kept my promise to him: that if one day he walked out and failed to return, I was to wait six months and then, presuming some fate had befallen him in the course of his employment with the Pinkerton Detective Agency, I was to return home to Edinburgh.

Ever since I arrived in May 1895, I had been confidently expecting an invitation to Orkney, perhaps even the suggestion that I make my home with them at Yesnaby House. The distant tone of Emily's infrequent letters, hinting that our grandmother, frail and needing extra care, was now living with them, made me suspect that only a sense of duty directed her to reply at all. Indeed, in moments of depression and doubt, of which there were many in those early days, I felt that she wished to banish all memory of the tragic circumstances of her only sister's return to Scotland.

As time passed, I often asked myself was I unreasonable to expect an immediate invitation to Hopescarth and I believe I could be forgiven for nursing bitter disappointment at not even the suggestion of some future visit.

Reluctant to think Emily heartless, I gave her the benefit of the doubt and assumed a total inability to express her emotions in letters or some pressing domestic anxiety of her own – which indeed proved to be the case.

To my anxious requests for more details regarding our grandmother's health, her replies were carefully veiled.

There was no mention of yet another relative, even older than Gran. A great-grandmother, whose existence had never been mentioned in our Orkney days.

Certainly, had I given the matter of Sibella Scarth considered thought, a simple calculation based on Gran's eighty-four years would have set her own mother's age at past a century, her bones presumably laid peacefully to rest long since in the local kirkyard.

But to return to Emily's eagerly awaited invitation.

It had arrived at long last, at what seemed the most opportune of moments. Summer had almost given up in despair in Edinburgh, rain and cold winds sought out every crevice in the stone walls of my ancient home in Solomon's Tower at the base of Arthur's Seat. Already there was a touch of mellow autumn in the slanting sunlight on harvest fields, an air of melancholy bringing with it the stealthy return of bitter memories.

This was the second anniversary of

Danny's disappearance and I was not yet reconciled to the inevitable conclusion. I still hoped – my faith undying – for his reappearance.

So many deep-rooted scars were miraculously healed in dreams. There was one where a door opened. Danny was there smiling, holding out his arms, awaiting our rapturous reunion.

The dream faded rapidly into a sad reality as, once again, I opened my eyes to an empty room, an empty heart and a door obstinately closed against the one person I longed to resurrect, totally ignoring what common sense screamed at me.

That I was willing back a dead man.

True, I had found another love. Detective Sergeant Jack Macmerry of the Edinburgh City Police. And Jack was growing impatient. His practical, logical mind could not accept that my desire not to commit myself was due to my deep-seated faith in Danny's return. Jack wanted marriage – now – and children – before it was too late. Reminding me that I was thirty-one years old, he believed that I was making an excuse.

Lately he had accused me of not wanting to settle down and be a policeman's wife. Perhaps he had guessed my secret, knew me better than I did myself, for I enjoyed my role as a detective.

I now had a logbook of domestic mysteries and hotel robberies which had called for utmost discretion. All had been successfully solved without calling in the police and losing the desired anonymity of the victims: in most cases, a wealthy bored married woman with a young lover or a well-kenned gentleman with a mistress or a taste for the seamy side of Edinburgh life, for whom disclosure and scandal would mean ruin.

There had also been two very alarming and dangerous encounters with murderers where my own life had been in deadly peril and I had narrowly survived, in part due to Jack's intervention.

However, as I have already remarked, Emily's letter was opportune. I needed an escape clause. I was between cases. With no clients for the past three months, I had begun to despair of unfaithful husbands, indiscreet wives, thieving domestics and frauds.

How Jack gloated over my lack of business, certain that this would persuade me to set the date for our wedding! He was heartily sick of our 'on-off' arrangement, for I was neither mistress nor wife. It was all too casual, too unconventional for him. He – and his parents – had set their hearts on a Christmas wedding.

And what was more important, it seemed that a wife would strengthen his chances of promotion. For some reason he believed that the board would look kindly upon the non-flighty, well-settled family man.

No wonder I fled! Too cowardly for a definite 'No' – yet I did not want to lose Jack. I loved him in my way, and as Gran was to point out when we talked later, I had every intention of having my cake and eating it! In that she was quite correct, without my adding 'as long as I can!'

But I did not doubt Jack's determination to bring the issue to a conclusion. When I returned Jack must have his answer one way or the other.

As we said goodbye, in the prickly manner of one who feels himself ill used, Jack said: 'You're not concerned about Thane, I trust.'

I smiled. The deerhound Thane, my strange companion for the past year, was the least of my problems. He needed no human carer. He had his own life. Long before we met – how long I had not the least idea – he had survived and would continue to do so, returning to the existence he had always known in the wild secret haunts, the hidden caves of Arthur's Seat.

'Three weeks and we'll be together again,' Jack had sighed as he kissed me. 'Don't worry, it will soon pass.' (This in a quite unnecessary tone of consolation.)

I forbore to mention that this was a holiday, one I was greatly looking forward to, as he continued: 'You'll be back home in plenty of time to plan everything. Everything, Rose.' The firm set of his jaw left me in no doubt of what he was getting at: to plan our wedding.

And so I closed the door of the Tower behind me, confident of my return, with not the remotest idea on that sunny morning of how a family visit to a beloved sister might erupt into danger greater than that involved in any of my Edinburgh cases.

Without Jack or Thane as a last-minute rescuer, delivering me from evil.

Or death.

Chapter Two

As I bicycled down the road to Hopescarth, my progress assisted by a stiff seaward breeze, I realized that this terrain was different to Kirkwall, the town where I grew up.

This was a new land, a foreign soil. I had forgotten there would be no trees, at least none worthy of comment or sheltering charm, like sturdy oak, horse chestnut and elm. Trees bold enough to inhabit these cold northern isles were timid sycamore and melancholy willow. Offering no airs of protection and benevolence, they hugged the shelter of house walls in a manner suggesting despair if not downright apprehension, their continual fight for survival clearly visible in twisted and distorted limbs.

Orkney may lack trees or mountains and display little of the grandeur of the Scottish Highlands or the tamed splendours of shady gardens in suburban Edinburgh, but there is adequate compensation in wild beauty and an atmosphere which is unique. Infinite space, the great sweeping confluence of sky, sea and rolling countryside, undulating hills in a sea-bitten, wind-torn landscape of greens, greys and peat browns, interrupted here and there by a patchwork of scattered crofts, few outwith sight or sound of the sea.

As I puffed up hills and soared down them again, the wine-clear air, so bracing and familiar, seemed to hold out a promise of recapturing the nostalgia of youthful days. Of returning to sunlight and long golden beaches from Edinburgh's close-packed smoky city, rightfully termed Auld Reekie.

That confused blur of excitement, tinged with sadness.

Goodbyes to Pappa and beloved step-brother Vince, clutching my memory of Mamma, a smiling photo, that last bedside farewell. The disbelief that she would not open her eyes when I kissed her. Or that the little wax doll at her side was the brother who would never run out into the street to play with Emily and me.

A merciful fate concealed from me that one day I was to have a waxen baby of my own to lay in a lonely grave lost for ever somewhere in the deserts of Arizona.

Here in Orkney, scene of carefree child- and girlhood, I was confident that I would again find healing, for Edinburgh still pressed hard upon me, scarred with memories of Danny unfolding at every street corner. This island was different, part of my world before Danny McQuinn.

Now Stromness lay a mile or two behind and fragments of that happier past began to return as I sailed effortlessly downhill for a while.

Eventually I stopped to wipe my nose, with a wry smile for cool breezes always had that effect on me. That little matter taken care of, putting away my handkerchief, I set off again with an increasing sense of pleasurable anticipation that I would enjoy every moment of the weeks ahead, that Orkney's magic of old would work for me, that a change of scene would be followed by clarity of purpose and faith in the future.

When I returned to Edinburgh, it would be to give Jack his answer for already I had to confess to missing him just a little. I imagined our returning here together and my introducing him to the places of my early life.

At that moment I had not any doubts. I could hear myself saying: Yes, I will marry you. And we'll honeymoon in Orkney.

Suddenly it was all easy, simple. Too simple. I was brought down to earth with a grinding wobble on my front wheel.

I had picked up a stone in the spokes.

Perhaps that was an omen, the first of many I should have heeded.

There was worse to come.

Removing the offending stone I discovered the front tyre was punctured. Cursing under my breath in a very unladylike fashion I took out the tin box containing the repair kit and stared at it blankly. I had never had reason to use this in Edinburgh with Jack always available.

At that moment I wished most heartily that I had him here now to make soothing noises, allowing me to stand by and marvel at his skill and dexterity while I told him he was so good at such things and I was all fingers and thumbs.

As I set to work, to crown all the rain began. Where was that lovely sunlit sky? Even the skylarks had taken cover in disgust. Wishing I could do the same, I dragged out my rain cape.

Suddenly, from the direction I had travelled, the road hidden by the top of the hill began to vibrate. Straightening up, I stared at the sky.

Thunder? And at that moment the most welcome sight in the world. Wheels and the broad blunt nose of a snorting asthmatic monster appeared over the brow of the hill, quickly reassembling itself into a motor car.

Wonder of wonders! The horseless carriage had found its way to Orkney!

Scrambling well aside, overwhelmed by smoke and fumes, I gave it ample room to pass on the narrow road.

The driver, goggled and helmeted, looked down, saluted me gravely. Then with a squeal of brakes the gleaming machine slid a few yards forward. A series of groans announced some misgivings as it came to a standstill and puffed more blue smoke in my face.

The driver jumped down.

'Having trouble, miss?' he asked, as if kneeling on the side of the road with a bicycle's wheel in the air was not sufficient evidence of trouble for an observant eye.

However, the question was encouraging. It suggested that help might be at hand so I smiled sadly and decided to be very feminine. Although nature decreed that I should be small with a cloud of yellow curls, appearances are deceptive. The role of helpless female does not come naturally, as many males, gentlemen and otherwise, have found to their cost. On this occasion, however, I decided that a measure of innocent deception would never have more reason to be called upon.

'I am indeed. I haven't had to deal with a puncture before.' I even fluttered my eyelashes hopefully. They are glossy black and thick, like my eyebrows, inherited from Pappa. Completely at variance with yellow curls, they were the continual despair of my sister-in-law Olivia who considered such eyebrows in particular were not only unfashionable but rather unladylike.

Shaking his head, the driver gazed down at me from his lofty height of six foot-something. Frowning, he gloomily contemplated the bicycle with its injured wheel whirring gently.

'It's these infernal roads, miss. They're a menace, nothing more than sheep tracks in places.'

I had hoped for more than this dejected appraisal but his tone warned me sadly that he'd also be helpless to deal with a punctured tyre. And at that moment what I needed was a man of action.

Of swift action, I thought anxiously, if I were to see Hopescarth, still ten miles of hill and dale away, before dark.

'Know anything about bicycles?' I asked hopefully while he continued watching the prostrate machine very cautiously as if it had just dropped mortally wounded at his feet.

'Never had the pleasure, I'm afraid.' Another shake of the head, a sigh. Had it been a horse at that moment, he would have undoubtedly advised shooting it, a mercy killing, to end its misery.

Another regretful sigh and holding out a leather-gauntleted hand palm upwards: 'The rain's getting heavier.' A slight bow. 'Permit me to give you a lift to where it is you're going – you'll do better under cover.'

A gallant offer. But were we going in the same direction? I presumed so as I didn't expect there would be more than this one main road, winding purposefully over the landscape and eventually leading to Hopescarth. I didn't want to discourage him at that stage or give him a chance to regret his offer, so with a breathless 'Thank you' I watched him seize the bicycle and anchor it firmly on to the luggage grid at the back of the motor car.

Then with an air of triumph, handing me up the step and into the passenger seat, he unfurled a gigantic umbrella.

'There you are. Where now?'

He could hardly throw me back on to the

road after all that. And he did sound like a gentleman.

'I'm heading for Hopescarth. Do you know it?'

He laughed delightedly. 'I certainly do. I'm going there myself.'

Here was fortune indeed! 'To Yesnaby House?'

He shook his head. 'Nothing so grand. Just as far as the village. Hold on.'

A great roar and the monster shot forward. We were away.

He chuckled delightedly. 'Excellent! Excellent – thanks be that you were downhill or I'd have had to rush past and leave you there, I'm afraid. Daren't stop on an upgrade or it's sheer hell – begging your pardon, miss. It's the very devil to get the old girl going again.'

He grinned at me. 'Let me introduce myself. Craig–'

I lost the rest as the engine went into a furious performance of moving forward. Noise, blue smoke, rattle and shake of every bolt and screw. All rather unnerving although the driver seemed happy and indeed positively glowed with pride.

I gasped out my name and in return received information suggesting that he was in charge of an archaeological dig. From Inverness. I gathered that the motor car was on loan, the easiest way, he explained, to transport delicate artefacts to the Leith steamer which would take them to Edinburgh where, I understand, eager antiquarians awaited to classify them.

At least I think that was what he said, since conversation was severely limited and carried on at the tops of our voices, competing with the engine sounds which suggested being in the middle of a pack of baying hounds heading for the kill.

After a couple of noisy miles I saw that the rain had stopped and the sky, blue to the horizon, was occupied by a few cumulus clouds, the ones known to us children as 'angels' pillows'.

The skylarks were all around us soaring into the blue, to be seen, but alas, not heard. 'Our Lady's hens', the Orcadians called them. How Jack loved that! Thinking of him brought back home and Arthur's Seat vividly, and the memory of running through the heather with Thane.

As we sped along the road this land north of Stromness was a new experience. All my Orkney years had been spent in the vicinity of Kirkwall. We rarely travelled west with

Gran, who regarded it with suspicion worthy of darkest Africa and headhunters. Now I realized I had not been quite prepared for the emptiness, wild and bleak, the increasing glimpses of a harsh seascape.

A land whose waiting was measured not in passing centuries but in the darker millennia beyond the ken of God-fearing churchgoing Presbyterians.

'The isles at the world's end', mariners called them, to be feared as the place of wreckers and the legendary home of the seal people, of mermaids and trolls.

Here and there man had been bold and, turning a blind eye on the vagaries of an unreliable climate, had planted houses perched uneasy as summer flies on hillsides and boulder-strewn terrain.

As I considered whether these new tokens of man's optimism were prepared to defy and withstand centuries of winter winds, the scene before us darkened, the rain began again, heavier this time. I put up the umbrella.

We were going to be very wet by the time Hopescarth came in sight.

A signpost loomed into view. 'Skailholm' – followed by a street of newly built stone houses.

Craig Whatever-his-name shouted: 'The local inn. We'll shelter until the rain stops. Lenny's also the blacksmith. He'll know what to do – he'll fix that tyre in no time.' He patted the steering wheel. 'The old girl doesn't care too much for this heaving up and down hills in the rain,' he said.

Neither did I. And his next words stole my heart for ever.

'Fancy a cup of tea?'

I grinned from ear to ear. 'What a brilliant suggestion.'

The old girl, as he called her, seemed pleased too. She stopped with a minimum of braking and what in human terms might be called a purr of pleasure.

Craig obviously knew Lenny well. The bicycle was handed over to man of immense dimensions in every direction. The blacksmith of legend, straight from Wagnerian opera, a modern-day Thor, throwing his lightning shafts across the sky. Through a thick black hatch of beard, a gleam of teeth became visible, a broad grin assuring me of care and instant success, and he lifted the bicycle into the air as if it weighed no more than a pot of ale.

Once inside the inn, I realized by the smacking kiss bestowed on the rather shrill lady who greeted us that Craig was also on excellent terms with Lenny's wife.

Introduced as Maud, she seemed an incongruous addition to my image of the Orkney female. Her ample bosom, swaying hips, vivid complexion and elaborate coiffure fairly reeked of the city and, indeed, would not have come amiss on the stage of one of Edinburgh's variety theatres.

Tea, bere bannocks and cheese were ordered and Craig helped me out of my rain cape. Removal of his gloves revealed a rather grubby hand with broken nails. This indicated a close acquaintance with the soil and a lack of personal vanity and soap, which I found quite endearing, thoroughly at odds with the handsome motor car.

'The old girl', his pride and joy I guessed, was still much of a novelty especially as I had seen only an occasional Benz snorting its way along Princes Street and severely frightening the horse-drawn traffic, as well as sending young children and nursemaids with perambulators into hysterics.

The bosomy Maud set our order before us, hovering closer to Craig than was strictly necessary and eyeing me sharply with that 'who-is-this-woman' question in her eyes. I was intrigued to know what had set her down to waste her abundant womanly charms on Orkney's desert air and Lenny, the local blacksmith. Despite those narrow-eyed glances in my direction, she didn't scare me in the least. At that moment, hungry and cold, overcome by the prospects of a warm fire, the sight and smell of a teapot made me all emotional and I wouldn't have cared if she had two heads.

'I didn't get all of your name,' Craig apologized. 'Too much noise at the time.'

'Mrs McQuinn – Rose,' I said.

He smiled. 'Pleased to make your acquaintance, Mrs McQuinn. I'm Craig Denmore.'

I was impressed by my new acquaintance. Suddenly Denmore and Inverness clicked into place. The 'Denmore' was Pappa's favourite whisky and a certain addition to every elegant sideboard in Edinburgh. His father Sir Miles Denmore, the local laird, owned the distillery and doubtless the borrowed motor car.

And as the lad I presumed to be his son removed helmet and goggles, I was in for the greatest surprise of all.

For an instant he wasn't a stranger.

I knew him. Of that I was certain. We had met somewhere before.

But where?

Chapter Three

Craig Denmore was no stranger.

Later I was to tell myself that was just a feeble excuse, wishful thinking on my part. He was an attractive, above-average handsome man. Tall, with the black hair, white skin and dark eyes of the Highlander, he could have been anywhere between twenty-five and thirty-five. His looks seemed to improve at every meeting as did that weird idea that we had met before.

This notion became an obsession which was to remain with me until I learned the truth.

I have an excellent memory for faces, but Craig Denmore didn't fit in anywhere. A passing acquaintance, perhaps, the friend of a friend, but I would surely have remembered the handsome Highlander.

And I was certain now that it had been in Edinburgh.

I was completely baffled. I had met Craig or someone very like him, but not quite identical. Memory threw out a message, a face slightly out of focus. Something different. A beard perhaps that he had shaved off. I would ask when I knew him better.

Oh yes, of that I was quite sure, that I was going to know him better, and what better opportunity than now to ask that burning question.

'Could we have met somewhere before?'

He looked puzzled, taken aback. For a moment his eyes narrowed then he recovered, said heartily: 'You know, Mrs McQuinn, I've been thinking the very same thing. That I know you already.'

'Edinburgh?' I said helpfully.

'That must be it,' he said eagerly. 'Some academic society?'

I was flattered but said honestly: 'I don't belong to any.'

He frowned. 'What about the antiquarian lectures? They're very popular.'

'You give lectures?'

A modest nod. 'Occasionally.'

But that didn't fit. 'I'm sorry.' Lectures weren't my thing at all.

'Some gathering of mutual friends then?' he said.

I looked at him. 'That must be it. Perhaps you had a beard then?'

That idea seemed to startle him. His eyes

widened and his hand wavered towards his chin, then he laughed. 'A beard? Not I – never!'

So we skipped through a series of names and drew a blank there too.

At last, laughing at the absurdity of it all, Craig took my hand, and in a voice that made me aware of my own heartbeat, said: 'It must be Fate intended us to meet.'

His mocking tone warned that he wasn't to be taken seriously and, frowning impishly, he added: 'Do you believe in reincarnation, by any chance? Perhaps we both lived here in Orkney before. Vikings – maybe I came and carried you off. Part of the rape and pillage programme.'

My heart beat even faster as I contemplated that particular vision. I decided there could be worse fates than being carried off by Craig Denmore.

And to be honest I didn't think rape would have been necessary. I would have gone with this particular Viking willingly, even eagerly.

Certainly the idea of ourselves as the ghosts of long-dead lovers had a romantic appeal. But alas, that didn't wash with me.

Reincarnation was all too pat a theory for the practical mind I had inherited from Pappa. There had to be an answer to everything, a purpose. And if it wasn't immediately obvious then it was sure to be somewhere. One had merely to search diligently to be justly rewarded for one's patience.

So although I pretended to believe Craig Denmore's theory, I knew that deep down I wasn't being fooled. The logical explanation was there swirling about in memory's depths. One day it would surely surface...

There was some mystery about Craig Denmore, and solving mysteries was my business. But realization came when it seemed too late, a sledgehammer blow from a future still mercifully veiled.

Meanwhile, over a second pot of tea while the rain streamed down the windows, keeping us captive in this cosy parlour cut off from the rest of Orkney, I answered his questions about Edinburgh.

Oh, how he envied me all those exciting facilities – theatres, concerts, parks. I gathered life on a dig was mostly rather dull.

'Surely you've found some exciting things?' I asked.

'Not really. Just a few beads, some coins and a brooch. But they are valuable – everything fits together and eventually a picture emerges.'

'Do you know whose grave it is?'

'We're not absolutely sure. There are a lot of burials in this area, but from the artefacts this one is relatively modern.'

'Really?'

'Yes. Almost certainly thirteenth-century from the coins.'

Thirteenth-century didn't sound very modern to me, but the coins suggested treasure trove.

Craig laughed at my exclamation and shook his head. 'No, Mrs McQuinn. Don't fall into the trap like most of the crofters hereabouts. These islands are full of stone sites, remains of Pictish houses, Iron Age cairns, stone circles, brochs. Reason is that there were no trees.' He paused. 'Can you guess why?'

I knew enough about Orkney to answer that one. 'Trees are wood and timber rots.'

'Correct!' An approving laugh, exactly the kind he would give a promising student 'And with no wood for coffins, bodies were placed in cairns. Some are too dangerous to dig in this area because of the occasional peat-bog burial.' He paused. 'Like Hope-scarth, you must have heard about that?'

And when I shook my head, he said: 'Don't you remember, the woman who had lain there for more than ten years? Fallen in by accident on her way home ten years earlier and lain there undiscovered until last year. October it was. Just before we packed up the dig for the winter.'

He smiled. 'Surely that was big news for the Edinburgh newspapers?'

'I'm afraid I must have missed it.'

I didn't add that I relied on Jack, an avid reader of newspapers, to keep me in touch with the world news or any important or exciting local items.

And Orkney was important. Jack would never have missed that one. I felt a sudden chill, a cold shaft of dread as if someone had walked over my grave. I knew its footfall well. It was called premonition.

Craig continued: 'Mostly they are old bones, often animals from a kitchen midden, that we discover, and once in a blue moon the hint of treasure trove. But that has never been our luck so far,' he added rue-fully. 'Just a bag of coins, hastily buried by some departing resident or invader, hoping to return and collect it but unable to keep that particular date with destiny.' He shrugged. 'And so it lies hidden through the passing centuries.'

I knew what he meant. Fifty years ago,

near Kirkwall, a silver hoard had been found by an unsuspecting crofter ploughing his field and unearthing a burial chamber with rich pickings. A queen's ransom was how the newspapers described it.

Ever since that day every crofter went out hopeful that when his plough struck the next long stone or boulder, this would be the entrance to another cairn with grave treasure intact, the burial place of some long-dead chief, unplundered by the Vikings who, according to the runic symbols they left behind, sometimes took six days to remove all the treasure they found.

The archaeologists were eternally hopeful too. The slightest signal of success and they moved in. While the poor crofter watched eagle-eyed from his window dreaming of a life of ease, the only rewards for the diggers were back-breaking toil with treasures for the academics confined to the realm of further knowledge about the ancients.

I continued to shiver. All this talk of burials.

Maybe I was taking a chill.

Maybe the dreaded footfall of premonition had already aroused the demon that lurked hidden deep within the confines of memory.

Chapter Four

Craig was saying: 'Iron Age and Picts are really exciting, but the thirteenth century is just like yesterday for us.' He sighed. 'But there's always the next one. That's what keeps us going, the hopes of some historic burial site.'

'At Hopescarth, you think?'

'Something like that. Have you heard of the Maid of Norway, by any chance?'

I had indeed. And so had everyone else in Orkney. Legends had been built on the heiress to the throne of Scotland, the seven-year-old princess shipwrecked in a storm on Orkney's inhospitable shore. Buried in 1290 in an unmarked grave, her dowry was certainly a queen's ransom, long sought but never found.

Lenny, our genial host, popped his head around the door. 'The lass's bicycle is fixed now.'

I thanked him profusely and murmured about repayment.

He brushed that aside and said: 'Don't

worry your head about that, miss, it'll all go on the gentleman's slate.'

Laughter all round and he departed.

I had no further excuse to linger especially as the voluptuous Maud was now alarmingly evident, feverishly polishing nearby tables and keeping a sharp eye on Craig.

For her special benefit, I gave him my most charming smile, my most lingering glance. 'Thank you,' I said to him. 'You have been most kind–'

He looked at the window. 'Wait until the rain stops, you have quite a bit to go.'

That was true. Grateful for his observation, I sat back and asked: 'Tell me, what makes you think you've discovered the Maid of Norway's grave? Wouldn't they have been likely to choose an existing burial chamber for her? There are lots of them about–'

'Put her beside the remains of some pagan chieftain, you mean? Never. The Church would never have allowed that. There would have to be masses said for her. Remember, she wouldn't have been making that sea voyage alone or with just a few close members of her household. The entourage would include high officials and priests.'

He shook his head. 'No question of a

burial in unhallowed ground. And unless there was already a holy building within sight of the shore, my guess would be that they gave her temporary burial, intending to return and deliver her remains to Iona, the resting place of the Scottish kings and queens.'

He paused and looked at me. 'Know much about the background, the politics of the time?'

I shrugged. 'Mostly legend based on rumour, or the other way round.'

He was dying to tell me. It was pouring down outside. I was in no desperate hurry, so I let him have his head.

'In 1284 Alexander the Third of Scotland's only son and heir died on his twentieth birthday. The year before, the king's only daughter Margaret of Norway had died giving birth to a daughter – also named Margaret, the Maid of Norway – and in the absence of a claimant to the Scottish throne this made her heiress-apparent.

'When she was three, the King of Scots remarried, to Yolande de Dreux. Six months later he was dead, thrown from his horse as he tried to ride out a storm and reach his young wife waiting for him at Kinghorn, in Fife. There was no heir forthcoming from that brief marriage and no enthusiasm for a Scotland ruled by a child and a jealous regency.

'So it was decided that Margaret should marry King Edward of England's son, a year her junior, and so unite the two kingdoms. Infant marriages were very popular among medieval royal houses, with consummation postponed until the children matured. After a series of negotiations, arguments and false starts, she set forth in the autumn of 1290.

'All we know after that is that she died from the rigours of the stormy crossing, but there have been more sinister hints that various factions did not want her as Queen of Scotland or were outraged that there was to be a connection with the hated enemy England. There were hints at poison, a favourite way of getting rid of unwanted royalty in those days.'

'What about her dowry – the fabled treasure trove?' I asked.

Craig shook his head. 'Who knows? It certainly existed. Some very illustrious persons have long been intrigued by the question of what happened to the contents of the treasure ship that set sail with her from Norway but according to rumour never returned.

'After her death it vanished without trace.

Very easy in those days for a ship to do just that, go down with all hands in a storm in uncharted seas, disappear off the face of the earth, or become the victim of pirates who were very good at disposing of all signs of their ill-gotten gains.'

'What do you think happened?' I said.

'I'm in favour of shipwreck as the most logical reason. Think of it – the November weather which had brought about the storm and changed the face of Scotland's history, could have been equally wild and the seas treacherous on the way back to Bergen. That is the way historians see it. But they are orderly folk and they like to tidy up the unruly times they are recording, and wherever possible draw neat lines under events.'

He paused to refill his cup from a teapot now tepid.

'Less trusting souls have put forward the theory that someone in authority secretly stowed away the dowry on the island. So what really happened is anyone's guess. Maybe the ship went down and the secret died with the plotter – or plotters – aboard. Maybe someone lived to tell the tale, because wind of that treasure has definitely been rife in Scotland through the ages.'

'You think the story is just a romantic

legend then, this sad story of a tragic young princess?'

He looked at me and smiled. 'I keep an open mind. I've learned through the years that behind every legend there are a few grains of truth. Add a few more grains for a treasure.

'All we know for sure, from the records of one Huw Scarth who lived here in the sixteenth century, is the rather improbable story that he pursued a rainbow across his field and at its end he found a pot of gold. With it he was able to persuade Black Pate, the notorious tyrant who ruled Orkney at that time, to let him remain here–'

'Wait a moment,' I interrupted. 'So you think this pot of gold he found might have been the missing treasure – the Maid's dowry?'

He shrugged. 'Very likely part of it – who knows? It certainly bought the poor crofter Huw Scarth peace in his time and the lands of Hopescarth. Do you know, eight generations of Scarths must have lived continuously in the palace he bought from Black Pate. Until Edwin Yesnaby tore it down a hundred years ago–'

'Yesnaby?' I interrupted. 'What happened to the Scarths?'

'The last one was childless. It went to the only remaining member of the family, on the distaff side. Under Scots law females inherit, as you know. If Erland Yesnaby has no children, it will pass to the next nearest kin.'

He paused and smiled. 'Fortunately he took the precaution of marrying his heiress cousin, Thora, now deceased.'

'Will you be wanting anything else – sir?' Maud was now very busy polishing the table next to us and showing a keen interest in our conversation, or, more likely, in the very presentable archaeologist.

Craig gave her his most endearing smile. 'The lady and I are just leaving, Maud.' And turning to me: 'Where was I?'

'The Yesnabys.'

'Oh yes. Your present destination, is it not? Well, the present rather dull house was built by his grandfather.'

'What a shame. I'm rather sentimental about old castles, however ruinous.'

He grinned at that. 'Me too. But some parts of the original buildings are there to this day.'

My interest quickened again. 'Such as?'

'A moat. Couldn't do much about that. Before the castle there had been a broch surrounded by a moat, which through hundreds of years remains as bogland, a treacherous place for the unwary. As I told you, a woman fell in and lay there for years.' He sighed. 'Peat has marvellous preservative qualities. She looked as if she'd just died.'

Again that shiver went through me.

'Quite a sensation for the Hopescarth policeman, who had never encountered anything like this before. His mind immediately turned to murder, especially as she was a local woman–'

'Lenny wants a word.'

Just as the conversation was getting really interesting and I wanted to know more, the sharp interruption was Maud again, pointing to the massive shape of her husband which filled the door of the room.

As Craig excused himself, Maud still lingered trying to decide what to make of me.

'Thanks for the tea. It was delicious,' I said, giving her my best smile.

She gave me a dour look. 'You're heading to Hopescarth, are you?'

'Yes.'

Watching Craig go across the room she said: 'They're a rum lot up there. I'd go careful if I was you. And I wouldn't bargain on staying too long. It's a treacherous place for strangers in the dark.'

I felt a tingle of unease. She might just be jealous, of course.

'Really?' I asked, hoping to sound casual. 'In what way?'

She shrugged. 'Bad things happen. People in peat-bogs and all that sort of thing. You just watch your step too...'

I looked round and had a glimpse of Craig and Lenny in earnest conversation with a newcomer at the door. The man, whom I couldn't see clearly as he was dwarfed by Lenny's massive shape, was obviously agitated. Occasionally a raised arm was discernible.

They were too far away for me to hear what was being said but I could see by Craig's face as he returned carrying my rain cape that this was some sort of crisis.

He summoned up a smile as he helped me into the cape. Thanking him for the tea, I said I'd be on my way.

He sounded relieved. 'It isn't far and the rain has stopped. Be a nice ride, most of it is on the flat.'

Despite these assurances I guessed his mind was elsewhere.

'I would take you in the motor car–'

'No, no,' I protested. 'I wouldn't think of it.'

He looked relieved again. 'Something urgent – to do with the dig. I have to see someone,' he ended lamely.

And escorting me to the door, watched by the beady-eyed Maud – I wondered where she fitted into all this – he stood by the bicycle, regarding it uneasily. His attitude suggested more confusion about what was good manners or expected of a gentleman in this instance. He might be adept at handing ladies into carriages or his father's motor car, but I was prepared to bet he had never faced the quandary of handing a member of the female sex on to a bicycle.

'It has been a pleasure talking to you. I do hope to see you again sometime soon.' A very nice smile and I was sure he meant it. 'Take a walk down to the dig when you have a minute.'

He saluted me gravely as I wobbled unsteadily away on the uneven cobbles, off down the road with a lot of questions that had to go unanswered.

Particularly concerning the identity of the woman in the peat-bog.

Chapter Five

Beyond Skailholm village where I had left Craig, the landscape was occupied by stones that had once been human habitations and now were shelters for sheep. The bitter record of man's losing battle with the landlords' greed lay in these skeletons of ancient crofts with sagging roofs and broken windows. Like eyes emptied of hope, each told its own tale of cruel days half a century past, of Clearances and the beggary that still stalked the Northern Isles.

In the bleakness the peat fields had taken over, stretching with the bog cotton in every direction, my road leading past crofters hard at work. Surrounded by enormous baskets they stopped their back-breaking toil to shout a greeting which I returned with a cheery wave as a somewhat wobbly acknowledgement.

Peat workers made me think about the lady in the bog, preserved in peat for years and years. How very nasty, I thought, quite gruesome. As it had happened apparently in the bogland near Hopescarth, I expected Emily would have all the details.

The clip-clop of horses' hooves on the steep road I had just negotiated indicated another traveller and I moved aside for a passing carriage whose occupant stared out at me in amazement. I could hear the unspoken thought: A woman on a bicycle! What were things coming to?

I wondered how they would react to Craig and his motor car. Horseless carriages, my dear, a mere fad. They'll never last.

Happy to have shocked, my departing wave unacknowledged, I remounted and free-wheeled downhill, relishing the ever-changing restless sky which was never the same for more than a few moments. There were more habitations, scattered widely, secret grey crofts crouched low upon the heath, and well-groomed horses – the sign that civilized man must be around somewhere – trotted across fields. Horses for pleasure and horses for labour.

I hadn't had any great success with horses or ponies. I remembered falling off and being terrified, much to Emily's amusement. She was proud that, although younger than I, she was a better rider, born to the side-saddle.

Now there were fields where black and

white cows grazed contentedly and sheep, long past glamorous and endearing lambhood, hopefully suckled mother ewes who were short on temper and long dry of milk.

The hedgerow bloomed with cow parsley and ragged robin, with garden escapes of cultivated flowers, pansies and lupins. The dark heath was spotted brightly with bog cotton's fluffy tufts, pink sea thrift and the shells of flag irises.

The constant traffic of seabirds, wheeling overhead and across the horizon, extended my awareness of the kaleidoscope of colour existing alongside muted shades of grey, blue and green.

I stopped to blow my nose again and took a few deep breaths. Very comforting and rewarding to sniff the air since gentle winds and warm days had brought into being the fragrance of innumerable small plants and wild herbs.

I listened, aware that on every blade of grass and in every ditch an army of stealthy insects winged in rainbow hues filled the air with vibrant music beyond the human ear's range. Overhead the skylarks, taking heart in another burst of sunshine, added their flute notes of joy. And flocks of birds too small to be recognizable, exhausted by nesting and rearing of young, would soon return home to a happy celibacy.

Acutely aware of the mystic natural fulfilment of life, I looked towards the sea and listened to that inescapable sound, night and day, storm and calm – the boom of wave upon rock and shore.

I was not of a religious turn of mind, as characterized by Sabbath-going Edinburgh folk, but nevertheless I fancied for one brief moment that in the sea's eternal song I was hearing the whisper of creation, beyond time itself.

The sea was far below me. The seals were there, following my progress with almost human intelligence. I remembered how they used to follow Emily and me as we raced along the cliff path. Inquisitive, eternally vigilant, with their round shiny bullet heads, sleek and grey, and shining eyes that looked strangely human.

Sometimes Emily was quite scared and, taking my hand, would whisper: 'Do you think they might be able to turn into people – shed their skins, like we hear at school?'

'Emily,' I said firmly, consoling her as befits the elder sister, 'it's only a fairy story.'

It was – then. We didn't know about Sibella Scarth then. Her existence was still a closely guarded family secret.

I was jolted back to the present by a horizon no longer a bleak line against the sea.

The headland was occupied by a building, stark against the sky.

Yesnaby House and my destination.

It was less inspiring than I had imagined, even remembering Craig's warning, and something of a disappointment.

The homes of the affluent in Edinburgh are all designed to resemble small Gothic cathedrals but this grey, square, solid-looking house had none of the frivolities dreamed up by builders, eager to please their clients by following the fashion laid down by our dear Queen.

Here the weather turned its face firmly against exterior ornamentation, adornments which would soon succumb to wild winds and frequent winter storms. Here survival was the chief concern, in that nothing had changed.

For centuries past local architecture had learned the lesson of concentration on no-nonsense walls, deep-set doors and windows offering protection against merciless storms in a style set down, and almost unchanged, since the brochs built by those mysterious first inhabitants, that unrecorded slice of the island's history.

Before me, the ground dropped sharply across a stretch of bright green grass. The bogland I had been warned about, the stone bridge a reminder that once upon a time this building high on the skyline had been a moated fortress against invaders from the sea.

As I crossed the bridge, on my right some twenty yards away I noticed a dingy rubble of broken, untidy stones, evidence of shovels, wheelbarrows and recently turned earth, plus a noticeboard warning: 'Dangerous peat-bog. No entrance without permission. Strictly private.' So this was Craig's archaeological site.

The sniff of history – but whose old bones would this group unearth in their search? What shards of an ancient cooking pot waited to be excitedly exclaimed over, noted and dated and sent importantly to their ultimate destination, a dusty shelf in an Edinburgh or Glasgow museum?

Small pickings indeed and far removed from the hopes and dreams of that legendary long-lost grave of the Maid of Norway Craig had talked about – that lure for enthusiastic archaeologists, the incentive to keep going, to keep on turning over the soil in what must have been a dreary monotonous task even in the best of weathers, made almost intolerable in driving rain and fierce winds.

Beyond the bridge, the approach to Yesnaby House, still concealed, was softened by a drive of somewhat unwilling trees, offering shelter rather than ornament. Fragments of ruined walls hinted at habitations which had not survived the battle with the elements.

At last I emerged from the replica of a drive and on to a cobbled forecourt whose antiquity suggested that it had its origins in some earlier era, and, in the interests of preserving my bicycle's tyres, I dismounted.

The front door opened and the next moment Emily had gathered me into her arms.

'Emmy!'

This was my sister at last, she even smelt like Emily, for each of us has our own distinctive smell, a not unpleasant odour that no amount of soap and frequent washing can eradicate.

But opening my eyes, somewhat misted over by emotion, I realized that this Emily was different. Oh, so very different to the Emmy I had last seen more than ten years ago.

'Rose – let me look at you.'

Held at arm's length, I saw the fleeting disappointment, quickly concealed, that this was not the sister whose image she had clung to through those lost years. For I saw mirrored in her eyes that I too had aged. The woman, now past thirty, who had married, suffered grief and loss, was not the carefree girl who had abandoned a promising career as a schoolteacher in Glasgow.

The girl who had thrown it all away to make real her dream of marrying Danny McQuinn.

'Rose!'

Gran appeared, slower than Emily of course, and carrying with her the familiar kitchen smell of warm baking bread, but lacking none of Emily's warmth of welcome as we hugged and kissed.

In that moment I was overcome by a new emotion. The clock had gone backwards, and for the first time in years I felt safe – my anxieties for the past two years had been groundless. Safe with my own kin at last, I sighed with relief, having feared the worst from Emily's vague accounts of our grandmother's frailty and need of extra care.

But Gran looked exactly the same, not one day older, not one white hair seemed different. The same sturdy frame and round rosy face I loved, the same cheerful smile.

As Gran put an arm around me and prepared to lead the way into the house, it occurred to me that the changes wrought by increasing years obey their own mysterious laws. Youthful beauty is fleeting, soon overtaken and obliterated by middle age. Then there is a slowing down, a less visible and alarming change from elderly to aged.

Suddenly Gran halted. Aware of the bicycle, she pointed at it with distaste.

'And what do you want done with that thing?' she asked in the same rather contemptuous tone that she might have used towards a dirty disreputable animal I had brought with me, whose presence would be an embarrassment she could not possibly tolerate in her well-scrubbed kitchen.

That thought, the comparison, so amused me that I exploded into sudden laughter. 'It's not a thing, Gran, it's a bicycle.'

Gran looked surprised and hurt. I shook my head, couldn't explain why I was amused and, hugging her again, I said I was so happy, so very happy, just to be with her and Emily.

Mollified, she listened, but her eyes were still on that bicycle regarding it sternly as if it might have a word to say for itself.

'We'll put it in the coach house, beside Storm – he's our carriage horse. I'm sure he won't mind having a bicycle for company.' She laughed. 'That's if you agree, Rose.'

I said: 'Of course,' and at Gran's sigh of relief for a dangerous situation averted, Emily and I were conspirators in a quick glance of suppressed amusement.

We seized hands, paused to hug one another again, and I thought that not for a very long time had I been as happy as I was at that moment.

Nothing – nothing would ever change it.

I should have waited... Just a little while.

Chapter Six

I followed them up the steps, in through the front door and across a handsome marble-tiled hall. Ignoring a grand oak staircase winding upwards, we proceeded down a corridor and into a huge kitchen. I looked around in amazement for it could have comfortably accommodated the whole of Gran's Kirkwall cottage in which Emily and I had grown up. Larger too, I guessed, than many a crofter's cottage in the area.

This was Gran's domain. It had her stamp on it. A central table set ready for supper. Bacon, eggs and pancakes and one of her delicious fruit cakes, kept for special celebrations, for the prodigal's return.

As I sat down eagerly, resolved to demolish this rare feast, Erland's absence was explained.

'He is away to Bergen,' said Emily.

'He has some business connections, to do with the shipping,' Gran put in anxiously as if I might be offended that he was not there to greet me.

'He'll be back soon,' said Emily. 'Any day now. He's looking forward to seeing you.'

Then with plates laid aside and appetites satisfied, on to our second or third cups of tea, we loitered by that mammoth kitchen table. The size of a room in a crofter's cottage, it could have seated twenty diners with ease, and had obviously belonged to a prolific Scarth, head of a large family and employing a dozen servants.

There was so much to talk about, so many questions, some hardly answered as we skipped on to the next one, trying to set bridges over the gaps, the long years apart inexpertly rafted by vague and infrequent letters.

I was first to be questioned. What had brought me back from America? Had I really wanted to return? I thought I had made that clear from my letters and got it over with as quickly as possible, Danny's disappearance in Arizona, my promise to him that I would come back to Edinburgh.

And the loss of our baby.

Gran exchanged an anxious look with Emily. I must have given a more moving account than I intended, sitting there with my back straight and my hands tightly clenched beneath the table.

They both wiped away tears, leaned forward, touched my hands, kissed me gently.

Gran looked at Emily. 'Have you told her your news yet, lass?'

Emily shook her head, smiled. 'I'm having a baby, Rose. Next year. In the spring. At last!' she added with a happy sigh.

I was taken aback. Emily had been married for so long that I had presumed she was to be childless especially as her husband was a middle-aged widower.

'Emmy – I'm so glad. This is wonderful news. Wonderful.'

Gran watched us, smiling. 'Aye, we think she'll be fine this time.' And I learned that Emily had had several miscarriages through the years.

As I had myself. The same pattern, except that the baby I eventually bore, strong and healthy at first, had to die of fever on an Indian reservation.

And this was a new Emily. All the time I had been watching her, conscious of some subtle change and as always mildly astonished that we were not in the least alike and that no one had ever taken us for sisters. I was less than five feet tall, small and rounded. An hourglass figure with a tiny waist. Emmy was half a head taller, with long straight black hair. She had never had any bosom to speak of and this was the bane of her life, especially as it was something I had – and my mass of yellow curls. A reason for sisterly wrath and resentment when we were girls, for moaning against Fate and the ladies' magazines who decreed that curls and curves were essentials as husband-luring material.

However, the fact was that although she was the younger by two years, people meeting us for the first time presumed that she was the elder. This had pleased her enormously when we were children. 'Everyone thinks Rose is the baby, my little sister,' she had bragged to everyone, compensation for a sibling with the curls she longed for.

Now there was a new bond between us. That of motherhood, my own so short-lived. But Emmy would be different, I hoped. For I had wondered often if there was a curse on the Faro women, the dread St Ringan's curse which made women barren.

Gran had only one child, Pappa. Had she lost several afterwards? I thought of middle-class Edinburgh families with at least three or four, and the poor women in those horrendous High Street closes sometimes raising broods of ten or more in one stinking room.

But not to the Faro women the biblical gift of multiplying exceedingly.

As for Emily and I being so dissimilar, although it seemed to worry others, it didn't seem odd to me. I took after Mamma's side of the family, as did our stepbrother Vince, while Emily was what people here called 'a throwback' – meaning she didn't resemble either parent.

But that was before I met Sibella Scarth, our great-grandmother, the seal woman.

Suddenly my eyes were heavy, fatigue was winding around me, a great inescapable cloud. From far away I heard Gran's voice.

'The poor lass. She's just about asleep.'

The first day was over. So many questions remained unanswered, but I let them lead me by the hand, unresisting as a tired child, upstairs to bed.

The guest bedroom was beautiful, elegant with rosewood and mahogany furniture, fragrant with lavender-scented polish. It was grand indeed compared to the dormer-windowed attic Emily and I had shared in Gran's Kirkwall cottage.

I was to discover that the interior of the house was a box of delights, far more attractive than could be imagined or expected from its square grey exterior.

There was even a bathroom.

A huge mahogany white-pillowed bed invited me to put down my head. I looked at it yearningly. Too tired to get undressed and blaming the crossing and the bicycle ride for my exhaustion, I pulled the covers over and snuggled down into warmth and comfort.

I'd just sample the luxury – for a few minutes – then I'd unpack, have a wash and get into bed properly…

I opened my eyes to birdsong and bright sunshine beyond the window. There were faint sounds from downstairs, a few echoing footfalls.

It was morning and I had slept for ten hours.

Guiltily I sprang up. The water was too cold for a bath, so it was the stand-up variety and a change of linen. Brushing my curls free of tangles, I stared out of the window with its glimpse towards the sea. The peat field and, just visible, the roof of a tiny isolated croft.

Downstairs I ran to warm greetings from Gran and Emily, who rose from the breakfast table with anxious questions. Had I slept well, been warm enough, was the bed comfortable? Meanwhile I tackled porridge and bere bannocks, and between mouthfuls a dozen other questions were all waiting for answers.

'That was a long way to come from Stromness,' said Gran, eyeing me anxiously. 'You had better take it easy for a day or two.'

'I'm fine. Slept like the proverbial log.'

I smiled. This was the Gran I knew of old. As one who had never travelled willingly more than a mile or two across the island since returning from Edinburgh after my policeman grandfather Magnus Faro was killed, she regarded a sea voyage from Leith as a frightful ordeal.

Despite my reassurances she continued to watch me doubtfully and I said: 'Anyway, I was lucky. Didn't I tell you, I got a lift in a motor car for quite a bit of the way.'

'A motor car!' Gran and Emily exchanged glances and Gran asked suspiciously: 'Who would that be?'

'Craig Denmore,' I said. 'The archae-ologist at the dig over there.'

'Him!' Gran exploded.

'He seemed very nice,' I said lamely in an attempt to placate her, but it was too late. The mention of his name was like waving a red flag before a bull and a not altogether inept simile for her face flushed scarlet.

She thumped the table. 'I don't hold with them digging on our land.'

It would have been inappropriate to show my reaction which was that the land wasn't hers but belonged to Emily's husband.

'Gran!' said Emily and put an imploring hand on her arm.

'Don't you Gran me, you know as well as I do that they should leave the dead alone. I don't hold with that sort of thing. It isn't decent. And him a laird's son. His father's got a title and all that money from the whisky. Getting his hands dirty. He's not even one of us.'

By which I presumed she meant a born and bred Orcadian.

'What's in it for him?' she demanded. 'He doesn't need buried treasure if the Maid's dowry is what he's after–'

Emily held up her hand. 'Gran – he's a Scarth after all.'

'On his mother's side,' Gran admitted grudgingly. 'But that was long before your Erland's family took over.'

'Wait a minute,' I said. 'You mean that he's related to us?'

Was that the answer? The reason for the feeling of certainty that we had met before? Was there a family resemblance but too fleeting for immediate recognition?

Emily's words changed that idea. 'He might be a remote cousin generations removed since half the folk here are Scarths, Rose. Don't you remember?'

I shook my head. It hadn't been important to be one of a clan in my school days. 'I liked him. He was very kind. Bought me some tea, as well.'

Gran sniffed disapprovingly and gave me a hard look. A gentleman, I was about to add, and changed my mind. They knew that already, so in his defence I said: 'He seemed very earnest and sincere about the dig, about finding the Maid's grave.'

'Her dowry, more like,' snapped Gran, through pursed lips.

I let it go. 'There was something else he told me about, far more fascinating than that old mystery. A modern one.'

Looks were exchanged again. Emily frowned and Gran demanded cautiously: 'What would that be?'

'A woman's body found last year, in the peat-bog. She'd been there for years and years and yet she looked as if it was just yesterday. What did you think about that? Is it true?'

There was a sudden cold silence, a

stillness as if the two women before me had been turned to stone. Their faces made me shiver as Gran looked at Emily and Emily looked at Gran.

I saw something else. A mute appeal in that glance…

'Who was she? Did the police ever find out? Missing persons and so forth?'

They both watched me in stunned silence as I buttered another slice of bread, spreading on the jam.

I blundered on regardless. I was in my element, already sniffing out some extraordinary story here, a mystery that appealed instantly to Rose McQuinn, lady investigator.

'Did they manage to track down her family? Who was she?' I repeated. 'Didn't anyone recognise her?'

Emily looked at me. She was no longer still. Her lips were trembling. 'Yes, Rose. We knew who she was.' Looking at Gran she shook her head.

'Well?' I said.

A strangled whisper, so soft I thought I had misheard.

'Thora.'

For a moment I lost the thread. Thora? Who was Thora? Then I remembered what Craig Denmore had told me.

Chapter Seven

For a moment I was back at Skailholm listening to Craig Denmore: 'Erland took the precaution of marrying his heiress cousin, Thora, now deceased.'

Horrified I looked across the table at Gran and Emily, their faces suddenly white and strained.

'Erland's first wife?' I whispered.

Emily nodded, looked at me, her eyes tragic. 'Yes, Rose. That's who it was.'

I leaned across and seized her hands. They were very cold, lifeless somehow. 'Oh, Emmy. I'm sorry – I'm so sorry. How absolutely awful for you. It must have been horrible.'

'It was very upsetting for Erland.' Emily sighed. 'You see, she had left home – here – one evening years ago and no one had ever seen her again. She just disappeared.'

Like Danny. I remembered how upset Emily had been when I was talking about it. How she seemed almost tearful and had clutched my hand.

No wonder. Lightning striking twice in the same family, another odd coincidence.

'We – Erland, that is – thought she had left the island and gone to Edinburgh or Glasgow. She wasn't very well – in her mind, you know. She didn't like Hopescarth and she was always threatening to go. It was terrible for Erland…'

Emily began to cry and Gran put an arm around her. 'There, there, lambie.' She looked at me sternly, reproachfully, as if this was all my fault, bringing up this painful subject.

'Terrible for this poor lass, too,' she said. 'You can imagine that. She was married to Erland and the poor chap had buried someone else in Thora's grave. He thought – we had all thought it must be Thora. A couple of months after she went away, terrible weather, and a woman's torso washed up off Marwick Head in the roarsts.'

'The roarsts?'

She paused at my puzzled expression.

'The tide-races that beat up on the rocks below the cliffs here at the Troll's Cave,' said Emily. 'They come up in a spout at high tide. Or in a storm.'

Her voice was thin and strained and she spoke slowly. 'No man or woman, or boat,

70

could survive in those terrible seas, dashed against the rocks. Like giant's teeth, they are.'

She shuddered and Gran said grimly: 'Aye, there wasn't much left of the woman we all thought was Thora. No arms or legs–'

'Gran!' Emily protested, her hands over her face, shutting out that horrifying picture.

But I could imagine it. Erland going down to identify 'what was left' of his missing wife, Thora. I shuddered.

There was another silence then Emily removed her hands from her face, straightened her shoulders. She was very pale as she looked at me and said: 'You know the rest, Rose. We got married.'

'Yes, of course.'

But something puzzled me. Where had I got the idea that Thora was an invalid, that Emily had nursed her until she died? And now I was hearing the real story.

'As Gran said, Thora wasn't well. You see, she was always a little unbalanced.'

'Aye, daft as a brush,' said Gran angrily. 'There was a history of it in her family – a brother and sister married not knowing they were related. Happens all the time in small communities–'

Emily shook her head. She didn't want to be interrupted. 'When the – the body was found, Erland presumed that Thora had committed suicide at Marwick Head.'

My detective instincts were taking over. 'Did he have some reason to think that she'd take her own life?'

Emily shrugged and Gran said: 'We were told she had rushed out of the house in a furious temper. So what else could the poor man believe?'

I ignored that. 'What about this other woman? The body they found. Did no one claim her?'

'No.'

'Don't the police keep a list of missing persons?'

'Apparently not.'

They both shook their heads, looking at me as if they had never heard of such a thing. Maybe I was expecting too much of a tiny community like Hopescarth, with the nearest police station in Stromness.

There wasn't much law to break – or much crime either, I was to discover. Nothing more than a little poaching, which hardly seemed to justify paying a policeman's wages.

I studied the little scene across the table.

Gran frowning, staring at the scrubbed surface and tracing patterns on it with a fork. Emily white-faced, touching her stomach as if to reassure the child she carried that all was well.

This kind of event was well beyond my Edinburgh experience of petty crime. It smacked of melodrama. The insane wife on the clifftop poised above a wild sea hurling itself against the rocks at Marwick Head.

Poor Emily and poor Erland. And it didn't take any great feat of imagination to hazard a guess that they were already in love with each other long before Thora disappeared. One could hardly blame Erland for being glad to be relieved of the domestic hell of an unbalanced wife. Or for his willingness to accept a decomposing limbless corpse as Thora. And who could blame him for suppressing any secret doubts and believing that he had seen the end of a bitter marriage, making sure that he and Emily could have a decent life together at last.

The story of Thora, her disappearance and re-emergence in the peat-bog ten years later, was also the explanation for Emily's vague and infrequent letters, a complete inability to describe in words the happenings at Hopescarth.

We all jumped when the horrified silence of our thoughts were shattered by the Westminster clock very melodiously striking the half-hour. Gran stood up.

'I'd better make a fresh pot of tea, Sibella will be here any moment, takes a walk every day, all weathers – rain, snow, wind or hail.'

I was glad of the diversion. Sibella Scarth, the first intimation of the great-grandmother I had never met and whose existence I had never heard of in all those years Emily and I had lived in Orkney. Pappa had proudly boasted that his grandmother was a sea woman, the past tense indicating that she was dead long ago. Logically one would presume so...

I did a rapid calculation and said carefully: 'She must be an incredible age.'

Gran smiled sourly. 'Aye, past her hundredth birthday.'

'How far past?'

Gran shrugged. 'We don't know exactly. You see, no one knew exactly how old she was when Hakon Scarth, your great-grandfather, carried her into the house, the year it was built she claims. 1795.'

'Incredible, isn't it,' said Emily proudly, 'but wait until you see her. You'll find it hard to believe–'

'Hakon had picked her up in his fishing nets,' Gran put in. 'They thought she was about two or three, but she could have been older. There was no way of being certain.'

'Hold on – fishing nets, you said?'

Watching my astonished expression and before I could ask how she got there, Gran went on hurriedly: 'Folks said she must have floated ashore from a Norwegian ship that went down in a storm two nights earlier. It was called the *Sibella,* so they gave her that name.'

'Poor little soul,' said Emily. 'Tragic, wasn't it?'

I agreed. 'But that didn't make her a seal woman, surely.'

Gran shook her head. 'Folk here have always got strange notions about the power of the selkies, the Finn folk, that sort of thing,' she added apologetically, remembering that I had been 'educated', as the local folk would say. Such education supposedly removed me from local superstitions in a society where the schoolteacher joined doctor and minister, elevated to higher ranks of respect and awe.

'What made them think she wasn't just an ordinary little girl who had been ship-wrecked, for heaven's sake?' I said, my logical mind taking in the absurdities of any other conclusions.

'There was no record of any small child on the ship that went down. That was how she became known as a selkie.'

'She could have been smuggled aboard,' I insisted.

Gran shook her head. 'There were a couple of the Norwegian sailors who survived and were brought ashore. They didn't have much English but both swore that they had never set eyes on her before or knew of any wee lass on the ship. So they refused point-blank to take her back to Norway with them. They were scared of her too.'

I ignored that. 'What about their shipping line? Surely they must have had records of the crew, even in those days. For paying them, and so forth.' And clinging to the logical: 'Sounds as if someone smuggled her aboard.'

Gran smiled grimly. 'Aye, right enough. Perhaps the ship owners didn't pay very close attention to what went on among their crew.'

'Seagoing wives, you mean.' I knew about wives who went to sea with their husbands on merchant ships. 'So it is possible, that she'd been there on the voyage and no one had taken any notice.' I felt a sense of triumph, as I added: 'The child could have come aboard with her mother who went down with the ship.'

'Right enough,' said Gran. 'But then a seagoing wife's name would be on the list with the rest of the crew. And the peedie lass's mammy might not necessarily have been there officially.'

Gran made a face. 'A lot of those kind of women went to sea those days and stayed out of sight.' She coloured. 'The company turned a blind eye on them. They were there for the – er, convenience of the men. Sailors needed female companionship on long voyages.'

Emily chuckled. 'Companionship! Come along, Gran. Rose is a married woman. You can say what you mean to her. That the sailors took their fancy women with them.' And to me. 'It was well known that some of the sailors had a wife and family on shore as well as one at sea.'

And thereby lay the answer, I thought. 'In that case it could have been very inconvenient for the child's father, if he happened to be one of the two survivors, to take home a small child to his legitimate wife. What a predicament!'

'Aye, we've often thought something like that might well have been the reason,' Gran said cautiously. 'Anyway, right from the beginning folks were scared of her. You see, it was Lammas time – August like now – if it had been any other time it might have been different, but the seals were on the move.'

'Remember, Rose,' said Emily, 'how we used to watch them. Those great colonies of Atlantic seals that move inshore and the racket they made all night.'

'It used to keep you both off your sleep,' said Gran.

I remembered now, night after night awakened by the roaring of the bull seals, barking like dogs. An eerie sound echoing, on and on in the moonlight streaming through our tiny attic window.

And unable to sleep, two frightened little girls clinging together and scaring each other to death with stories about the seal king rising from the waves to snatch a human girl and carry her back to his kingdom of coral and pearl...

To be his wife for a year and a day.

'There are lasses hereabouts you still couldna pay to walk by the cliffs alone at

Lammastide, even in this day and age,' said Gran. 'I was her only bairn, you know, the only one to survive, that is. Sad it was. I had a brother Peter but he drowned.'

I'd never heard of a great-uncle Peter either and presumed he must have been a small child when the accident happened.

I shivered again. Sibella Scarth sounded just a mite strange and I was no longer so eager to meet her.

Imagination was painting weird, sinister pictures.

Scary pictures of the wicked witch who haunted childhood stories now made manifest in a seal woman.

Chapter Eight

As if she read my thoughts, Emily said encouragingly: 'Sibella's sharp and bright as a button, interested in everything and everyone that's new.'

'Aye, she loves young folk about her and is prepared to listen to what they think about it all. Even Wilma Flitt, Meg-at-the-post-office's bairn who's never out of my kitchen.'

Gran's sour tones suggested that this young visitor did not meet with her approval.

'Sibella's a wonderful old lady,' said Emily proudly.

Gran sniffed. 'That's just because you're the apple of her eye. She's sharp enough with any that cross her.' Again Gran's voice hinted that she and her strange mother did not see eye to eye.

'Oh, you two will get along grand, Rose. I just know it,' said Emily. 'I bet the first thing she'll want to know all about is that bicycle. She loves new things, not like some folks here. Another four years and we'll be into a new century and they still cling to the Dark

Ages. I suppose it's different in Edinburgh,' she added wistfully, picking up her knitting needles.

A shawl, delicate as a spider's web, no doubt for the new baby. I said a silent prayer.

'There are still some superstitious people even in Edinburgh, Emmy, who hold on to strange ideas. You'd be surprised,' I said, wondering how they would react to the story of Thane, my strange deerhound who roamed the heights of Arthur's Seat.

'So when do I meet Great-grandmamma?' I asked.

'Very soon,' said Emily. 'And incidentally she likes to be called Sibella. She doesn't care for the Great-grandmamma image.' And with a teasing glance in Gran's direction: 'Doesn't care to be reminded that she has a daughter who is past eighty.'

Gran winced a bit at that. 'Aye, we've got used to it over the years, but it does sound a mite disrespectful to folk who don't know her odd ways. She fair dotes on Emily, hardly lets her out of her sight.'

I detected a touch of envy in her voice as she added: 'They have a lot in common. Don't let her hear you calling her Emmy, though.'

'Oh, Gran. She doesn't like shortened names either,' Emily said apologetically.

'Doesn't she stay with you?' I asked, thinking of all the rooms in this vast house I had still to explore.

'Not likely,' said Gran. Did I hear a suspicion of relief? 'She lives on the far side of the peat field over yonder. Has her own peedie croft over the hill. You can just see it from your bedroom.'

Peedie? I looked up. That word again. How long it was since I had heard the almost forgotten Orcadian word for small. Gran continued with a sigh: 'Doesn't want to live in the house with us, but she's never away. That's because of Emily, like I've said. She had little to do with the family before that,' she added, just a touch resentfully, I thought.

'What happened, Gran? Why on earth has she been kept such a secret from us all this time? Why did we never meet her? I can hardly believe it – all those years living here with you and we never knew of her existence.'

I looked at Emily for confirmation and we both turned to Gran. 'Why didn't you tell us?'

Gran gave an uncomfortable shrug.

'Surely Pappa must have known – as a

child – about his own granny?'

'No. Especially not my Jeremy. Him most of all. We agreed when he was a bairn that it was best he should think she was – no longer with us,' Gran added delicately.

With a despairing sigh she looked across at Emily who nodded. 'Yes, Gran. You'd better tell her what happened.'

There was a long pause and I thought of the secrets my visit was unearthing and why Emily had been so long in sending that invitation.

Now I sympathized. Not too easy to explain, Erland's first wife Thora preserved for ten years in a peat-bog, a seal woman great-grandmother and a family feud everyone wanted to forget.

Except me, of course. I wanted all the details.

'Go on, Gran. Rose'll have to be told sometime. Right from the beginning,' she said, and to me: 'You remember, Rose, how Grandpa went to be a policeman in Edinburgh.'

I knew the story, how he was killed on duty by a runaway cab and Pappa years later had tried to prove it was murder, connected with the discovery of an infant's body in the wall of Mary, Queen of Scots' apartments in

Edinburgh Castle. A tiny mummified corpse wrapped in cloth of gold who might well have been the real Jamie the Sixth of Scotland, future King James the First of England.

Rumour had it that the Queen had been delivered of a stillborn Prince and that the Countess of Mar who was her midwife and pregnant at the same time had substituted her own son, thereby throwing the entire Stuart succession in jeopardy.

But what I was hearing from Gran had nothing to do with that ancient mystery, long ago investigated by Pappa.

Gran's story was going to be the usual mother-in-law squabble. Grandpa Magnus didn't take to Sibella even before he married Gran. And his feelings were reciprocated, because he laughed at what he called her witches' tales of trolls and hogben and her Finn folk. Magnus didn't hold with the supernatural, or with her alleged nativity. In his opinion she was a Norwegian sailor's bastard, saved from the sinking ship. And what was worst, he tried to convince everyone else.

'He had to explain everything logically, as he called it, and that made Sibella a liar. Things went from bad to worse then one

84

day he did prove something – I dinna ken what, but he pointed out that she had tried to fool people. He had proved her wrong, made her look small and shamed her in the face of all these folk who trusted her cures and went to her for advice as the local white witch.

'But my Magnus was so sensible, honest and down to earth, he just had to tell the truth, come hell or high water, whatever it cost. There was a terrible row and he threw her out of the house. From then on her name was forbidden. He was going to be an Edinburgh policeman, he was so proud of that, and in mortal fear in case any of his colleagues heard that he had a silly old mother-in-law pretending to be a seal woman.'

Gran sighed. 'He was ambitious, my Magnus, clever too. If stories about seal women got around, he'd be laughed to scorn and never get promotion. He just put his foot down, refused to be reasoned with.'

Another sigh, a sad shake of the head. 'I had to choose and I chose my Magnus, so Sibella went away, back to South Ronaldsay. Our Jeremy was a peedie bairn at the time. We kept quiet about it, and if he had heard rumours about her, we let him believe his granny had died long ago, before he was born.

'And when I brought him back to Orkney after my Magnus was killed, I never got in touch with her. I never wanted to see her again, I know it's awful but I couldn't help it.'

'So you never said a word to us either,' I said. 'All those years of being with you here on Orkney,' I repeated reproachfully. 'And not even a whisper.'

'I know it was wrong, I should have told you, but I put her out of my mind. As far as I was concerned she was dead. I wanted to believe that. If ever I had a pang of conscience as the years went by, I told myself it's a fair distance to South Ronaldsay and I've never been a good sailor. I'm even sick on the ferry.'

She paused to give us both a glance of mute appeal. 'There was only once I started to feel bad about hating my own mother and being ashamed of her. And that was when I brought the two of you back to live with me and I saw the way you both missed your Mamma and wept for her.'

She shook her head. 'But then I remembered my loyalty to my Magnus so I went on doing what he would have wished.

'Then one day just after you got married,' she said to Emily, 'I heard rumours about her marvellous cures. I knew then she was still alive and I had to make my peace with her. I went down, one look told me she was very ill. Neighbours said she was dying and I knew I couldn't let her stay there, die alone.

'Erland was so very understanding, he insisted we bring her here to Yesnaby House. He arranged it all and she was too far gone to refuse.' She shrugged. 'Somehow, and without any of her magic remedies, I nursed her back to life again.'

She shrugged. 'Maybe it was just being loved again, maybe being part of the family gave her a reason for wanting to stay alive. And I was glad to be at peace with my conscience at last, when I saw how grateful she was. No reproaches, not one word. It was just as if we had never quarrelled all those years ago. She seemed to have lost her old fire too and right from the moment she set eyes on Emily, she took to her, although she was very wary of Erland–'

She stopped, glanced at Emily, seemed to change her mind about what she was going to say.

Emily looked up from her knitting and

smiled. 'I can't think why. Erland is so good, so kind to everyone and to her in particular.'

Gran shrugged. 'A couple of years ago she was as active as either of us, but she has to take it easier these days, she needs an afternoon rest–'

'Just like me,' said Emily with a laugh.

'And she canna guddle about in the kitchen the way she did before her hundredth,' said Gran with just a touch of satisfaction.

I felt Gran would have no time for any female, seal woman or no, who could upstage her in her own domain, as she continued: 'Says her feet aren't what they were. But she never had good feet like the rest of us. They were almost more like – well–'

She was cut short by a sharp frown from Emily who interrupted hastily: 'She'll want you to see her croft, won't she, Gran? First place she'll take you. It's a fascinating place. Out of a fairy tale about Red Riding Hood. Crammed with bottles and books and old birds' nests – just about everything–'

'I've only been across the door once since she came here,' said Gran. 'I just wanted to tidy up and clean the place for her. Give her a hand. And that set her off. She was blazing mad at me. So I'm no longer welcome,' she added bitterly. 'That's the privilege of the very few. Like Emily and that Wilma.'

Emily smiled and put a hand on Gran's arm. 'We appreciate it. We like the house as it is, spiders and all.' And when Gran shuddered, she looked across at me: 'You'll just love it, Rose. I know you will.'

As dust and spiders were my constant companions in Solomon's Tower, where my daily life did not include intense activity with mop and duster, I had a natural fellow feeling for weird houses, a bond with Sibella.

'I can't wait till she sees that bicycle of yours. She'll probably want to have a go at it.'

'You won't let her near it!' warned Gran.

That seemed quite unnecessary as I could hardly imagine a century-old seal woman on a bicycle. I laughed and Emily said:

'And she'll be delighted to know that you need it to investigate crimes in a wicked city like Edinburgh.'

I hoped Emmy hadn't exaggerated the humbler version of my career as Gran sniffed again and gave me a hard look, a frown which clearly indicated her rather transparent thoughts. That such things weren't nice for a young woman to think about never mind to get involved in. Crimes were sordid, dirty and disagreeable, there was something contaminating about them.

And hadn't her own darling Magnus been a murder victim? That she could never forget, not would she ever forgive Edinburgh for allowing such a thing to happen to one of its policemen.

As for her darling Jeremy, our Pappa, she had never understood why he didn't stay in Orkney and do a nice clean job behind nice solid walls. He had been clever even as a little lad, the teachers said he would go far, he could have worked in a bank in Kirkwall or taught in the local school.

However, I knew that Gran had been placated over the years by a policeman son who had reached the dizzy heights of chief inspector in the Edinburgh City Police. Even, it was whispered, being called upon to be the Queen's personal detective at Balmoral Castle. Now that was something not many Orkney mothers could boast about.

The Westminster clock chimed again and Gran stood up with a sigh to attend to the teapot and set the table.

'She'll take very kindly to you offering to walk with her,' said Emily. 'Instead of me, that is! As long as you don't mind walking a bit slower – but do it tactfully, I know you'll never hint that she needs a helping hand up banks and the like. Sometimes her feet make her a little unsteady,' she added with a glance at Gran. 'We do worry a bit when she goes out and stays away for hours, without telling us where she's off to. Sometimes she just wants to sit on the headland and stare down at the sea, but mostly she has cronies in the village, likes tea and a gossip. People are like that here, remember, Rose?'

I smiled. 'Indeed I do. If you're out and passing a door and someone sees you, in you go for tea and bannocks. And whatever your urgency, you're never too busy to see anyone passing, open the door and give them a cup of tea.'

Emily smiled, the bond of Orcadian hospitality between us, then continued with a frown: 'We worry a bit about the hill. It's steep and these rough paths are for the fleet of foot, although she says she's walked rough roads all her life and they don't scare her.'

Gran said: 'She gathers fresh flowers from the hedgerows. She can't manage the steep steps down to Erland's garden now, but most of the arrangements about the house are hers. I havena the time.' For the first time Gran sounded grateful.

'She's a great reader,' Emily added. 'Only took to glasses for reading when she was ninety – and she can still hear the proverbial pin drop. By the way, if you want to be on her good side,' she said, taking another cup and saucer down from the dresser, 'don't look too surprised about the mittens.'

'Mittens?' I asked.

They exchanged glances and Emily said hurriedly: 'One of her little fads. She always wears them. Otherwise you'll find she's quite normal.'

I may have seemed prejudiced but 'quite normal' wasn't how I would ever have described Sibella Scarth.

A sound of light footsteps on the path outside. A shadow passed by the window.

'Here she is now. For heaven's sake, don't hint that we were talking about her. And try not to look startled – because she's so old, I mean. We might think it's an incredible age,' Emily added in a whisper, 'but she just hates to be reminded that she's a very old lady.'

Despite their reassuring words, I steeled myself for my great-grandmother's appearance.

I expected the saurian, skeletal face of any

centenarian fortunate enough to appear in a photograph. The sunlight was behind her and I was totally unprepared for the doll-like figure who sat down, dwarfed by the high-backed Orkney chair.

White hair, pink cheeks, bright eyes. At a glance she could well have been Gran's younger sister, a well-preserved seventy-year-old.

'So you are Rose. I've heard such a lot about you, my dear.' And as she held out a small mittened hand, her fingers exquisite as ivy, I was aware of the emanation of some power beyond the ordinary.

I suspected some magic at work, to be so old, to have survived all her contemporaries. Though she was frail as glass and slow-moving, the miracle of longevity remained. If her eyesight and hearing were as good as Gran and Emily claimed, so too was her memory and I remembered the old saying about first meetings. 'Look well upon the face of friend or foe at first meeting for you may never see them as clearly again.'

And I knew then that there was something odd about Sibella's appearance. The sloping shoulders, the short neck, the very round, almost contourless face were something of a shock.

I did not wish to consider the image she evoked, what Sibella's shape reminded me of!

Chapter Nine

Our first meeting was brief indeed. We had exchanged no more than a few words before the pleasant domestic scene in Hopescarth's kitchen suddenly dissolved.

The sound of a carriage on the drive, doors closing, voices.

'Erland!' said Emily.

The master of the house had returned. In that moment everything changed and Sibella disappeared as if by magic.

One second I was looking at her in the Orkney chair. Then my attention was diverted to Emily and Gran, now on their feet, Gran hastily tidying the table, touching her hair, smoothing her apron.

When I looked back at the chair Sibella was gone.

In that one instant I had learned something. Either she didn't like Erland or he didn't like her. Or was it mutual, a repetition of Sibella and Magnus Faro?

As for the newcomer, I didn't know quite what to expect. An ogre of some kind perhaps, terrifying children and old women.

But the Erland Yesnaby who flung open the kitchen door and fathered Emily in his arms was undoubtedly one of the most ordinary men I had ever met.

Tall and bony with sandy hair, going thin. A perpetually puzzled expression and the most benign of blue eyes behind thick glasses. The curious thing was that I was prepared for an elderly widower but Erland didn't look much older than Emily. I was to find out that there were fourteen years between them but the gap looked much smaller than that. Perhaps the reason was that Emmy didn't look particularly young for her age.

Erland bowed over my hand in an almost old-fashioned gesture, and bade me welcome to Yesnaby House. And then I knew his secret. His was one of the most beautiful voices I had ever heard. Deep, musical, tender – the kind that suggested he should be singing instead of speaking. The kind that had he recited the letters of the alphabet and Bradshaw's train timetables, they would have sounded like Orpheus and his lyre.

No wonder Emily had fallen in love with him. All she had to do was close her eyes and listen.

'Yes indeed. I have heard a great deal about Emily's lovely sister,' he was saying. The voice had a nice smile too. 'I do hope these two ladies of mine are making you at home.'

(Mark the omission of Grandmother Sibella!)

Gran was obviously delighted, she giggled a lot when he talked to her. A new coy, girlish version of Gran that made me raise my eyebrows. I was to discover she found it difficult to keep her hands off him too. In passing, she would touch his sleeve, his shoulder, his hand. All terribly maternal of course.

As if he were a little boy. And of course, that was another aspect of Erland's charm. A beautiful voice and the slightly bewildered expression of a small boy who doesn't know quite how to deal with the world or the day's problems. I could imagine him forty years ago, at school, with a slate in his hand, trying to do his sums. He probably had a fine voice even before it broke, the pride of the church choir.

I realized I was sitting there with a silly smile on my face and hardly listening to the conversation, which concerned his business trip, anyway.

He was anxious about Emily, stroking her hair back from her forehead and hovering close by, his arm around her shoulders in a very nice protective way.

Then I was being asked about my journey. How was Edinburgh?

Emily said: 'Rose brought her bicycle. Came on it all the way from Stromness.'

He looked at me and said: 'How very exciting. I've never ridden a bicycle,' he added in such a wistful tone that I immediately said: 'Please feel free to try mine.'

His eyebrows rose over that high clever forehead. 'May I really? That is very good of you.' He stood up. 'If you'll excuse me, I have to go to my study. Things to sort out.'

And in answer to Gran's question, was he hungry?, he patted his waistcoat. 'I had a huge breakfast, thank you. Just a sandwich will do nicely.'

Turning to Emily, he smiled and said gently: 'Time for your rest, love. Off you go.'

I followed her upstairs. No longer used to being with people all day, I needed time on my own, time to relish that lovely bedroom with the glimpse of the sea.

Closing the door I stacked away my few clothes in the depths of the huge handsome wardrobe, smelling of lavender. Then I placed my reading matter on the bedside table. I'd brought along Emily Brontë's *Wuthering Heights,* deciding that that tale of passion and vengeance could equally well have originated in Orkney, and had added her sister Charlotte's *Jane Eyre* for company. I wondered how my friend Nancy was coping with the widower Gerald Carthew's children in Fife.

Nancy was kin to Mrs Brook, Pappa's former housekeeper at Sheridan Place. I had been instrumental in getting her a situation as nanny in Edinburgh. By one of those odd facts of life, she and Jack had known each other as children. For a while my thoughts had turned to matchmaking, especially when I realized she was in love with him. But the feeling was not reciprocated. Jack wanted me.

Things happened, bad things, a tale which doesn't belong to this chronicle. I put them out of my mind very firmly as, at the back of the lavender-scented drawer, I secreted well away from these two respectable Brontë sisters several pamphlets originating from women's suffrage which I was anxious to study. Two were written by Emmeline Pankhurst, and I hoped Gran would not come across them in her 'tidying'.

Glad to be alone to consider the past twenty-four hours, I found it scarcely believable that only yesterday I had arrived in Stromness. Already Edinburgh seemed part of another world I had left long ago. And I realized that this had been the pattern, even in childhood. Once we were back in Orkney after the summer holidays with Pappa, Edinburgh retreated quickly into the past.

Was that the secret of why Emily's letters always seemed so vague? Perhaps Edinburgh wasn't a real place to her either after so many years.

Certainly, for a peaceful holiday, the events had been momentous since I arrived. The meeting with Craig Denmore, an exciting interesting man, one whose further acquaintance I was already eager to cultivate. In that respect I must confess that his association with Edinburgh and the numerous learned societies was very encouraging. It gave rise to secret hopes of a promising friendship which would not end when in three weeks' time I left Hopescarth.

How lightly and impersonally he had told his tale of the peat-bog woman, never guessing, of course, that I was related to

Erland's second wife. Had I known her identity, I certainly would have shown more tact in bringing up the matter.

I shuddered at the recollection. How utterly awful, the worst possible experience for Erland, and I wondered whether it was the reason for another of Emily's miscarriages. It must have been an appalling shock for them both.

I took my chair to the window and, sketchbook in hand, I drew the scene. My conscientious habit of recording every new place resembled, according to Jack, the way a dog circles round his basket before settling down.

Dear Jack. I had so much to tell him – but later. A pretty postcard…

Time passed and I was content, finishing my sketch with the silence broken only by occasional distant footfalls below stairs and far-off voices.

I must have dozed, for I awoke to the sound of a carriage driving off across the cobbled yard.

Erland had gone out again. I looked at the clock on the mantelpiece: Emily would by now have had her hour's rest and would be waiting for me downstairs.

But Gran was alone in the kitchen doing

the ironing.

'Emily? She's away out with Erland. They've gone to Kirkwall. Business things.'

I was a little put out at that information as I would have loved the chance to go with them, see Kirkwall again. But obviously Emily had never given that a second thought.

My face must have shown it all, as Gran said: 'They didn't want to disturb you. Thought you'd be needing your rest.'

And I felt vaguely irritated at being treated like an elderly invalid worn out by the exertions of travelling from Edinburgh.

Gran knew me too well not to notice that scowl and, patting my hand, she said: 'Don't take on, Rose, there's a good lass. Erland likes to have Emily to himself. After all, he's been away a week, a long time apart. And they just want to be together for a few hours. On their own.'

So I swallowed my disappointment along with one of Gran's well-buttered scones. How food soothes the troubled breast and triggers memories. The sight and smells of Gran's kitchen carried me straight back to those early days when Orkney had been my home.

From Gran's questions, I realized that she

too was rooted in the past. She talked of people we used to know whose names I had long forgotten as well as the faces that fitted them. Gossip about neighbours revealed that I was still 'peedie Rose Faro' and any interest in my present life was sketchy in the extreme.

But Gran who gossiped about everything, great and small, never once mentioned Thora or referred to our earlier conversation with Emily. A curious omission, I thought at the time. Almost as if it had never happened, or I had dreamed it – a particularly unpleasant nightmare!

I watched her bustling about the kitchen absorbed by the normal daily preparation of the evening meal, peeling vegetables, rolling pastry. Gallantly I made the offer to help which thankfully she declined.

'You go out, lass. Get some fresh air while the weather holds,' she said.

That sounded like a good idea: it was time to explore Hopescarth. Gran continued: 'And if you meet Sibella, she'll be glad of your company.' She gave me a shrewd glance. 'Folks about here will be curious to meet you. They'll invite you in for a gossip. Remember the way it was in the old days?'

I did indeed. 'I haven't forgotten.'

And I repeated with her that childhood lesson: 'Unless it's a matter of life or death, you are never too busy to see a neighbour passing by, open the door and offer a cup of tea…'

It was on the tip of my tongue to say that it wasn't quite the same with some neighbours, like Craig Denmore. I couldn't see Gran flying to the door and asking the laird's handsome son from Inverness and the whisky distillery to come and sit by her fireside for a cup of tea.

Chapter Ten

Half an hour later, with warnings not to get lost, I was sailing down the hill on my bicycle across the stone bridge to Hopescarth.

Not that there was much to explore. A dozen grey stone houses all huddled together and staring into each other's windows across a rather dull winding street. A square grey building heavily railinged and carefully segregated, 'Boys' and 'Girls' carved in stone lintels above the entrances, marked the local school.

The rest of Hopescarth consisted of a few scattered opulent-looking houses keeping themselves to themselves behind high walls leading towards the village church.

A kirkyard promised a melancholy but interesting study, so I decided my first stop would be to acquaint myself with some Faro ancestors.

And there they were, Faros and Scarths all carefully filed away, peacefully resting together under stone slabs and crosses, some leaning at curious angles as if the incumbents were trying to carry on conversations with each other.

The graves went right back to the mid-seventeenth century. A memorial to a Faro who had left Orkney to fight for Prince Charles Edward Stuart and had died at Culloden. A large number 'Perished at Sea', sad indication of the fate of a whole boatload of Scarth sons. Many tiny slabs were for infants under two years old and others mourning tragically young mothers who had died giving birth or from unspecified complications afterwards.

I stood back and surveyed this scene of aggressive mortality. I had made one discovery: there were enough branches of Faros and Scarths for a family tree. Pappa, of course, had never had either the time or the interest to indulge in such speculation but I was sure my stepbrother Vince, now resident in London as junior physician to the royal household, as well as his wife Olivia, would be fascinated. So I might as well take a look at the parish register in the church.

My path passed near the Yesnaby vault, neatly railed off with a memorial tablet to 'Thora Yesnaby, beloved wife of Erland, died 1885. Interred 1895.'

That inscription would intrigue future generations, I thought as I walked away sadly aware of the reason for Emily's lack of communication. Such happenings would be very difficult to explain in letters and she had enough nightmares to be lived through every day in Hopescarth without a widowed sister in Edinburgh on her conscience.

Suddenly I realized I wasn't alone. There was another interested spectator.

'I'm Wilma,' she said. 'You must be Missus Rose.'

So this was the awful child who haunted Gran's kitchen. At first glance I could have mistaken her for someone of my own age. A skinny child, tall as myself, with one of those 'born old' plain faces that never manage to look childlike even in infancy.

She pointed to Thora Yesnaby's memorial. 'Did ye know, Mr Frank who found her is my Ma's lodger,' she said proudly. 'He let me see her.' Her smiled waited for comment.

Giving me a moment to think of some suitable reply and disappointed no doubt that none was forthcoming, she added importantly: 'After they dug her up, you know.'

And shaking her head in a grown-up manner: 'She didna look as if she had been lying there for years and years. She wasna like a skeleton or the bodies they dig up over yonder.'

A nod in the general direction of the archaeology dig.

A solemn shake of the head. 'She looked awfa like a real person who had just died.' Another pause. 'Like my aunty who had a bairn and died of it. She's over there. Do you want to see her grave? I can show you it, if you like,' she added eagerly.

I gave her a non-committal smile. She looked disappointed. 'Bet you've never seen anyone dead.'

It was a challenge and I replied carefully: 'Not very recently.' Not very true either, but I declined to enter a morbid conversation with a twelve-year-old who was revealing a profoundly macabre streak as she continued proudly:

'Oh, I have seen lots and lots of dead folk. There's no need to be scared of them, you know. They canna touch you. And Ma lets me go and have a look before the coffin's closed.'

She stopped to hold up her fingers. 'I've seen nine,' she counted, closed her eyes. 'No – ten, I'd forgotten Grandfaither. I didna like him much. He wasna pretty like my little cousin Vera.' She laughed. 'But then I didna like him much when he was alive either.'

Pausing, she regarded Thora's memorial with a frown. 'But that lady there – she was different. Mr Frank, our lodger, was awfa upset – and real scared. He went on and on about it. Ma was fair fed up. I go and see the doctor sometimes,' she added proudly, with a quick defensive glance. 'That's Dr Craig. It's no' medicine like our doctor, he canna even cure a cold. It's to do with digging dead folk up. And Ma lets me go and watch sometimes.'

She gave me a triumphant smile as if I might raise some grown-up's objection: an attitude suggesting that most of her requests were greeted by a firm 'No, you can't.'

'Dr Craig lets me have a trowel to dig with them.'

'Really? Have you found anything exciting?'

She nodded eagerly. 'Once he let me hold a skull.' She closed her eyes ecstatically. 'That was real thrilling. He likes me because I see things. I can tell him where to look.'

The words were in a whisper, staring beyond me as if there was something I couldn't see. It reminded me strangely of Sibella.

'You must be a great help to him then,' I

added carefully.

Wilma smiled, relaxed, and her approving look told me I was on her side, not one of those wearisome adults who said no to everything.

What an extraordinary child, I thought. No wonder Gran didn't care for her. I decided to leave the parish register for another day and headed towards the gate while Wilma skipped alongside and pointed to my bicycle resting against the railings.

'Everybody knows about that. It's yours, isn't it? That's how I knew who you were,' she added triumphantly. 'Ma told me to watch out for you.'

She made that sound quite like a warning as she stroked the handlebars, as if it was a particularly nice but not very trustworthy pony.

'I wish I had a bicycle, Missus Rose.'

She sounded so wistful that I took a quick look up and down the road. No one in sight. And a straight broad path bordering the kirkyard. I had a strange feeling that this particular child didn't have much to celebrate in her life and on an impulse I said:

'I'll teach you to ride, if you like.'

She clapped her hands, jumped up and

down with delight. 'Oh, Missus Rose. Would you really? I'd do anything–'

'Come on then. Up you go. One foot there – and the other. Now press down on the pedals. That's right. Off we go.'

I ran alongside – a few wobbles, fewer I have to say than I made the first time I rode back from my friend Alice's house in the suburbs of Edinburgh across to Arthur's Seat and Solomon's Tower.

'I can do it,' she shouted. 'I can do it! Look at me. Oh leave go – leave go.'

'No – you'll fall.'

'I won't – I won't.'

'Sure? All right.' I ran close behind ready to grab her. But the amazing child was wheeling along the path and back to me as if she'd been born in the saddle. Stopping and getting off were tricky: I expected trouble, but she managed, and quite gracefully too.

'You were wonderful,' I said. 'Congratulations.'

'Oh Missus Rose, that was the most exciting thing I've ever done in my whole life. Can I – can I do it again?' she asked wistfully as she relinquished the machine.

'Of course you can. Come up to Yesnaby House and we'll have another go.'

'When can I come?'

'Any time I'm there. Tomorrow morning, if you like.'

Again she danced up and down, clapping her hands.

'Lovely, lovely!' She was so eager that I wondered what I was letting myself in for.

Suddenly her face fell. 'Missus Rose, would you – I mean, can you keep a secret?'

'Cross my heart,' I said solemnly.

'You won't tell Ma?'

'Of course not.'

'She'll skin me alive – she'd never let me–'

I touched her hand. 'I've promised, haven't I? This will be our secret.'

'Oh thank you, thank you.'

The church clock belled the hour and Wilma shouted: 'I'll have to go. I was taking a message for Ma – she'll kill me.'

And she was off, skipping down the road, turning occasionally to see if I was still there as if our encounter had been just another of her childish fantasies. Another wave and she disappeared.

I smiled. It seemed that the bicycle had found me a strange new friend.

Returning to the church, relatively modern and therefore rather uninteresting from a historic point of view, I saw upon closer inspection that it had been built on an older foundation. Carved stones, grave covers and lintels were piled untidily against the walls: materials scavenged and left over, no doubt, from the ruined castle Erland's grandfather pulled down.

The interior was bleak despite one stained glass window, donated by the Yesnabys, of course. I thought I was alone until a shadow moved and a voice called:

'Hello – so we meet again.'

Craig Denmore. Delighted to see him so unexpectedly when he occupied a sub-stantial measure of my thoughts, I felt an inappropriately girlish blush creeping across my cheek. I told myself to stop being so silly as we shook hands and he murmured conventional pleasantries regarding my settling down and so forth.

'I was watching you giving young Wilma a try of the bicycle.' He paused and then said approvingly: 'Well done, the pair of you.'

And pointing towards the stained glass window: 'Just exploring, were you?' It didn't need a reply and he went on: 'I come here often to consult the old records that Yesnaby left regarding the castle. Parish documents are relatively modern, anything before the 1820s that is.' He looked round. 'Otherwise there's not much of interest architecturally.'

I had to agree and he pointed to the baptismal font. 'That's pretty modern, fifteenth century.'

I was tempted to smile at his description of modernity.

'Just looking round, are you?'

'My purpose is the same as yours. Old records, if they exist.'

He smiled. 'Great minds do think alike.'

We wandered outside, our ways to part once again.

'Come and have a look at the dig sometime,' he said, giving the Yesnaby vault a rueful glance. 'I'm afraid I'm not on the visiting list, *persona non grata.*' He gestured towards Thora's memorial tablet. 'There was a terrible furore. I was away in Edinburgh when Frank and the lads discovered her. They had no idea she was Yesnaby's missing wife.'

And with a sideways glance to see how I would take it: 'This discovery was a considerable embarrassment since he had buried an unknown woman believing it to be Thora and proceeded to take a second wife, ten years earlier.'

He paused as if expecting comment. And then with a shrug: 'Not quite the ticket to have wife number one appearing from the dead on the scene no matter how fleetingly. I got a distinct feeling that they blamed us for finding her. That we should have let dead wives lie,' he added ruefully.

'Especially when no one ever discovered the identity of the woman in the first wife's grave.'

He shrugged. 'Well, we'll never know that now. Too many rough seas have flowed past Marwick Head since then.'

'But doesn't it intrigue you? Who she must have been?'

Again he shrugged. 'Some poor soul, I guess. She could have drowned anywhere up the coast. Fallen overboard from a ship – who knows?'

'Doesn't it bother you?'

He smiled vaguely. 'I'm afraid my interest in corpses, drowned or otherwise, belongs to past centuries.'

'You know that wife number two is my sister Emily?' I said sharply.

He gave me a wide-eyed look. 'Well, I never.' It was his turn to be embarrassed. 'Now I understand your interest. Forgive me – oh, dash – I thought – oh, never mind what I thought.'

And with a more intent glance: 'Sisters, eh?' A shake of the head and that phrase I always knew to expect. 'Well, well. You're not the least bit like sisters...'

And there the conversation ended as a man wearing a clerical collar hurried down the path towards us.

'Dr Denmore. I am so sorry to have kept you waiting.'

I was introduced and greeted cordially. Reverend Mullen didn't make the same mistake as Craig since Emily had told him her sister was coming on a visit.

'I hope we shall have the pleasure of seeing you in church on Sunday, Mrs McQuinn. Have a good holiday with us.'

He gave a slight bow and turned to Craig. 'I have some papers for you, sir.'

I made my excuses and decided to return to the house. Walking towards my bicycle I was aware of someone waiting under the shadowy trees outside the kirkyard.

It was Sibella.

Chapter Eleven

Sibella walked towards me, holding a tiny bunch of flowers.

She leaned forward, presenting a cheek to kiss. 'You are looking rested, Rose. You slept well last night?'

When I said yes, she smiled. 'I am just about to take a walk back up to the house. I'd be glad of your company.' She glanced apologetically at the bicycle. 'If it wouldn't be too much trouble, that is.'

'Not at all,' I said, relieved that Emily had been wrong and there was no suggestion that Sibella might request lessons like Wilma.

'A moment – I have to give Hakon his flowers,' she said.

Was Hakon the minister? I wondered, following her back into the kirkyard. But when she bent over the Scarth graves, I realized from the dates and 'Drowned at Sea' that this Hakon was her very late husband.

Sibella was smiling, her lips moving in a silent greeting. Laying her hands tenderly on the grave, she turned to me and said: 'I was telling him about you.'

I tried not to look surprised as she straightened up, a little unsteadily at first, but needing no assistance from me. Remembering Gran's warning, I suspected my help would not be welcomed in any case, as she went on:

'I am so pleased we've met this morning, Rose. On our own. It's a chance to get to know you.'

The same thought had been in my mind as we walked a few hundred yards down the road.

Sibella paused by a grassy bank, obviously a favourite place, with the whole wealth of the islands spread out below in the glory of late afternoon sunshine, the land calm and welcoming. Skylarks soared heavenward on the field at our back and the house dominated the hill, towering high against a cloudless sky.

And there in the peace that was older and more serene than any I had experienced since childhood days in Orkney, Sibella seemed eager to tell me her own story.

'I expect they told you where I came from?'

She wasn't expecting a reply and, as I wanted to hear her version of Gran's extraordinary story, I smiled vaguely.

This seemed to satisfy her. 'I wasna born here.' A gesture took in the landscape before us. 'I don't know where I came from but they all said I came from the sea and the folk hereabouts still don't know quite how to take me, because of that. Even after nearly a hundred years.'

She laughed sharply. 'My ancient years are seen as witchcraft – black or white magic.' She paused to see how I took that. 'Yes, Rose, they think I'm a selkie. In this day, I ask you, can you credit that? Don't folk ever learn?'

I felt that was for my benefit as she looked at me as if expecting a reply, a denial.

I shook my head. I didn't care to mention that in many places, on both sides of the Atlantic, witchcraft – a belief in the power of the occult, of good and evil – had never gone out of fashion. People had always wanted to communicate with the dead even in big cities. In Edinburgh spiritualist societies and mediums were doing a roaring trade and making their fortunes out of a gullible public. Every evening the bereaved, the grief-stricken crowded into dark rooms and dim halls in the hope that the spirits of their beloved dead might materialize for a brief moment. They were longing to hear and pay for a few reassuring words. And I suspected not only for comfort but to sweep away feelings of guilt. The audiences were mostly female – daughters and widows – those kept awake at night, haunted by feelings that they had not done enough, had not loved with all their hearts an ailing parent or spouse.

Desperate for Danny in those early days, I went once. 'Yes, your dear husband says he's happy. You're not to worry. It's a lovely place.'

The message was so unlike Danny, I wanted to laugh.

But I stayed and listened to the same words, the same pattern being handed out to the bereaved, a panacea for those still raw wounds. Consolation. That was what they came for and paid for.

'I don't know when or where I was born,' Sibella was saying, 'but I was carried into the house up yonder as a peedie girl – I well remember the day.'

Closing her eyes as if she could still see that picture clearly, she added: 'So I must be a year or two past one hundred. There are those who sniff and say that someone couldn't count properly. But they cannot deny that the builders were putting the last slate on the roof in 1795 when Hakon Scarth carried me from the sea, wrapped in his coat. I was shivering, like a half-drowned puppy, he used to tell me. By my size, they reckoned I was no more than two when he asked his Ma who was housekeeper to the Yesnabys to take care of me.'

I have a long memory inherited from Pappa and I asked: 'Don't you remember anything before that?'

Even as I said the words I realized that very few people do remember their first two years. Most often tales of those very early days are related by parents, so vividly that they are incorporated into memory and a child can grow up actually believing he or she remembered.

Sibella shook her head. 'I remember nothing before Hakon lifting me out of the boat, and the smell of fish.'

She paused and said: 'They couldn't get me to eat it. I just sicked it up and I still can't digest it, even to this day. Isn't that extraordinary? Everyone but me eats fish on Orkney.'

Then she laughed. 'Hakon thought I was one of his catch at first. There was seaweed wrapped around my legs and he got a terrible shock. Thought he'd caught a mermaid.'

She sighed softly. 'All I recall is that it was like someone lighting up with a searchlight what had been total darkness. Like being born. That's the only way I can explain it. Coming from a dark womb,' she whispered. 'I can't remember anything about being on that ship they told me about, the one that went down with all hands. Or whether I heard the poor drowning folks shrieking when it hit the rocks and went under the waves. That's what they told me in Hopescarth about the wreck and I tried to remember seeing it, but all I know is Hakon Scarth gathering me, cold and shivering, into his arms.'

She smiled at the memory, clasping her hands, her eyes suddenly narrowed, far away as if she saw Hakon before her.

'I never thought I was different from other bairns. But when I went to the school they all whispered what their fathers who were fishermen had told them. That the month before he rescued me, Hakon had found an injured seal pup. Their fathers told them how it had been caught in his nets and was badly cut. It was cruel to keep it alive, suffering like that, and they said the kindest thing would be to hit it on the head, throw it back into the sea again.

'But my Hakon wouldna do that. Even as a lad, he was always daft on animals. They all came to him, you know, just like they come to me these days. Wait till you see my croft – I have a barn full of sick creatures.'

She paused, looking round for a moment bewildered, and I had a strange feeling that sometimes past and present joined hands and were one and the same for Sibella.

'Where was I? Aye, my Hakon cared for the little seal and when its wounds were healed, he returned it to the sea. Now, there's a story among the Finn folk that onc of their kind spared to the sea is three spared to the land.

'And so it came about, just like that, for he was out fishing with his father and brother. A sudden storm and the roarst dashed their boat to pieces on the rocks, but the three of them swam ashore. A miracle,' she said with a shake of her head. 'No one ever survives the roarst, but they did. And not even a scratch on them. Folk were pleased but they didn't believe in that kind of miracle. They said it was a selkie's magic. Because Hakon had rescued a seal lass.'

She sighed, gazing out towards the ever-moving restless sea. It was almost high tide and huge waves were streaming towards the rocks.

'I just wanted to be like other lasses, but then it got me respect – and fear from other bairns at the school. Mostly they were terrified of a look from me and when I grew up, where I came from never bothered the lads who came to court me.'

She smiled. 'But I never wanted any but Hakon Scarth. All the lasses wanted him too, for he was the handsomest lad on the island. He was fourteen when he took me from the sea and when I was sixteen and him a man of thirty, still unwed, he asked me to marry him, for I was the one he had been waiting for all these years. He had saved up and had his own boat and promised me a bonny house in South Ronaldsay. The other lasses were mad jealous!'

She laughed, clasping her hands together. 'He wouldna listen to his family or his friends either who said it was dead unlucky to take a seal woman to wife. Had he not read the old stories? That some day Sibella would be called back to the Finn folk. That I'd bring him a bright summer but it would end in a woeful winter.'

She tapped her chest, thin under the shawl.

'But here I am and I never wanted to go back to the sea, I was in mortal fear of it. Why, I wouldna even paddle my feet in the water, like the other bairns, without screaming.'

She sighed. 'And it was the sea that took my Hakon from me. Maybe the Finn folk were jealous of our happiness.'

She was silent, looking at the sky, and suddenly I took the mittened hand in mine.

Sibella turned to me with that bewildered look again as if she'd just returned from a distant place.

'You're a good lass, I can feel your goodness. You'll be happy too and lucky, because you love people right.'

And I thought guiltily of poor Jack, waiting for my reply that I'd marry him, as she said: 'Now, where was I? Ah yes, my Hakon, we were happy as the summer was long and we had a long life together. I gave him two bairns, strong and healthy. Peter – and Mary, your grandmother.'

She shook her head sadly. 'The sea claimed my bonny Peter, such happiness as mine and Hakon's required a sacrifice and I suppose it was the right of the Finn folk to claim our first-born.

'Hakon was good to me. Folks hereabout said he should have put me back in the sea long since, especially when despite my human appearance, for I looked a real peedie lass, I was as dumb as any animal.'

'Dumb?'

She shook her head. 'No voice, not even a whisper. No one heard me speak a word. Although most bairns two or three can speak I couldn't say anything. I had to learn to say even simple words and then I just croaked like a frog. Even when I went to the school I wasna much better but there were people who whispered that in the circumstances it was quite normal – in a selkie.'

She paused dramatically and looked at me. 'They said I had traded my siren's voice, the one mermaids used to lure sailors to their doom, when I took on human form.'

'Your voice sounds fine,' I said weakly, aware that was expected of me.

'Aye, but I had to work on it. Hakon understood and we weren't like other folk, sometimes we went days and days without saying a word and knew exactly what each other wanted, or what we both were thinking.'

Pausing, she frowned. 'I sometimes worried about Mary when she was a bairn, a late talker, she was too. But she's made up for it since.'

126

With a laugh, she added: 'Aye, she has that. Her tongue never stops wagging except when she's asleep.'

We had reached the stone bridge and I wondered if she would be coming back to the house with me, but she shook her head and said: 'Off you go, Rose. We'll talk again.'

She took my hand, held it to her lips briefly, an old-fashioned gesture of farewell.

I watched her go, observing that under the shawl her chest was completely flat and her body long and quite pear-shaped. This would be no surprise in someone past a hundred where age might be expected to have brought radical changes to the female form. But Sibella's legs were quite short and, remembering what Gran had told me, about the trouble with her feet, I had noticed that under the trailing skirt she dragged her legs. That too could be mistaken for age, but when she walked, although she moved quite smartly, she slid her feet along the ground, as if–

As if–

No. As I wheeled my bicycle up the drive, I firmly resolved to banish the image Sibella evoked.

It just wasn't logical. Or possible.

Chapter Twelve

Erland and Emily had returned from Kirkwall.

Walking towards the coach house, I could hear Erland talking to the carriage horse.

Taking the bicycle from me, he set it against the side of the stall and said: 'Here's your new companion back again, Storm old chap.'

As the horse nuzzled his shoulder Erland grinned at me and said: 'It's going to rain soon.' He looked up at the cloudless sky with a countryman's inborn knowledge. 'The trees are waiting for it. See how still they are.'

Giving Storm a final pat, he led the way out of the coach house. 'May I show you the garden, Rose? The next storm and it'll be laid bare until spring. The last of the summer flowers are just holding on.'

Orpheus and his lyre, I thought again. In this case a superb human voice and that beguiling invitation could have led me anywhere.

The garden lay to the east of the house, down a flight of steep stone steps, invisible from the drive. Signs of earlier habitations were marked by pieces of broken wall and as we descended I looked at the vast array of colourful flowers.

An old world garden from an ancient painting, it was carpeted with plants carefully chosen for longevity and resistance to the elements and sheltered by the house.

'Given our climate, it's a marvel that anything survives at all,' said Erland. 'All I need to maintain is the pattern my grandfather laid down. Do you know there is hardly a day when I can't find some quiet spot out of the wind to smoke my pipe. There's a place for all seasons, and a windy day in August is quite different from a windy day in April – I've learned a lot from my garden,' he added proudly and, pausing to light his pipe, he watched the curl of smoke absorbed by the air. 'Well, Rose, what do you think of it?'

I looked around in amazement. 'It's beautiful. Hard to believe that there's a bleak landscape stretching for miles just across the wall.'

He laughed, pleased at my observation. 'There's another reason for the soil's fertility. This land has been inhabited continuously since man first came to the island thousands of years ago.'

He tapped his foot on the ground. 'In medieval times, this was the kitchen midden. On this exact spot, animal bones, human excrement and waste deposit from countless generations have been recycled and poured into the earth to grow again into the garden you see here.'

A scene of perfect tranquillity. Timeless, it suggested sunlight and birdsong, flowers radiant in summer glory. 'If ever gardens were haunted, then this one must be,' I said and Erland smiled.

'A very benign kind of haunting. A feeling of comfort, don't you recognize it?'

I agreed and he said: 'Think of it, every person who ever lived here who has laughed and loved and died here through the passing centuries has left some part of themselves. In essence, they are still with us in spirit,' he added gently.

And suddenly embarrassed by this display of emotion, he puffed at his pipe and the aroma of an excellent tobacco joined the other fragrances.

'I like to think they watch over the present generations and the ones still to come. Pity we can't get tall trees, but we have the birch and alder and the willow.' He pointed. 'And over there is a hornbeam. Hornbeam,' he repeated. 'Now isn't that a grand name for a tree?' I smiled, he made it sound like music.

'And over yonder, that's the last of our hazels, doesn't produce nuts any more, the poor old thing. Come and look at these.'

I leaned over beside him and looked down at the tiny patch of green.

'Here's our little treasure, the *Primula scotica* which would be just as happy growing on the grassy sea cliff a mile away. It rarely survives cultivation so perhaps it was here – like these wild orchids – and firmly established before man invaded.'

As I knelt and touched the tiny petals, he said: 'What does it remind you of – that little face?'

'It looks like a tiny monkey.'

'Right. And that's what it's called: *Orchis simia* – the monkey orchid.' He straightened up with a groan. 'We don't advertise our rare flowers, so keep it to yourself. In a few years they will be extinct and there's some would come all the way from Edinburgh and Glasgow, and even further afield, to harvest our rare specimens.'

He sighed, narrowing his eyes suddenly.

131

'Can't you just imagine how all this must have looked before the first people came and set down their roots? They must have seen and ignored so many plants and delicate flowers which are now only a memory, or have evolved into something tougher and less beautiful to survive.'

Shaking his head and knocking out his pipe on the stone wall, he sighed. 'That was long before man knew enough to appreciate and record them. Just think of the perfumes of exotic flowers and plants lost to us for ever.'

And sniffing the air as if some fragrance still remained: 'And the bird plumage lost for ever once they had to forgo their brilliant colours and evolve into dun greys and browns to keep them safe from their chief predator – the hunter Man.'

I tried to see it through his eyes, through that beautiful voice, trying to paint greens and yellows and browns into rainbow shades.

'Somewhere in the house, in the attics I suspect, there are old drawings and I think, a watercolour done by my grandmother, of the garden. Do you paint, by any chance?'

'Yes,' I said, the artist in me aroused for here was a theme that challenged and

132

pleased me. I would take time and record this garden, go back to earlier days when I had painstakingly drawn botanical specimens. It would be an absorbing, rewarding task on a holiday which offered little else but the ability to take time to relax.

Or so I thought. So wrongly, I was to discover.

'Over there is the vegetable patch. You'll find the perennials have been name-tagged. The metal tags are the originals, engraved by my grandfather.'

Our path led past another vivid flower bed, bright with the faces of late pansies. With an exclamation, Erland bent down and picked off a head.

'Dratted slugs, at them again.'

I offered my remedy. 'I have a hedgehog in the garden. She polishes off slugs for breakfast. And as she has a large family of young to support, they all troop out after her for a saucer of bread and milk at bedtime.'

I smiled at the memory of Thane watching over this scene, huge, but ignored by the hedgehogs. Perhaps he was too large for them to encompass, or perhaps there was another benign reason that they knew they need not fear him. He was on their side.

'Hedgehogs are relatively recent incomers

to the island. Did you know that, Rose? Introduced by a minister's sons from the mainland just twenty-five years ago, 1870 it was. They seem to have flourished and multiplied with biblical zeal. I must see if I can lure one, or kidnap one, more like.'

'I think I should warn you that they won't come to anyone's bidding, or stay. They have to do the choosing.'

'I'll get Sibella on to it, see what she can magic up for me. She seems to be a magnet for all living creatures.'

He looked quite solemn as he said it, as if he realized her power. He had turned suddenly quiet as he led the way back to the stone steps. Above us rose the house. With the sunlight on it, I saw now that some of the stones looked exceedingly ancient.

I pointed to them and said: 'There are some carved stones like that I noticed outside the church. Were they from the original castle?'

'Older than that, Rose. Some of them originated from the broch down by the shore. And these stones in the garden walls and on the sills are from the Earl's palace which occupied this spot in the sixteenth century – the garden is built on its foundations.'

I remembered Craig Denmore telling me

how Erland's grandfather had replaced it with the present building.

'You'll know all about Bad Earl Robert, of course.'

I nodded vaguely and he went on. 'Mary, Queen of Scots' half-brother and a complete disaster. Everything that ever went wrong with the island, past or present, was laid at his door. The palace here belonged to his son Patrick, the sinister Black Pate as history records him.'

He stopped and smiled down at me. 'Sibella will tell you his ghost still haunts this place, but take no heed of that, Rose. Sibella has an answer for everything,' he added shortly.

I wasn't going to let it go at that. 'Tell me more, I'm intrigued. There are plenty of ghosts allegedly haunting Solomon's Tower and Arthur's Seat, where I live. And I haven't seen one yet.'

He laughed. 'Well, if you should ever find you are being followed by a black-cloaked rider, riding fast on a black horse, you just get on to that bicycle of yours and ride like the wind.'

We both laughed at such absurdity and Erland said: 'The Stewarts weren't the first to colonize Hopescarth. Before them came

The Bu, the Norse earl or headman's homestead.'

I remembered tales of The Bu, house of the Wolflord of Orkney, the convivial Viking drinking hall, as he went on: 'I dare say my diligent grandfather uncovered layers and layers of past history in his building operation. If you're interested there's a load of dusty papers in the attic that I've never had time or wish to read. Those would be the important documents. I expect a lot more went into the rubbish dump. Those lads hadn't arrived on the scene with their spades and riddles,' he added with a wry nod in the direction of the archaeologists.

'Grandfather was a practical man and when he inherited the estate and decided to be a farmer, he had no grand ideas about living in a palace packed with ancient history. All those years at sea, sailing the oceans of the world, he had dreamed of a modest comfortable home to defy the elements, with a sheltered garden.

'As for the palace, it had been a costly ruin for two hundred years and the family had gradually retreated from leaking roofs and falling masonry into one draughty crumbling wing where every winter took off a slice more.'

He smiled at me. 'Even if you are sentimental about old castles, this one would
have been hell to live in. But there is a
painting of it somewhere in the house. Ask
Emily. She'll find it for you.'

'I will.'

'It's in the glory-hole up in the attics. Its
rightful place is in the local museum.
However, to give Grandfather his due, he
did leave one tiny piece of the original
palace, so he had his sentimental moments
after all. Come along.'

As I followed him, I asked: 'Talking
history, have you any theories about the
Maid of Norway's grave?'

He stopped walking, bit his lip and looked
thoughtful. Then with a sigh he nodded in
the direction of the unseen archaeological
dig. 'Not really.'

'You don't think she's buried over there?'

He shook his head, said 'No' very firmly.
And then holding up his hand: 'Rain! I
knew it.'

Hurriedly we retraced our steps. 'My
orchids will be grateful. Quickly – over here,'
and he took my arm. 'Let's test your powers
on my other treasure.' He led the way to a
patch of ground near a compost heap: an
unlikely place for a tiny orchid reverently

framed by chicken wire.

'This one looks like a skull, white with a yellow helmet – it reminds me of the ghost of Hamlet's father.'

A triumphant laugh from Erland. 'Know your Shakespeare too,' he said approvingly. 'That's one thing I miss here in Hopescarth. We have no theatre. I have to take Emily to the mainland for that.'

He touched the tiny flower. 'You were right again. It's the Ghost orchid, because of the skull and those pale translucent flowers and the fact that it lives on decaying matter in the soil surface.'

Sheltering the tiny orchid was an ivy-covered stone wall. Erland pushed back the foliage, which had almost taken over, to reveal a stone seat somewhat inhospitably lodged in a small embrasure, an ancient carving in the lintel.

'You'll see this in the painting. It belonged in the palace herb garden but I reckon it's much older than that. Most probably Pictish. There used to be a series of stone lintels like this, in the garden walls, each with its own coat of arms of the various branches of the Stewarts and their royal connections.'

'It must have been very grand,' I said,

trying in vain to imagine the huge palace, vast herb and flower gardens, dovecots, now reduced to one tiny piece of wall, the only evidence of the once massive foundations occasionally erupting as broken fragments of stone walls.

I looked closer at the stone carving. Ancient, storm-weathered despite the protective ivy, its design was almost obliterated by the elements.

A mermaid wearing a crown and holding a mirror.

A ghost of memory twitched. Somewhere I had seen it before.

'Is this one quite famous?'

Erland shook his head. 'I doubt it. I expect it should also go to the museum, in Kirkwall, like the others. But we're inclined to be hoarders, as you'll see when Emily takes you on a tour of the attics.'

I considered the stone again. 'Then I couldn't have seen a photograph of it somewhere?'

'I doubt it,' Erland repeated and when I said it seemed familiar, he smiled. 'You've probably see the same design on runic stones in museums. It's traditional Pictish and that's about all anyone knows of its origins. The suggestion is that the mermaid was a fertility symbol.'

Was that a wistful note I heard? Was that why the Yesnabys hung on to it?

As we walked away, the stone bothered me.

I was certain I had seen it before, but not in any of the contexts Erland suggested.

I racked my brains. The mermaid on runic stones, yes, but this was different.

The crowned mermaid and her mirror. I had held something like it in my hand. And that meant jewellery.

I have an excellent memory. My one weakness however is total lack of interest in the normal feminine acquisition of rings, brooches and necklaces. I have never coveted precious stones or desired any adornment but the wedding ring Danny put on my finger years ago in Arizona.

The crowned mermaid and mirror did not belong anywhere in American Indian cultures so if it was jewellery, then it had to be Scottish. And that meant, for me, it must be Edinburgh.

But when and, more important, why?

Chapter Thirteen

Erland left me in the hall, retired to his study and closed the door. In the kitchen Gran was bustling about, her hands covered in flour.

'Where's Emily?' I asked.

'Having a rest. Kirkwall tires her out.' Gran made it sound like a day in the big city. She noticed my amused expression and said sharply: 'Erland insists.'

'Is she – well, is she going to be all right this time, Gran?' I asked anxiously.

Gran looked at me, smiled reassuringly. 'Of course, she is, lass. It's just that with her past history – I think Erland's more scared than she is. Having a son will mean such a lot to him.' She shrugged. 'After so many failures, perhaps they both feel this will be the last time.'

'She's only twenty-nine, Gran. Lots of women get married long after that and have children.'

Gran paused in her pastry-making and gave me a shrewd look. 'What about you,

Rose? Isn't it time you married, had some bairns? Are you going to marry that nice policeman you were telling us about?'

I had hardly mentioned Jack Macmerry, but Gran's matchmaking instincts were acute as ever.

I smiled. 'I don't know. Maybe there are too many policemen in our family – and I've lost one already,' I added bitterly. 'Do they make good husbands?'

I was thinking of Pappa, but she bristled. 'My Magnus was the best in the whole world. There was no one like him.'

'I'm sure he was.' Tactfully I didn't remind her that she and Grandpa had been married only a year or two before he was killed. Maybe if, like Pappa, he had gone on to long service and promotion in the Edinburgh City Police there would have been a different story.

I guessed from his conversation that Pappa always felt guilty about having neglected Mamma. Maybe that had put him off a second marriage to his writer companion Imogen Crowe – of whom Vince, Olivia and I all heartily approved as an excellent choice of stepmother.

'You shouldn't turn your back on a good chance or let a good man go past you, lass.'

How often had I heard Gran's warning words in my girlhood years. Solemnly handing me a fresh-baked scone, she added with an impish smile: 'Here you are, lass. Can't have your cake and eat it, you know.'

Eager to change the subject, I asked if there was anything I could do to help her.

She declined my offer firmly. I was on holiday, I was here to enjoy myself, not to work.

'Go out and get some fresh air, lass.'

I had a feeling I was going to be very replete with fresh air by the time my holiday came to an end.

'Erland has been showing me the garden.'

Gran beamed. 'Aye, he has right green fingers.'

'I saw the mermaid stone,' I said.

Gran paused in her baking activities to look at me. 'Well?'

'Could I – could I ever have seen it before? When we lived in Kirkwall?'

Back to the rolling pin, she sighed: 'How could you, lass? We never came to Yesnaby.'

'I realize that. What about school outings?'

'There were never any as far away as Yesnaby.'

'Maybe you had something like the mermaid stone – an ornament or a picture,' I persisted.

'No, I never did. I liked pictures that were decent and had clothes on them, not naked bosoms,' she said firmly. 'What did you think of Hopescarth?'

So I told her about the church and the family graves, tactfully omitting any mention of the memorial to Thora Yesnaby and wondering why she was so edgy about the mermaid stone. Was her prim reaction to that 'naked bosom' the only reason why she changed the subject so quickly?

'Next time you go down past the village shop you could bring me a packet of salt, if it's no trouble. And some more butter. It's a fair trail for me these days,' she grumbled. 'All that way down the drive is bad enough without that hill up to the shops and back again. It seems to get longer as I get older.'

And I suddenly remembered that Gran was past eighty, a matter of reverence and awe in city life where age is a matter of importance. To country folk, however, as long as one had good health and good heart, is able to obey the dictates of the four agricultural seasons, increasing age goes unnoticed and unworthy of comment.

I said: 'I'd love to do your shopping, just keep a list handy. It'll be easy with the bicycle.'

At the word 'bicycle' she gave me a doubtful look as if her groceries might be contaminated by association with an alien machine. But mere mention of 'a trip down to Hopescarth' and Gran could immediately produce an arm's-length list of things that were urgently needed.

'I met Wilma,' I said, 'wandering about the kirkyard. She's very interested in the dig.'

'Spends every spare minute there. It isn't natural in a child her age,' said Gran.

'Yes, she's certainly strange.' I wasn't going to mention the bicycle episode, having made my promise to Wilma, but I hoped I would be around when she came to have the offered riding practice.

I said I had walked back with Sibella.

'I suppose she told you her whole life story. Never misses an opportunity of impressing folk,' said Gran, disapproval hardly suppressed.

I laughed. 'I like her, Gran. She's fascinating.'

'Hmph,' said Gran sourly, indicating that the subject was closed.

As she rushed back and forward to the oven, my presence was obviously no longer needed and, looking out of the window, I saw that Erland's promised rain had come to naught. With the mermaid stone still weighing heavily on my mind, I decided that Craig Denmore was the most likely authority on the subject.

Walking back down the drive and across the bridge, I came upon a busy scene of scratching and scraping.

Craig's fellow diggers looked up curiously, there was a rapid series of shouted introductions, polite smiles, and they all went back to trowelling and riddling.

All except Frank Breck, Wilma's mother's lodger, who looked as grey and dry as the ground he was working on.

'Good to see you, Rose,' said Craig. 'You've come at a great time. We've just made a discovery,' he added proudly, smiling at Frank.

'The Maid's grave?'

'Not yet,' said Craig ruefully.

'But we're very hopeful,' said Frank earnestly, watching Craig put a grimy hand into his pocket. With an air of triumph he drew out a coin and handed it to me.

Most of the dirt had been removed but it was still indecipherable. 'Roman?' I asked.

Craig shook his head.

'Viking then?' I said.

He laughed. 'No. Probably thirteenth-century Scandinavian. Don't you see, Rose? Finding this coin right on this spot could mean that it formed part of the Maid's dowry.'

He looked at Frank who forced a wry smile and added solemnly: 'It almost certainly suggests that she was buried in this area.'

I could understand their enthusiasm but it didn't seem convincing. I didn't want to dampen his optimism when I said: 'Weren't there other travellers from Bergen – I mean just ordinary sailors trading with Orkney? After all, they'd been doing that for years.'

Frank's heavenward glance of disgust clearly indicted that this was a Miss Know-all. With a curt nod to Craig he went back to his digging.

I watched him go. I had upset him but surely archaeologists were used to this sort of thing, to examining all finds logically, considering all the possibilities.

Craig looked quite crestfallen. With a sigh he pocketed the coin and indicating a fragment of ancient wall said: 'Won't you take a seat? It's all we can offer, I'm afraid – and my back's breaking.' I made room for him and he went on:

'You may be right about the sailors. But I hope you're wrong and that the next find will be something that indicates the Maid's grave is right here.' He tapped his foot on the ground.

'And Huw Scarth's pot of gold?'

He knew I was laughing at him. 'We've already found some coins of Earl Robert Stewart's personal denomination. Not content with a reign of terror by sword, fire and torture, he changed the old laws of the island guaranteed by the Scots Parliament and made some new enactments including his own currency. Free lieges of the monarch were banished and their property confiscated, or they were allowed to remain on condition they yielded up their heritages to him. Where these two methods of piracy failed, they were left to rot in prison without trial.'

He paused with an apologetic grin. 'Is that enough for you, or shall I go on? First thing about any archaeology project is to know all the history of the area. Everything that happened before you came along. Right!

'Earl Robert compelled lairds and liefs to entertain him and his household in a royal progress, I quote "to the number of six and seven score persons with adequate and great cheer at their own expense." As he had nineteen children each with a private army of retainers, even a short visit led to their hosts' immediate penury and the inevitable transfer of their property into the earl's hands or to one of his brood who had cast a greedy eye on it.

'He also claimed rights to all common moors and pastures and forbade the burgesses to trade except by his leave and licence. Even churches weren't exempt as they had to hand over their benefices to him. The most sinister form of subtle oppression was the increase of bismer and pundler to his own specification.'

He stopped and looked at me. 'Bismer and pundler – the ancient Orkney weights?' A smile. 'No? A bit before your time at school here. There was no escape by death either, since by his law dead men could be charged with old crimes.

'They were condemned in effigy and their goods confiscated, which left a neat margin for appropriating anything that took his fancy. And old Robert showed a surprising depth of imagination, we must give him that. As for the live inhabitants, another law: none should leave Orkney and Zetland in order to make complaint against himself. And so all ferries were stopped and people had to have a licence to leave.

'When I looked into Earl Robert's notorious rule, I realized that the activities of the wreckers which had always seemed a discreditable part of Orkney's history now shone by comparison, a virtual necessity for survival.'

I said: 'I'm beginning to see the significance of Huw Scarth's rainbow and the pot of gold.'

'Good girl! One thing stands out like a sore thumb in this story and that is how Huw Scarth's pot of gold brought him peace in his time. When you think about it, this one man managed to achieve wealth and security and Black Pate's blessing and he was able to remain here. In a Stewart palace.'

He paused and rubbed his chin thoughtfully. 'Could this pot of gold be the Maid's dowry? If so, I'd hazard a guess that it vanished without trace into the Stewart Earldom long ago. We'll never know. But there was already interest in the dowry even before Earl Robert came on the scene.

'The Stewart kings were always short of cash and when Robert's father, King James the Fifth, visited Orkney, the hint was that he had heard of "monies" there. Someone certainly passed on the word to Edinburgh because Queen Mary's gift to her half-brother was not quite as altruistic as it sounded.

'Robert Stewart was a great crony of that sinister young man, her second husband Henry Darnley. We gather it was at his insistence that Robert was given the preferment of Orkney: "that there was much to be gained thereby".

'When Mary's reign ended disastrously with Darnley's murder and Bothwell's flight to Orkney, Mary wrote to Gilbert Balfour who was then Governor and lived at Nordland Castle, beseeching him to do what he could to help and to "raise monies and treasyrs in particular the Maid's dowry."'

I knew the rest of that sorry story. Bothwell wasn't allowed to land and, outlawed, went to his end to die eight years later, mad and chained to a pillar in a Denmark jail.

I still wasn't convinced that the pot of gold had been squandered long ago. Perhaps Craig read my thoughts as he said:

'A pipe dream maybe, but no one on Orkney can resist the thought of buried treasure even if our main concern as archaeologists is finding the Maid's grave.

Anything else is just a bonus.'

And then he changed the subject. 'How are you enjoying your holiday?'

I was about to mention the mermaid stone when there was a shout from the dig.

'Craig!' It was Frank. He rushed over holding up his hand, shouting excitedly. 'There's something else!'

Chapter Fourteen

Frank was shouting: 'One of the lads has found another coin.'

Craig sprang to his feet. 'Excellent! You see!' he said to me triumphantly. 'I really think we are on to something.'

I smiled. 'Then I'll leave you to it. But before you go, can I ask you both something? It may be important for your discoveries.'

That got their full attention.

'Erland was showing me their garden. Have you seen the mermaid and mirror stone in the little arbour?'

Frank looked at Craig who shook his head. 'The garden is strictly out of bounds to us archaeologists, I'm afraid.'

'Too many precious plants and flowers we might trample over with our muddy boots,' said Frank contemptuously.

'What about this mermaid stone?' asked Craig. There was an exchanged glance between them, an air of excitement.

'I thought you might know its origins.

Erland showed it to me – it's a carved stone on a little embrasure beside one of his orchids. He hinted at runic stones.'

They were both watching me, listening intently now.

Craig said cautiously: 'Yes, that could be,' and Frank echoed: 'Yes, indeed, it could be.'

'You obviously were impressed, Rose. Was it important?' asked Craig smiling.

'It is to me. You see, I am sure I've seen something very like it before.'

'Oh, and where would that be?' asked Craig gently, still smiling.

'That's the problem. I don't know where. I thought maybe you could help. That you might have some ideas where it could be. In a museum collection, perhaps.'

They looked disappointed. There were perceptible shrugs which left me feeling suddenly very foolish as Craig said: 'If it's runic then that's too early to have any significance for our explorations.'

'But could you have seen one like it – in Edinburgh somewhere?' I insisted and Craig's head jerked up at that.

'In Edinburgh?' Then: 'No, of course not. What makes you think that?' he asked sharply.

I shook my head. 'I don't know, Craig. It's

just an idea.'

He looked at me thoughtfully. 'There could be something like it in Edinburgh, but I'm not familiar with it.' And he turned to Frank. 'What about you? Come across a mermaid stone in your activities?' he asked lightly.

Frank continued to watch me, his gaze brooding and intent as if he was trying to read my thoughts. Then he shook his head. 'Not that I can think of. And there aren't many Pictish remains in Edinburgh.'

I thought of Arthur's Seat and all the evidence of runrig agriculture, but I wasn't going to argue with authority.

'What about your antiquarian societies?' I asked Craig.

'Can't say I've come across any mention of such a stone in their papers.' He paused. 'Why are you so interested?' he asked curiously.

'I know this sounds foolish but as soon as Erland showed it to me I had this feeling that I had seen it – or something very like it – before. I know it sounds ridiculous but I have actually held something with that symbol – the crowned mermaid and mirror – in my hand.'

'And when would that be?' Craig asked.

155

'All I know is that it must be fairly recently. Since I came back to Edinburgh.'

Craig stood silent, Frank at his side. Both tall men, they towered over me in what seemed a suddenly intimidating manner.

Then Craig smiled, a polite smile. 'Sorry we can't help you, Rose. But if we think of anything…'

He looked at Frank who nodded eagerly. The little group were staring at us, impatient to discuss the possibilities of this new find. 'Back to work, eh, Frank?'

'Perhaps this is your pot of gold,' I said.

'Hope so.'

'Good luck,' I said rather lamely and made my way back along the drive and up to the house.

I was full of unease, certain that there was something I had mislaid, for I have an exceptionally good memory – have to have, it's in the nature of my investigations.

So why had I lost the mermaid stone?

Now it seemed I must wait until I got back to Edinburgh to find out.

But I was to have the answer very much sooner than that.

Emily was in the sitting room with her knitting, her feet up, when I returned.

To my anxious question, she smiled reassuringly. 'I'm perfectly fine, really. Erland just insists on me taking a lot of rest. He makes such a fuss and I do it to keep him happy. Anything for a peaceful life. Erland tells me you liked our garden,' she added proudly. 'And that you were very knowledgeable about hedgehogs.'

'I rather fell down on orchids, though.'

She laughed. 'Did he show you his pride and joy, the Ghost orchid?'

I told her how it had reminded me of Hamlet's father and her eyes widened. 'Erland would love that. The story is that the Maid of Norway brought some of the most precious and delicate plants from her garden to remind her of home.'

Erland hadn't mentioned that and I said: 'If that's true, Emmy, perhaps that is what gives rise to the legend that she was buried at Hopescarth.'

'I suppose so.' Emily's deep sigh told its own story: that she had heard the story of the Maid of Norway at least a hundred times and, as far as she was concerned, that was ninety-nine times too many.

Laying her knitting aside rather reluctantly, she said: 'I promised Erland I would look out the botanical prints and the old watercolour to show you. If I can find it. Like to come?'

'If you're not too tired,' I said although there was little sign of the baby beyond a slight thickening of her waistline.

'I've told you, Rose. I'm very well.' She sighed wearily. 'Please don't join the chorus of those who want to watch over me as if I'm an invalid or a piece of Dresden china. And as if having a baby isn't the most normal event in a woman's life. Think of the poor tinker women who give birth by the roadside, or those who have to go back to work the next day. I'm very lucky to be so cherished.'

Touching her stomach in a gesture I was to find very familiar, she said softly: 'I assure you the little chap is doing fine and as I'm well past the danger time, you can expect to have a grand little nephew next spring.'

As I let her lead the way across the hall and up the handsome oak staircase with its fine carved balustrade, I remembered that every night I prayed for what concerned me most.

Her safe delivery. Of either the son Erland longed for or a pretty little daughter.

In daylight with the sun slanting through the stained glass window, I noticed lighter squares on the walls where presumably picture frames had been removed.

'What happened to all the paintings?'

Emily shook her head. 'They were so dreary, those old family portraits. Very plain indeed, the lot of them, but they did like to be immortalized. Their gloomy presence depressed poor Erland, walking up and downstairs under the eagle eye of his ancestors, so they have been banished to the attic.'

Pausing half-way, she indicated the empty walls. 'We are about to celebrate by decorating the staircase and hall with some nice new wallpaper. I fancy roses, big flowers. What do you think, Rose?' she demanded excitedly. 'We had a quick look in Kirkwall this afternoon, but I don't trust Erland's ideas. I thought we might go together,' she added eagerly.

I said I'd love that. I was very willing to look at wallpapers although I wasn't any kind of judge. The modern taste for bucolic patterns, I found rather threatening. If I'd had to live with them I'd have felt rather like a small insect pursued across a garden full of predatory flowers.

Tapestries on Solomon Tower's walls – to keep out the cold draughts – was as far as it went with me.

She led the way along a corridor which housed the main family bedrooms and a bathroom, that delightful addition to the modern age, then we climbed another, less imposing, staircase. Linoleum-clad creaky wooden steps led to the attics on the third floor, which Erland's grandfather had originally intended to house maids and nannies for the future Yesnaby dynasty.

I looked round and Emily was toiling after me a little breathlessly. I waited for her and we went up the last flight hand in hand.

This part of the house looked dusty, it smelt disused and rather damp. At last she opened a door into a room with a sloping ceiling and this was accompanied by what I thought of as a familiar scurrying sound of mice and insects of the larger species.

Our entrance raised a cloud of dust from the floor and Emily sneezed. 'Sorry about the mess, Rose. It's a glory-hole for everything Erland doesn't want but won't throw away in case it is valuable. He wasn't the first Yesnaby to suffer from that disorder either.'

I believed her. Trunks covered in dust and cobwebs bore faded labels from far-off places in the Empire, no doubt carried by seagoing and soldier Yesnabys who had travelled to more exotic lands than Orkney. There was a rocking horse, a broken Orkney chair and, partially hidden by a sheet, a beautiful carved cradle.

Emily seized upon it with a cry of triumph. 'So that's where it got to. Erland bought it in an antique shop in Edinburgh – it's supposed to be seventeenth-century.' Her touch sent it rocking gently. 'He brought it home the day I lost the baby – that was when I was expecting our first. We had such hopes,' she added with a sigh. 'Poor Erland was distraught, worse than me really. Women are used to such things and I always believed we'd have a baby soon. But Erland cried and cried, although he pretended I was the one so upset. Anyway, he couldn't bear to see the cradle in our bedroom, a terrible reminder…'

I could see Erland, so sensitive to gardens with their flowers and plants, being heartbroken at Emily's miscarriage. 'I lost two more after that, you know, but now…'

As she pulled the cradle into the light, I rushed forward. 'You are not taking that anywhere.'

'Just downstairs,' she said.

'Not even across the landing, Emily.' I gave it an exploratory shove. 'Solid oak – it's far too heavy. Leave it to Erland.'

She smiled wanly. 'Perhaps you're right. Best to leave it until the baby arrives this time. I don't want to upset Erland.'

'For heaven's sake, don't be daft. You'll need a month or two to make blankets and have everything prepared. I could give you a hand while I'm here.'

She shrugged. 'I know. And I appreciate the offer. But Erland is terrible superstitious this time. He doesn't even want to talk about it without crossing his fingers. Poor Erland – it would break his heart – I don't think I could bear it either if – if…'

I put my arm around her. 'You're not ever to have such thoughts. You've told me yourself you're past the danger time and you'll have a strong healthy baby. Believe it – have some faith.'

'You really think so, Rose?'

'I know so – and remember I'm the one in the family with the second sight too.'

We both laughed at that long-standing joke.

'Remember how the girls at school thought you had magic powers to find their missing pens and lost handkerchiefs, Rose? And you generally were successful. It amazed them.'

'Nothing magic about applying some logic

162

to a situation, Emmy.'

'Logic – something you inherited from Pappa, I expect.'

'I suppose so.' Important in my chosen career, logic had also landed me my very first case with my friend Alice who had remembered that I could solve mysteries at school. 'All I ever made them do was to back-track, think where they had last seen or used it.'

'It generally worked.' Emily paused. 'Sibella thinks the baby will be all right,' she added but something in her voice scared me.

I didn't know why then.

Chapter Fifteen

Emily looked around the dusty attic.

'Over here!' Triumphantly she pointed to a stack of frames. 'Now is your great moment. You can be introduced to most of Erland's solemn ancestors. But first of all...'

And she pounced on a faded folder, blew off a great quantity of dust and said: 'These are the botanical prints – but where is the watercolour of the garden? Yes, here it is. Oh, the glass has broken and the frame is cracked. What a shame.'

As for the painting, it was pretty enough and rather what I expected. A pleasant amateur effort and I could just imagine the lady of the house sitting in the warm sunshine, paying meticulous attention to every bush and flower, anxious to include each leaf and petal.

'Do you think the prints have any value?' asked Emily doubtfully, opening up the folder. 'They're mostly of Erland's precious orchids, but you know something about watercolours.'

The botanical drawings were brown-spotted, foxed with damp. Pointing it out to Emmy, I told her they were beyond repair and of little value.

Laying them aside I considered the painting of the garden critically. For there was the mermaid stone, clearer, brighter, before it was overgrown with ivy.

'You should hang this one. Definitely.' And as I said the words, again that irritating twitch of memory.

'Emily, had you ever seen that stone–' I pointed to it – 'before you came to Yesnaby?'

'Of course not, Rose. How could I?' Her response was immediate and a bit impatient like Gran's.

She gave a little laugh. But I'm sensitive to atmosphere and I wondered what Emily had against the mermaid stone that she wasn't willing to talk about it either.

There was that sudden change of subject too. 'The painting's not very good, is it?' She had gathered that from my reaction.

'Never mind that, Emmy. The painting is part of the house's history and that is what matters.'

She watched me thoughtfully. 'But you could do a much better painting while you're here. I'm sure of that.'

'Mine would be quite different. The Yesnaby lady did that with her whole heart, a painting of her own lovely garden. She didn't care whether it was valuable or not, or even if no one in the family wanted it after she had gone. She did it to please herself and possibly even as a present for her husband.'

'Very well, I'm persuaded.' Emily smiled. 'I'll get Erland to have it repaired and perhaps a new frame too. Then it can hang in the breakfast room. But I'd still like your painting – the house perhaps or some other aspect of the garden, and Erland would love that too,' she added wistfully.

As she moved it back against the wall, I was suddenly aware that the temperature had dropped.

It was cold. I wanted to go downstairs again to that warm, comfortable – safe – kitchen.

I'd had enough of the past. But not quite…

Emily saw me shiver and smiled.

'A quick look at the rogues' gallery then you'll have earned that cup of tea,' she said. 'Although I suspect they were all too dull and boring to be anything else but harmless.'

I had to agree. The oil painting Erland had

mentioned of the original castle was black with age, depressing and, I suspected, worthless. As for the portraits, they all looked as if they had been the work of an unskilled artist better at painting doors and windows than the human face.

'Had enough?' Emily laughed.

I said yes. 'But is that one we've missed – over there against the wall?'

Emily looked at me. 'That's a portrait of Thora,' she whispered hurriedly as if she could be overheard. 'Erland was so upset by – by all that happened he couldn't bear to look at it.'

That was hardly surprising, but I was very curious to see what Erland's first wife had looked like as, somewhat reluctantly, Emily turned it to the light.

A woman with dark hair and hard eyes in the fashionable dress of the 1880s.

She was at the mantelpiece of the drawing room downstairs, so that her reflection was in the mirror behind her. She looked over her shoulder towards the artist, her thin lips slightly parted, her hand raised against her bare neck.

'What do you think of it?' asked Emily. 'I think it might be valuable. It was painted by one of the Glasgow School.' She mentioned a painter whose exhibitions I had seen in Edinburgh. 'He's quite famous now – if Erland ever wanted to sell it, that is.'

But I was hardly listening. My eyes were riveted to that long swanlike throat and the locket that adorned it.

A heavy gold, rather ugly locket.

In its centre a crowned mermaid, her tail studded with blue stones, possibly sapphires. The mirror she held, pearl-rimmed.

And this was an exact copy of the mermaid stone I had seen in the herb garden.

'What do you think?' Emily asked.

'That locket!' I gasped.

'The Yesnaby family heirloom,' she said sadly. 'It's supposed to be about two hundred years old, handed down to the wife of the eldest son and heir. Not that I'd care to wear it,' she added hastily. 'I think it's rather ugly, don't you?'

'Where is it now?' I asked.

She shrugged. 'At the bottom of the peat-bog, I imagine. You see, Thora always wore it. She adored jewellery and Erland said she was wearing it the night she disappeared.' Emily sighed. 'I'm afraid it has gone for ever.'

'Gone for ever? No, Emily, it can't be. I'm sure I've seen it somewhere–'

'Indeed? And where would that be, Rose?'

It was Erland. I hadn't heard him come upstairs and he stood by the door watching us.

Emily gave him a startled glance and hastily thrust Thora's portrait back against the wall.

'I thought I'd find you here,' he said.

'You're just in time to take the cradle downstairs,' Emily said firmly.

'If you're sure.'

She smiled. 'Absolutely sure, dear.'

Erland bowed and turned to me. 'I interrupted something. You were saying, Rose?'

'Just that I don't think your Yesnaby jewel is lost for ever.' I waited but there was no delight or anticipation in Erland's expression as he said quietly:

'And what makes you think that?'

'I'm certain I've seen it – that locket. And definitely more recently than ten years ago.'

Erland studied me silently for a moment. 'Indeed, and where would that have been?' he asked carefully.

I shook my head, confused. 'That's the problem, I don't know. Somewhere in Edinburgh, I expect.'

'Indeed,' he repeated coldly.

I looked at him, bewildered. He had

known about the missing locket when we were in the garden and I asked him about the mermaid stone. Surely he might have mentioned the Yesnaby jewel then, but he hadn't said a word.

Emily was telling him: 'Rose doesn't think it disappeared. Do you think someone could have found it?'

Erland made an impatient gesture. 'For goodness sake, Emily, are you suggesting that Thora dropped it in her flight and someone – someone from here, from Hopescarth – stole it?'

It was Emily's turn to look bewildered. She shook her head and Erland said sharply:

'You realize that anyone finding it here would have returned it to the house? The only other explanation is that a thief carried it to Edinburgh where Rose – believes she saw it.'

My mind was racing ahead. The only thief or thieves could have been from the archaeology team.

They had both turned to me for some explanation.

'Do you think that is what happened, Rose?' Erland demanded.

Even as he spoke, I knew that the Yesnaby

jewel had never been stolen by thieves and taken to Edinburgh, nor had it disappeared into the peat-bog with Thora.

In a sudden rush of enlightenment, memory flooded back, complete in every detail.

I had seen it before. In an Edinburgh hotel room.

Last year. On one of my clients.

And the face in the portrait I had just seen triggered into memory–

For the woman who had sought my help and called herself Mrs Smith was beyond any shadow of doubt the same Thora Yesnaby who had disappeared from Hopescarth eleven years ago.

Chapter Sixteen

Edinburgh. October 1895.

Having just completed the second of my
discreet investigations into matters ladies
and gentlemen with reputations at stake
preferred not to put into the hands of the
Edinburgh City Police, I had received an
invitation to the opening of a smart new
hotel and restaurant on Princes Street
overlooking the Castle.

As it was unusual for respectable un-
married ladies to be invited without a
husband or a male relative, I realized that
this new establishment must be very
modern indeed or else, ever hopeful, that
there was a client in the offing.

The postman brought a note from Mr
Brightwell that the hotel carriage would
collect me and as I dressed with more
thought than I usually devote to my daily
toilette, I wondered if the invitation had
been suggested by Mrs Alice Bolton, one-
time school friend, now rich and influential.
We had met again on my return from

America and Alice was, I suspected, hell-bent on introducing Mrs Rose McQuinn, widow, into middle-class Edinburgh society.

I had just managed to tame my mop of yellow curls, with the frequent stabbing of many hairpins and unladylike curses, when the carriage arrived. Adorned in my one tea gown (inherited from my tall elegant sister-in-law Olivia and much shortened), I felt very vulnerable being whirled towards the hotel in solitary splendour.

Obviously I could have invited Jack Macmerry to escort me, but the presence of a detective sergeant of police partaking of a polite afternoon tea at what I expected to be a predominantly female occasion, would have been inappropriate enough to arouse one of Jack's famous scowls. Theatres and concerts were a different matter and he was not averse to having a widowed lady on his arm, but Brightwell's Hotel at four in the afternoon was a very different matter.

Gliding up the handsome staircase to the drawing room, I observed middle-class Edinburgh matrons were well to the fore and I was relieved to be greeted by Alice, who rushed over to introduce me to Mr Brightwell. He bowed over my hand his sleek macassar-oiled head, the high forehead already beaded with sweat which extended to his hands, doubtless the effect of a rather too tight waistcoat.

Whatever Mr Brightwell's discomfort he stayed by my side, his mission in life at that moment apparently to make me warmly welcome. I was impressed. His introductions included several titles and a lady whose name I gathered was Mrs Smith.

Urgently summoned by a harassed-looking waiter, Mr Brightwell, bowing profusely, left us and I was uncomfortably conscious of the elegant Mrs Smith's steady gaze. Although she was no longer young, she was slim, her appearance striking under the veiled hat. Her escort was a handsome man, considerably her junior, tall and sleek, black of beard and moustache. He bowed in my direction and, side-stepping an introduction, quickly excused himself.

As though his departure left Mrs Smith vulnerable, she glanced after him nervously then said with a grimace: 'Business matters, you know. Young men find these gatherings rather tedious.'

I could sympathize with that. However, we couldn't stand there gazing at each other so I broke the silence to ask politely: 'Do you live in Edinburgh?'

'No.'

I had anticipated that reply as her accent was one I had long been familiar with. 'You are not from these parts, are you?'

'I am merely a guest in the hotel,' she said coldly, her manner indicating that further information was not forthcoming.

Her origins were her own affair, after all, so I changed course and asked politely: 'Are you enjoying your stay?'

She looked across the room. The young man was hovering by the door. There was no doubt that she was relieved at his reappearance as she excused herself and neither of them appeared at the afternoon tea, when we were served dainty sandwiches and cakes.

I have been hungry too often in those pioneering years with Danny to be self-conscious about second helpings and as my solitary life in Solomon's Tower tends towards the spartan, I did full justice to each passing plate.

With little to contribute to conversations on topics dear to middle-class Edinburgh matrons, problems with servants and children's education, I was relieved when Alice drifted over.

'The carriage is at the door, Rose. Can we

set you down at Solomon's Tower?'

As we went towards reception for our cloaks, weaving towards us was Mr Brightwell. Bowing, he asked if I could spare him a moment.

I indicated Alice and he said quickly: 'We will provide a carriage for Mrs McQuinn.'

As Alice smiled assent he turned to me again. 'If you could oblige me – a matter of great concern.'

He looked flustered and rather put out. Saying I would be with him directly, I told Alice who whispered slyly: 'Of course I forgive you, Rose. You were on my guest list, but perhaps your fame has spread already. Judging by Mr Brightwell's demeanour, all is not well…'

Mr Brightwell was pacing the floor impatiently and I followed him into his office where no expense had been spared in the very modern décor. Pot plants, handsome gilt-framed oil paintings, plush sofa, all were there.

Inviting me to take a seat, with profuse apologies for having delayed my departure, he said: 'I trust I am not taking too great a liberty with your time. I already knew of your excellent reputation as an investigator and it was nothing short of providential when Mrs Bolton introduced us.

'I will come to the point, Mrs McQuinn. One of my guests has lost a valuable piece of jewellery. It happened this morning, while Madam was out of her room – in the bathroom.'

Mr Brightwell was inordinately proud of this modern addition to his hotel, stressed so glowingly in his opening announcement in *The Scotsman*.

'Madam returned to her bedroom to discover that the item left on her dressing table had disappeared.'

'Was her door locked during her absence?'

Mr Brightwell looked scandalized at such a suggestion. 'Mrs McQuinn, this is a respectable establishment,' he said huffily. 'Considering the high reputation of our hotel, Madam did not think that necessary. She was leaving her room to cross over the corridor, a few steps to the bathroom. Madam was absent for a few minutes only.'

His pause and delicate cough indicted that she was availing herself of the water closet.

'Were there any other guests on the same floor?'

'None who were present. There are four other bedrooms, two are unoccupied until Friday and the two couples occupying the remaining bedrooms were out of the building. You have my assurance on that, since their keys were deposited at the reception desk, and I saw them leave myself.'

'Is it possible that any of your guests had seen the lady wearing this valuable piece of jewellery and had been tempted?'

And I thought of the possibilities, that any of these absent guests might have re-entered the hotel, crept up the staircase and into the victim's bedroom.

Mr Brightwell's eyes rose heavenward, his furious exclamation indicated outrage at such a suggestion. 'Mrs McQuinn, I cannot imagine what you are suggesting, that any of our guests would behave in such a low fashion.'

'It does happen sometimes, even in the best hotels,' I reminded him gently.

'Not in my hotel,' he declared hotly. 'Our guests are quite impeccable, persons of privilege, even of the nobility. You have my assurance on that. Besides the lower classes could not afford to stay here,' he added with an air of satisfaction.

But having made his point he simmered down. 'As for Madam, newly arrived, she was in the dining room for luncheon, her key handed into reception at that time.

There were few other diners so we may safely dismiss the idea that Madam's necklace might have given cause for envy and temptation,' he added firmly.

It was my turn. 'If this is a valuable piece, Mr Brightwell, surely this is a matter for the police.'

'It is indeed. The piece in question, a locket I am told, is a family heirloom. But there is a complication, and that is why I need your service as an investigator, Mrs McQuinn.'

He paused and then said guardedly: 'Madam has personal reasons for discretion.'

'An assignation?' I asked delicately, remembering the young man I had seen with her who was so eager to avoid an introduction. 'A gentleman who is not her husband, perhaps?'

Mr Brightwell wheezed a sigh. 'Exactly.' And with a despairing gesture. 'You understand the situation.'

I did indeed. It formed the basis of many of my cases.

'Did the lady unpack her valise on her arrival?'

'Of course not. When ladies are not accompanied by their own personal maid, this is the duty of the hotel chambermaid.'

A little light was beginning to dawn and I said: 'I think at this stage, it would save time if I could see the lady's room and speak with her personally.'

He smiled at last, relieved. 'I will be indebted to you if you would do so, Mrs McQuinn, for this incident could not have come at a worse time for my hotel's reputation.'

I followed him upstairs and as we halted at Room 2, he whispered: 'To have this made public, to have it in the newspapers, would mean ruin. You have already met Madam – I introduced you–'

Before he could say more the door opened.

The lady who stood there was Mrs Smith with whom I had recently shared a somewhat vague social conversation. The young man was not in evidence.

Mrs Smith invited me to be seated, her gesture to Mr Brightwell indicating that his presence was no longer enquired. Bowing, he withdrew and I produced my card.

Mrs Smith read it carefully. 'Thank you for seeing me, Mrs McQuinn. I am in a desperate situation. This piece of jewellery, a locket, is a family heirloom and I am quite distraught.'

She shook her head. 'Its theft adds to the state of crisis in my life at present. I left my husband some years ago – the details need not concern you, but let us say that I took the locket as a matter of insurance, in case of financial need.'

She paused, her lips tightened. 'I allowed my husband to believe that I was dead, that I had taken my own life. Alas, that was a grievous mistake. In fact,' she added bitterly, 'our whole life together had been a mistake, a marriage of convenience. We were not suited to one another and he was in love with a younger woman and wished to marry her.'

She regarded me intently, hesitated and then went on: 'I now find that I need money desperately. I cannot sell the locket because it might be recognized and as I took a family heirloom without my husband's permission, I could be prosecuted for theft.'

'A moment,' I said. 'As his wife, surely the locket belongs to you?'

She shook her head. 'Only as long as I am his wife. It is passed down through the generations.' Her eyes narrowed as she continued: 'So I had decided on a plan, the reason why I am in Edinburgh at the moment. I am en route north to where my husband lives–'

Listening to her, I heard again that familiar accent.

'Are you from Orkney, by any chance?' I asked.

She froze. 'Where I am from need not concern you, Mrs McQuinn. Now may I continue? I intend reappearing, alive and well and asking for a divorce and the payment of certain debts I have acquired, so that he can make his own bigamous marriage legal. In return for the locket. A bargain, don't you think, especially as it is not only priceless and of sentimental value to the family, but of historic importance.'

As she judged my reaction to this piece of information, she added: 'We can be sure his new wife would not wish me to put in an embarrassing and very public reappearance after ten years, especially as this would make any heirs they might have had illegitimate.'

I asked the obvious question: 'There were no children by your own marriage?'

'None,' she said. 'I do not care for children, particularly dynastic ones – that it is a wife's duty to provide.'

At closer quarters without the veiled bonnet, her eyes were hard, her lips thin, and it was at that moment I decided I did not like Mrs Smith. But then I do not have to like my clients, I thought as she added anxiously: 'Is there any way you can possibly recover the pendant for me? It is only hours since it disappeared so it cannot have travelled very far.'

Perhaps I was not concealing my feelings of distaste for this assignment too well, for she leaned forward impulsively, touched my arm and said: 'Please, Mrs McQuinn – I will pay you a great deal of money for the locket's return. My whole future depends on it. You see, I have also met someone else...'

I told myself that my clients' morals are not my concern otherwise I would be out of business. I was perfectly aware of the less agreeable facts I might have to face when I became a lady investigator, discretion guaranteed.

'It was a great stroke of fortune that you were a guest here this afternoon. I have Mr Brightwell's assurance that you are quite remarkable,' she said, hoping flattery would work.

And it did. That promised 'great deal of money' was also irresistible.

'Very well, Mrs Smith. I will do what I can. When do you leave Edinburgh?'

'Tomorrow – as soon as I have the locket in my possession. Otherwise my whole plan – my whole future must fall apart.'

'Will you tell me exactly the state of the room when, as I understand it, you left it briefly to go to the bathroom.'

She frowned. 'The chambermaid had unpacked my valise and hung my clothes in the wardrobe. The locket had caught in my hair as I was removing my dress and I asked for her assistance. I then took it off and placed it beside my jewel box on the dressing table.'

'Was the maid still in the room when you left it?'

'No. She said she had to fetch extra towels from the linen cupboard. I saw her there on my way to the bathroom.'

As I made notes, Mrs Smith watched me intently. 'Is there anything else you wish to know? I have told you everything as I remember it.'

'Thank you, Mrs Smith. You have been very helpful. Now I wonder if you could do me a rough sketch of the locket?'

She sighed. 'I'm not very good at drawing but I'll do the best I can. It is gold, you know. On a chain.'

'I just need some idea, size, design, jewels and so forth.'

She produced paper and pencil and while she drew I had a quick look round the room.

But I had already solved the case. She had given me enough information to guess the thief's identity and it was unlikely that the locket was hidden anywhere in the room. Time was of the essence for I suspected it had already left the hotel.

Wishing all cases were this easy, I promised Mrs Smith that I would do my best to recover the heirloom with all possible speed. She was grateful and, taking out her purse, handed me ten guineas. 'There is another ten for you if you can recover the locket.'

I accepted gratefully and hurried downstairs where Mr Brightwell was waiting in reception, delighted and relieved that I was willing to make a desperate bid to save his hotel's precious reputation.

'I should like to speak to the chambermaid who was on duty when Mrs Smith arrived, and who helped her unpack her valise.'

Mr Brightwell gave me a despairing look and shook his head. 'On that matter, I have made some progress while you were talking to Madam. I understand from the housekeeper that Maeve, one of the Irish maids I took on – with excellent references, I assure you – attended to Room 2. The girl said that she must return to Ireland straight away and tried to borrow money for her fare from her future wages. It seemed that her mother was dying, or so she said.'

He paused and looked at me significantly. 'I understand that the girl hasn't been seen since and never returned to her other duties–'

'You are presuming that she isn't likely to return?'

'I think that is rather obvious, Mrs McQuinn, especially as Mrs Rowe informs me that the maids' bedroom has been cleared of her possessions.'

I guessed those possessions would be few and this was confirmed as I followed the housekeeper up to the dreary attic room where the less fortunate staff of the opulent hotel had their quarters.

I had already concluded that if the Irish maid needed money urgently, the most likely place for a knowledgeable Edinburgh domestic to turn stolen jewellery into cash was at a local pawnbroker.

The first that came to mind was one Jack Macmerry had pointed out in the High Street. A fence for stolen goods, no questions asked, he was under surveillance by the police – and Jack.

There was no time to lose. As I was leaving the hotel, I had another glimpse of Mrs Smith's young lover who was entering and held the door open for me. Acknowledging me with a brief bow, he had tactfully made himself scarce during my talk with his mistress.

I wondered if he could be involved and then thinking this was highly unlikely I made my way to old Jacob's shop.

He greeted me politely but guardedly when I showed him Mrs Smith's sketch of the missing locket. Handing him my card, I knew before I asked: 'Have you seen such a piece' that he had it in his possession.

The next move was on his part. If he knew it was stolen property, valuable and unique, then he would keep it well hidden until an opportunity arose to sell it to some foreign traveller who would take it far from Edinburgh.

'Have you money to pay for such a piece, an unredeemed pledge, madam?' he asked, smiling.

I explained that the locket had been stolen and the lady who owned it would give twice as much as he had paid the person who had pawned it.

He was immediately defensive. 'The young lady said it belonged in her family and she needed the money for her fare to return home. She sounded genuine enough. She was very distressed and I had not the

187

least idea that she had come by the piece by dishonest means. I do not want to get into trouble with the police–'

It was a standard reply and he went on: 'I gave her five guineas for it,' he said, opening the drawer and producing the locket.

Mrs Smith's drawing had not done it justice. It was a large oval, heavier and less attractive than I had imagined.

I would never have worn it. The gold casing embossed with a crowned mermaid and mirror, outlined in coloured stones and pearls, did little to enhance what I considered an ugly piece of jewellery.

'It is as well the young person brought it to an honest dealer – I doubt she knew its real value,' he added ruefully.

Not mine to reason why, thank goodness. I put the locket in my pocket and returned to the hotel.

Mr Brightwell was overcome with relief and gratitude but his emotions were nothing compared to those of Mrs Smith, who handed me a further ten guineas for my trouble.

I went back to Solomon's Tower very happy indeed, and thrust my finer feelings aside, totally unrepentant at having been a party to Mrs Smith's blackmailing intentions regarding the locket. I told myself her husband was most probably a very unpleasant man and I was on the side of wives who often have very raw deals with brutal husbands especially where property is concerned.

In addition I was glad that the young chambermaid would not be prosecuted and that she was safely in Ireland with her family again.

Naturally I did not tell Jack any of this. I do not tell him everything, and besides, to have betrayed Mrs Smith's confidences would have been outwith my role as a discreet investigator.

Next day, my conscience was cleared by a note from Mr Brightwell saying that the postman had brought a letter containing the pawn ticket. To be forwarded to Mrs Smith to recover her locket.

'As this is no longer required and Mrs Smith has left the hotel, I have destroyed it,' wrote Mr Brightwell.

The case was closed.

Chapter Seventeen

Back in my bedroom, staring out over the sea, I considered the nightmare situation I had found myself in.

Thora Yesnaby could not have lain in the peat-bog for ten years, to be conveniently discovered last year.

Last year, calling herself Mrs Smith, she had been very much alive with a young lover in an Edinburgh hotel. A prospective client...

Thora had made her way back to Orkney with the Yesnaby locket, which I had recovered for her from the Edinburgh pawnbroker. I was aware that she was to use it to blackmail–

Yes, that was the word – to blackmail her husband Erland into divorcing her and paying dearly for the privilege, thus avoiding the scandal of bigamy and leaving him free to legally marry my sister Emily.

There was only one terrible conclusion.

Her unexpected arrival in Hopescarth had upset someone so much that she had been murdered–

Murdered. And her body disposed of in the peat-bog to be discovered by the archaeology team.

This had none of the marks of a crime of passion, of sudden anger and despair resulting in violence. This crime had all the marks of premeditation and conspiracy for it could not have been carried out efficiently by one person alone.

Emily had not noticed my confusion as we left the attics and was chattering happily. On the landing, excusing myself, I went into the bedroom, closed the door and leaned weakly against it.

Thora Yesnaby had been murdered. And the chief suspect even at this distance had to be the one with most to gain by her death.

Her husband Erland – my brother-in-law.

Or – the dread whisper of logic – my sister Emily.

And the truth could not be avoided.

Thora had been murdered by either of them. Or both.

I could not see the gentle, rather vague Emily assisting Erland to kill Thora and deposit her body in the peat-bog. But was I being completely honest without consulting the motives?

Emily had been pregnant again with the

baby they both longed for. Was she to allow Thora to ruin their lives by coming back from the dead? To reclaim her rights of inheritance, to break Erland's heart by declaring their marriage bigamous and the coming child illegitimate.

What if Thora's inconvenient arrival had caused Emily to miscarry and sent Erland into a murderous rage? There were other men, seemingly mild-mannered, who had been driven to acts of violence *in extremis.* Had Emily been present, a mute observer of Thora's murder?

Before any condemnation I had to put on their shoes, metaphorically speaking, and walk around in them, share that time of nightmare.

And a little honest soul-searching brought me directly to Danny McQuinn. I could make a comparison here, certain that Emily loved Erland as much as I loved Danny, and had I been called upon to do so, I might well have sacrificed my immortal soul and committed murder to save him.

So, having set aside the moral issues, what did I do next?

The obvious, most comfortable answer was to ignore it, to forget the whole thing, pretend I had not recognized the mermaid pendant in the painting. Forget the Edinburgh incident and pretend that 'Mrs Smith' was merely Thora's double. Leave it at that, continue my holiday, happy and carefree.

And I knew that I could not do so.

Whatever the outcome of this case, the most devilish and personally distressing ever likely to come my way, I had to know the answer. I had to know the truth. Even, I told myself, for my own satisfaction if it was one that must ever remain a secret between me and my conscience, never to be revealed without destroying those I loved most.

One thing I was well aware of. The vagueness of Emily's letters that had so annoyed me since I returned to Edinburgh. Now I could forgive her all. Considering the load of anguish and perhaps even guilt she carried about Thora's body newly discovered near the gates of Yesnaby House, the needs of her sister safe in Edinburgh paled into insignificance and could never have rated high on her list of priorities.

I looked out of the window, conscious that Orkney and its sentimental past had changed for ever. Nostalgia for this longed-for holiday had evaporated like morning mist over the sea. My horizon was now occupied by the grim purpose ahead of me. One I must conceal at all costs from Emily, especially in her present delicate condition.

But where to begin?

With the grim discovery of Thora's body shortly after she left Edinburgh. Then an interview with the doctor who had so cleverly diagnosed that death had actually taken place ten years ago, her body amazingly preserved by the peat-bog.

I would be very interested to meet that gentleman. Could it have been incompetence relating to death certificates or devotion and excessive loyalty as a family doctor which had led him to keep silent about his suspicions?

As for the local policeman, even if he had known anything about the science of preserved bodies in peat-bogs, which is doubtful, he would have hesitated to question the word of the higher echelons of Hopescarth society, namely the doctor and the local laird.

I went downstairs, my legs shaking. I was going for a walk, I said, the effort of producing a normal smile a considerable strain on my facial muscles.

They looked up at me, Emily and Gran, all as normal as I had pictured them in so many happy memories of childhood and girlhood days.

194

Now I feared I had lost them for ever. The grim reality of what I was about to discover surely meant that I would never again regard my dear ones in this tranquil innocent light.

But my sense of horror was well disguised. They didn't notice what I feared was written all over my face.

They smiled. 'Be back before dark, lass,' said Gran. 'And if you're going on that thing' (meaning the bicycle) 'be careful.'

'Just some fresh air this time, Gran.' I added a convincing deep breath, managed another smile.

My first inquiry would be at the dig.

Once outside I hurried down the drive anxiously watching as it came in sight, in case Craig and his team had finished for the day.

Craig was there alone, packing up his tools.

I was just in time, he said, the others had already left. He seemed surprised and, I thought, pleased by this unexpected visit. Puzzled too perhaps when, without my usual care, or any pretence at polite chatter, I launched on to the subject of the peat-bog woman, hinting that it had been discussed at a teatime conversation I had just left.

'It is so intriguing. Has it been written up anywhere?'

Craig turned the key on the last of the day's specimens in a wooden box, and regarded me quizzically, so intently that I wondered if he could read my thoughts.

'The local newspapers made quite a thing about it. It even got a mention in *The Times*. I expect *The Scotsman* took it up as well.'

That was true. It was certainly unique enough to receive a mention in the Scottish newspapers while the other nationals would follow suit.

But I hadn't noticed it because I relied on receiving copies from Jack and didn't always have time to read them. Most likely I was on a case at the time or mention of Orkney surely would have stirred my interest. However I doubted if I would have made the connection with Mrs Smith and the mermaid locket.

Craig went on: '*The Orcadian* will have it in their files. Worth a visit to their offices next time you're in Kirkwall, if you're still interested.'

I shrugged, trying to indicate that it wasn't really important. 'You must have found it a rather nasty experience. Digging for old bones and finding something only ten years old.'

He nodded. 'The peat-bog is the very

reason we suspect that the Maid's grave may have been hereabouts. That and the coins. That's exactly why we don't give up, why we keep on digging so persistently, year after year. We're certain there is something here – and in time, we will find it.'

'You think a body might have survived for six hundred years?'

He shrugged. 'Possibly.'

There was a pause and I said: 'You must have been very disappointed at finding the late Mrs Yesnaby.'

Craig shrugged. 'I wasn't here, alas, at the time. Just my luck, I'm afraid. A momentous discovery and I was away in Edinburgh at an antiquarian society giving a paper when Frank and the lads found it.'

I was disappointed. I had hoped for some valuable first-hand information from Craig. I said: 'How did they react to the discovery? It must have been something of a surprise.'

'Shock is the more appropriate word. As you can imagine, they all thought when a hand suddenly appeared from the ground–'

'Where exactly?'

He smiled, obviously thinking I had a very morbid turn of mind. 'Over there, just below the bridge. Come and I'll show you, if you like.'

I followed him along the well-worn path above what had been the moat.

'The exact spot, as Frank told me. Down there, a somewhat muddied but very well-preserved hand appeared above the surface.'

He paused dramatically. 'As you might imagine, panic all round. They thought that they had discovered a murder victim. The local constable was summoned. The local doctor sent for...'

At last, that was what I needed to know where to begin my inquiries.

Chapter Eighteen

'There was quite a stir in the village, I can tell you. Nothing as dramatic as that had ever happened in living memory. In everyone's mind was the same thought, was there a murderer abroad in Hopescarth? Or was the victim from somewhere else, planted here?'

He paused and said: 'Poor old Frank was shattered. It was worst of all for him. You see, he recognized the body. He knew Thora well. The lady of the manor had been very kind to him especially after Lily stopped coming to the dig each summer.'

'Lily?'

'Mrs Breck.' He smiled. 'Frank's wife.'

I shook my head. I'd never have guessed Frank was married. To me he seemed the crusty old bachelor.

'What happened?'

Craig shrugged. 'The usual story. Lily was a city girl.' He smiled. 'From Edinburgh, as a matter of fact. He'd met her when she came on holiday to Orkney. Anyway, she was swept off her feet. Thought archaeology digs were so romantic. They got married and she used to spend every summer here at the dig.'

'No children?'

Craig shook his head. 'No, they never had children. Well, the year Thora Yesnaby disappeared it was a particularly bad summer. No doubt Mrs Breck was keen to see the back of the dig, which had been even less productive than usual. She ran a small lodging house in Edinburgh. When they packed up as usual, Frank told the rest of the team that his wife wouldn't be coming back to Hopescarth in future.'

I looked at him quickly, but his expression was inscrutable.

'You think there was more to it – someone else, perhaps?'

He nodded. 'All this happened before I came to Hopescarth but from Frank's rare hints, I suspected that Lily had someone else lined up in Edinburgh. No one could blame her. Frank was always more dedicated than the rest of the team. Even when she was here, I suspect he spent every minute at the dig. His family were from Orkney and Meg – our landlady – who likes a gossip once hinted that he fancied the lady of the manor.'

Craig sighed, remembering. 'No wonder he was so upset when he dug her out of the peat-bog. Not a very pleasant thing for the lord of the manor, either,' he added ruefully. 'His late wife turning up like that, a bit of a shock when he thought he'd already buried her ten years earlier. As for your sister, poor lass, it must have been dreadful. Especially as she was...'

Suddenly realizing you didn't say 'pregnant' to a lady, I put the word in for him.

'I expect you know that she lost the baby. My doctorate doesn't cover medicine but the shock maybe had something to do with it.'

So I had guessed right. I felt suddenly chilled as I asked: 'Did they get the Fiscal on to it?'

'I expect so.' Craig looked vague. 'I was away when it happened and then I went on a lecturing tour. So by the time I came back it was old news. The sensation was over and Hopescarth could breathe again. They weren't looking for a killer in their midst after all.'

He looked at me. 'In our business, as I've told you, we know that peat can have extraordinary preserving qualities and the doctor verified that, when he said it was most likely she had lain there since the very night she disappeared.

'I gather Erland remembered that it had been a wild night, stormy, when she left the house. She must have stumbled and fallen, I suppose.'

He paused, biting his lip, hesitating as if he was unwilling to continue. 'I'm not sure how much you know about the lady but, again from Meg, I understand that she was – well, a little unbalanced to put it mildly. Overfond of the whisky too. Her behaviour could be completely irrational. Not an easy person to live with,' he added sadly.

'No one had the slightest notion about where she went after she ran out of the house that night. One theory was that she took Frank's fishing boat, which he kept in a shed down at the harbour and which went missing. A few days after Thora disappeared, it was washed up in one of our roarsts – these terrible seas produced by the tide-races and the unevenness of the rock beneath them. It was almost unrecognisable, reduced to matchwood, and the same thought was in everyone's head that Thora might have sailed off that night with some insane notion of heading across to the

202

mainland, especially when the woman's torso was washed ashore.'

He grimaced. 'There's a place called the Troll's Cave, on the cliff edge, where it funnels up at high tide. I must take you there sometime. It's spectacular – and quite lethal if you're in the vicinity. Anyway, Erland identified the body but in the circumstances I suppose a bereaved husband can be forgiven at not looking too closely at the remains of a woman who has been in the roarsts for a few weeks.'

I kept thinking of that unknown woman. Who was she? Where had she come from so conveniently to be identified as Thora?

Doubtless the police wouldn't be too eager to keep the body around either. I wondered were there other cases of missing persons at that time. If not, then they would have been only too relieved to close the case on the missing Mrs Yesnaby.

'Didn't it seem rather odd – Thora taking a boat out on a wild night in the first place? Rather surprising?'

'No one who knew her was surprised. She was an odd person, totally unpredictable. A creature of impulse and every time she had a row with Frank, which was often – he told Meg – she'd come down and sulk at the dig, and demand that he took her over to the mainland.

'Born and bred here, Frank was the only good sailor in the team. Meg said sometimes Thora would persuade him take her out. Lily didn't like that much either, especially as she was violently ill crossing over on the steamer each year.'

'Have you any theories about what really happened?' I asked. 'Obviously she didn't take Frank's boat, so who did?'

'There were rumours that it had been cut adrift deliberately by one of the local lads whose family had a long-standing feud with the Brecks. They weren't popular and local fisherfolk thought Frank had got above himself, being friendly with the laird's wife. However, Frank said Thora was gone and to let it drop. It didn't matter.'

'So it's anyone's guess what really happened that night?'

Craig sighed. 'Eleven years is a long time. The general idea was that in her highly emotional state – she had been drinking heavily – she had taken the short cut down to the shore, missed her footing, fallen face downwards into the bog and smothered.'

He was silent for a moment. 'And, well, that was that. A dreadful way to go,' he added grimly.

Dreadful indeed, I thought, and most unlikely. Not to say downright unbelievable, especially as the place Craig had pointed out to me was near the bridge.

I'd have favoured Frank's missing boat rather than the story that Thora alias Mrs Smith, strong and healthy when I last saw her in Edinburgh, vengeful and determined to destroy Erland – and Emily – had come to Hopescarth and, knowing the perilous terrain surrounding Yesnaby House, had succumbed to such a convenient accident. Unless she was very, very drunk and incapable.

And what had become of her lover from Brightwell's Hotel? That bothered me. Hadn't anyone at Hopescarth been aware of him? Had he come back with her to Orkney? If so, why had he disappeared into thin air? More likely, I thought grimly, as a witness to Thora's murder, he had been killed and his corpse disposed of far from the peat-bog.

And if he had not accompanied her, but was aware of her destination, had he not read the newspapers and guessed that Mrs Smith was Thora Yesnaby, 'dead these past ten years' according to the official reports?

And that being so, would he not have confided his suspicions to the police, who would then have set an inquiry under way?

'You're very interested, Rose.' Craig jolted me back to the present. 'Is this just the detective in your blood coming out?' he added with a laugh. 'I hear that your father is the famous Inspector Faro Orkney is so proud of.'

I hadn't told him that I was a professional investigator. I thought it would put him off me. It might have that effect on a lot of men, so I side-stepped and said: 'Mysteries always intrigue me.'

'Even on holiday?' he laughed. 'You should give them a rest,' he advised gently.

I ignored that. 'Were any of the present team here when the discovery was made?'

Craig shook his head. 'Not the two young ones. They're new. Frank was in charge. He was the only senior while I was away, we mostly take on students in the summer. Often foreign students.'

He paused, thinking. 'We had two lads from Germany that summer.'

I could hardly demand their addresses, attempt to track them down at this stage.

He looked at me. 'You could ask Frank tomorrow, see if he can tell you more about it, but I don't think he'll have anything new to report that wasn't in the papers.' Another pause. 'I should warn you, he doesn't like to be reminded, doesn't like talking about Thora Yesnaby.'

The church clock struck through the silence, a pleasant peaceful sound that carried a fair distance on still evenings.

His manner suddenly urgent, Craig said: 'You must excuse me, Rose. I have to go – and clean up. I'm meeting someone at seven,' he added rather self-consciously. 'I'll see you tomorrow.'

As he indicated his motor car, accommodated in a disused barn at Sibella's croft, I wondered whether he was meeting the innkeeper's wife who had shown such a proprietorial interest in him.

I was left with a strange feeling that Craig Denmore was relieved that he had been absent when Thora's body was discovered.

Chapter Nineteen

Somehow I got through that evening, so pleasantly domestic, observing Emily and Gran busy with their respective knitting projects, the baby shawl and Gran's socks for Erland.

And in the Orkney chair, Sibella sitting very upright, saying little but absorbing all that was going on. Often I would find her eyes on me, watching me narrowly, which increased my feeling of guilt that she was reading my mind.

Erland had supper with us. Most evenings he departed to his study, but tonight was different. We were to be honoured with his company – at least the suggestion was that I was to be honoured.

The four of us were to play cards.

I looked at Sibella who shrugged. 'I only read the cards, I don't play games.' She stretched out a hand. 'If you wish Rose, I may tell your fortune.'

I pretended to make light of her offer, although I would have welcomed some expert knowledge of what my future held. But not this night. This night I was afraid. I had too many family secrets weighing heavily upon my mind.

We had a few hands of whist, Emily and I playing against Erland and Gran. Erland won.

'As usual,' whispered Emily. 'He always wins.' And turning to me: 'But you were always so good at cards. I thought you'd be a match for Erland.'

At this hint of a reproach from my partner for lack of concentration, I apologized.

'I'm a little tired,' I said, 'or just out of practice.'

'Do you want to continue?' Erland asked politely.

My mind was certainly not on the cards, but on a much deadlier game whose outcome I could not bear to contemplate, but realizing Erland had arranged all this as a special treat for me, I did not want to disappoint Gran and Emily, who both loved card games.

And so the game continued. As I watched the three players getting so excited and eagerly counting their tricks, I did my best but frequently forgot what was trumps, threw away my best cards, making more serious mistakes and provoking Emily's exasperation at my incompetence.

Nor were my powers of concentration helped by awareness of Sibella's steady gaze on me. What was she thinking? Was she aware of my misery? I avoided contact with those strange round eyes that I felt could drag out my soul.

My whole concern in all the world at that moment was to prove that my own sister had no knowledge of Thora's arrival in Hopescarth last year and that she had not been an accessory to her murder. Such was my desperation that I would be perfectly willing to commit perjury. Especially when I remembered that the outcome of the grim discovery had brought about a miscarriage and destroyed the child that Emily and Erland longed for.

Erland had produced a bottle of wine to add a note of celebration to his sister-in-law's visit.

I had a feeling that Erland liked me. He was delighted to find that we had much in common. I had warmed to him in that tour of the garden only yesterday. Now he was going out of his way to reward a welcome guest who was, in fact, considering him as chief suspect in his first wife's murder.

At last the evening was over, the cards put away and recriminations laid aside. Emily continued to gaze across at me, asking anxiously was I feeling all right.

Trust Emily, I thought grimly. And when I said more sharply than was necessary: 'Of course, why do you ask? I told you I'm just a little tired, that's all', she smiled.

'You were so good at winning. Don't you remember, Gran always said: "Lucky at cards, unlucky in love."'

I laughed. That was in the days when I was desperately in love with Danny, sure he'd marry someone else before I grew up. But time and fate had proved me wrong.

Sibella left her chair unaided, though rising with the deliberate care and stiffness of age. Declining Erland's offer to see her home, she pointed at me, smiling:

'I should like Rose to come with me. There's still enough light and she hasn't seen where I live yet.'

Goodnight hugs and kisses followed and Sibella was solemnly presented with a large brown paper bag, which according to Gran's murmurings held the day's left-overs. I wondered how Sibella could possibly tackle them as we set off down the drive, and she tucked her arm in mine.

'There now, dear. We'll walk quicker like this. Don't let me lean too heavily on you.'

Her arm was thin, weightless. And cold too.

It was just a step across the stone bridge near the spot where Thora's body had emerged from the peat-bog. I knew I would never look at it again without shuddering.

A short distance past the dig lay the little croft I could see from my bedroom window.

When she opened the door, I was taken aback. It was all so ordinary, neat and tidy, one large room with a bed, a table and two comfortable chairs before a peat fire.

At my side Sibella chuckled. 'Not quite what you expected, is it, Rose?'

Remembering Emily's version, I was embarrassed. Wagging a finger at me, she said: 'What have they told you about me? That no one ever knew what Sibella might conjure up or if the mysterious stranger passing by and seeking shelter might reveal cloven hooves and a tail? You expected a house from "Hansel and Gretel" and you find just a dull ordinary croft like you'd find anywhere on the island. There is one difference though.' She pointed. 'Over there.'

And pulling aside a curtain, she revealed a table and a deep shelf full of bottles of assorted colours. In the central position, very important-looking, was a large black leather book. She took it down. It had a brass lock. 'What do you think this is, Rose?'

'A book of spells?'

'Not quite.'

'The Book of the Black Arts?' I whispered and she laughed.

'That's what folk believe, and it ensures that I never need to lock my door. Actually I lost the key years ago.'

And touching the book she smiled. 'This contains nothing more sinister than some of my best herbal cures and recipes. I had it with me when your grandmother brought me up to Hopescarth, when I was feeling poorly. That was before Emily and Erland got married. When Emily came as companion to Thora.'

She turned those luminous eyes upon me as if expecting a reaction at the mention of Thora. There was none and she smiled.

'Your Gran did well out of that marriage. He persuaded Emily that he needed a housekeeper as well. And Mary Faro was nothing loath to leave Kirkwall. She liked the idea of living in the grand big house.'

She laughed. 'Anyway, when I first came to live with them, I didn't have the croft and

I'd swear Erland never knew a moment's peace while I had what he thought was the Book of the Black Arts under his roof. Here, hold it for a moment.'

I took it from her carefully. It felt very heavy and very old.

'No, my dear. This is not the real manual of magic printed in white characters on black pages, which gave its owner unlimited power. However, as with all the Devil's gifts there was a snag. The owner of the book, dying, could be carried straight to hell. Only for a smaller coin than was paid for the book could it be resold and anyone young and inexperienced could be forgiven for thinking the peedie black man at Kirkwall Fair was giving them a great bargain.

'Rumour had it that once wicked Earl Robert eagerly accepted it as a gift, ignoring its opening page: "Cursed is he that peruseth me." I often wonder if he realized the load of destruction he had in his possession, since a witch of that time had placed him under St Ringan's curse, used only by those who had suffered intolerable wrongs without other means of punishing their oppressors, a curse richly deserved by the earl and his sons.'

'I seem to remember being told at school

that it cursed an entire family with sterility.'

I didn't add my own fears for the Scarths and Faros, their bad luck with child-bearing, miscarriages and infant deaths. And the fact that neither female Scarths nor Faros seemed capable of producing vast broods of children.

Sibella had opened the book and put it on the table. 'There are some very interesting cures here, for every mortal illness. The ones for curing bleeding noses with pig dung are still in great demand and you'll find farmers still using cow dung poultices for bruised limbs.'

Smiling she turned the page, to more ancient writing. 'Here's one: sweetened urine for jaundice, and milk in which sheep droppings have been boiled for smallpox. I've tried some of those myself although I draw the line at this one, mice roasted for whooping cough and snails dissolved in vinegar for rickets.'

She closed the book with a shudder. 'Many are just plain common sense, or what would be better referred to as "uncommon sense". But there are other cures I prefer not to dwell upon.'

I regarded her thoughtfully. 'How good are your spells? Are you still in business?'

'I'm getting rather old for the staying power that is needed these days. A lot of concentration, you know, and I soon get tired. But in my time, I've done my share of exorcizing toothaches – I used to be very good at that. And I could cure a child's ringworm and get rid of warts by placing special stones in a bag and throwing them into the sea. There isn't much scrofula these days but the trick was to place white money – silver, that is – upon the sore and for a bad eye, a piece of gold,' and she smiled wistfully as if living again those lost days of the seal woman's power.

'Doonfa'-sickness, as they call epilepsy here, is still with us. Parents believed that if I pared the poor bairn's nails and cut off a lock of hair during one of the fits, buried both on the spot where he or she had fallen, the epilepsy would vanish.'

She sighed. 'Miracles they said I could work, but miracles are the work of the good Lord. A lot of my success was making folk have faith in themselves and faith that their prayers would be answered too.'

Pausing to look out of the window, she said: 'You'd better be going back to the house, Rose. I promised you'd get home safe in daylight, but there's one thing more I'd like to show you,' and she led the way into the garden to a large wooden shed next to the barn where Craig kept his motor car.

There wasn't a sound coming from it but as soon as she opened the door, all hell broke loose inside.

And I discovered that Sibella's compassion for the island's population extended to birds and animals, none of whom feared her approach for she talked to them constantly.

Ignoring my presence, those who were able fluttered or jumped down from straw-lined ledges and came right up to her feet. There they sat staring up at her trustingly, waiting patiently for titbits. Now I understood the reason for the left-overs from Gran's table.

Every inch of space in the hut's dim interior was occupied by cage or pen, row upon row, shelf upon shelf, where sick birds and an assortment of wild creatures had a health-giving but raucous convalescence. Packed full of herbs and medicines and ointments as their condition demanded, here many that would have found their way into the local cooking pots remained alive, nurtured and cherished by Sibella until the day they either expired or made noisy pleas to resume their lives back in the wild.

She led me to the edge of the tiny garden

which looked down on the shore with its rocks gleaming black in the gathering twilight.

'Down there,' she pointed. 'That's where I came from, Rose. See, by that big rock. That's where Hakon carried me ashore from the sea and that's where he'll be waiting for me – when I'm ready to go.' She turned and smiled at me. 'Some days, you know, I feel he is very near. Especially now. I feel his love like a cloud around me.'

She didn't have far to stretch to put her arms around me and gently kiss my cheek. Her lips were cold, papery, but the heart was warm as she said: 'I'm glad I had the chance to meet you before I leave Hopescarth.'

'I'm glad too, Sibella,' I said, thinking, If only I could confide my fears in you, you might provide all the answers.

But such terrible knowledge was not for Sibella and my eyes suddenly brimmed over as, waving goodnight, I made my way back to the house and the family who waited for me.

And the terrors that swirled like demons in the growing dusk.

Chapter Twenty

I wasn't sorry to find the kitchen deserted. Emily, Erland and Gran had retired. That was the general rule in Hopescarth. 'Down with the sun and up with the larks.'

Thankfully I went upstairs to my room, lit the lamp and, preparing for bed, I tried to reorganize my thoughts and make some sort of a plan.

Even as I did so, something deep inside said: Why not forget all this, forget that you met Thora alias Mrs Smith in Edinburgh. Pretend it was just someone like her and that mermaid lockets are a popular form of Scottish jewellery, like the luckenbooth and thistle.

I knew that would have been the sensible thing, but as Jack Macmerry never tired of commenting, taking the easy way had never been one of my characteristics. If there was a mystery to solve, I had to go into it headlong, regardless of the consequences or the destruction that might lie ahead.

Of course, Jack was right. I began my list.

The first person to see was Frank who had been on the site when the body was found.

The second was obviously the doctor who had so incorrectly stated the date of Thora's death.

Third, the local policeman. I would have to handle that with skill, a tone of casual curiosity, on the lines of: an interesting thing to happen, it must have been an exciting time for you, etc., etc.

Would he suspect that I had any ulterior motive for my inquiries?

At ten o'clock, there was a tap on my bedroom door and guiltily I thrust my notes out of sight.

The door opened and there was Emily.

'I saw the light on. Thought I'd just look in and say goodnight.'

That was an excuse. I knew my strange behaviour had been worrying her as she added: 'You aren't even in bed yet. You were so tired downstairs. I thought you'd be asleep before your head hit the pillow.'

I smiled. 'That was a long time ago, Emmy.'

Emily sat down on the bed. 'Well, and what did you think of Sibella's wee croft?' she giggled.

'Smaller than I imagined.'

'And less tidy. Gran is forbidden to step over the threshold. On her last foray with mop and bucket she moved some of Sibella's precious bottles. Sibella was furious, said keeping her croft clean was her business and no one else's.'

Emily sighed. 'Poor Gran. They are often at loggerheads and I seem to be piggy-in-the-middle. Gran was put out by Sibella's animal sanctuary too, as you might imagine. However, we got around that as it appeals to her sense of waste not, want not where the left-overs and the vegetable peelings are concerned.'

I said I was very impressed by the little hut and its occupants and Emily smiled. 'Sibella never kills a living creature and that drives Gran mad too when the doors and windows have to be opened for wasps and bees and spiders to depart all in one piece. I have to say I don't feel quite that way about spiders.'

She leaned back against the pillows. 'Do you know, until a year or two ago when she was a lot stronger than she is now, she wasn't past wading out to the rocks to bring back a seabird with a broken wing, or clambering over the rocks to rescue an injured sheep. Or some old ewe bleating in distress and like to die in the lambing. She has an amazing affinity with animals. None of the rest of us have inherited that.'

She paused and looked at me. 'I remember you were absolutely terrified of big dogs. There was one round the corner from the school who used to bark at us...'

For a moment, I almost denied that and I wanted to tell her about Thane. Then I realized that without proof of his existence such a confidence was inadvisable. And I had enough trouble and complications without a deerhound who might or might not exist.

She patted my hand. 'You are quite comfortable, aren't you?'

'Of course. It's a lovely room. Thank you.'

When I stifled a yawn, she said anxiously: 'I'll get you some milk.' And taking my hands: 'Rose, is everything all right, are you sure?'

I hadn't fooled my sister. She suspected something was amiss and sounded so concerned that I pointed to the table and said: 'Of course, but I must write to Jack. He'll be worried about me.'

That wasn't true but Emily nodded as if she understood and I went on: 'I have postcards to write. One to Mrs Brook. And my friend Alice – and Nancy. Nancy is a relative of our Mrs Brook,' I explained. 'She's nanny to the children of the explorer Gerald Carthew in Aberdeen.'

Emily was very interested in Mrs Brook. We talked about the old days in Sheridan Place and her marvellous cooking for a while and then she went off to bed, reassured that I was not falling victim to some fever or malaise.

I slept fitfully, full of strange dreams of Sibella and her animals and the portraits of long-gone Yesnabys.

Morning came with its chorus of seabirds and, after another of Gran's nourishing breakfasts, I set off to the post office with the inevitable list of her grocery needs, in the hope that I might waylay Frank on his way to the dig.

I was in luck. There he was trudging up the road looking as grey and dour as ever. Wondering if he ever smiled or if his face was set permanently in that state of melancholy, I felt sudden sympathy for the wife who had left him. Frank could not have been much joy to live with at the best of times but after long hours digging in mud and cold and fierce winds, I could not imagine him being a loveable – or passionate – fireside companion at the end of the day. As for Lily, after several years of enduring miserable summer digs, I wasn't in the least surprised that she had elected to remain in Edinburgh.

As Frank approached I greeted him, cheerfully. 'Craig was telling me that you discovered the peat-bog burial. How very exciting.'

He gave me a scornful look. 'All in a day's work, Mrs McQuinn.'

'Surely not!'

He shrugged. 'These things happen,' was the non-committal answer.

I was genuinely surprised. 'Really? I imagined you would be more used to dealing with Pictish burials. How did you spot it?'

He looked even more unhappy, if that were possible, at this question and I felt guilty that I was being relentless, especially recalling Craig's statement that Frank had been sweet on Thora.

He sighed deeply. 'Local bobby thought we had a murder on our hands at first. He was a bit disappointed, I can tell you. Didn't get much excitement beyond the local salmon poachers.'

'Were you in charge of the dig at the time?'

'Denmore should have been but he'd gone gallivanting away to a conference as usual.'

He sounded bitter. Encouraged I asked:

'Have you been with this group long?'

'Umpteen years, if you call that long. On and off, every summer and for all the finds we've made it's been time wasted. Especially as the professor–' he stressed the word heavily – 'always claims them as his own.'

So there was no love lost there. 'Then why do you stay?' I asked gently.

He glared at me balefully. 'Because this is where I belong. I've always lived here apart from a few months every year in Scotland.'

He made it sound like a foreign land, I thought, as he looked towards the sea. 'My wife still lives there, but I hate cities. And that includes Edinburgh,' he added with a malevolent look. 'All I want is to know what happened to the Maid all those hundreds of years ago. Just as my father did before me. But we were just plain crofters, scratching a living from the soil, and it was me that made the first find – a bronze ring. However, we weren't educated enough, the authorities didn't trust an ignorant crofter's son who had never been to the university, so they called in their own folk to take over–'

'Do you go back to Edinburgh for the winter then?' I asked innocently, knowing from Craig that he didn't any longer.

'No. I'm happy here – this is my life!'

'Your wife must miss you.'

He grunted at that and I realized I was treading on forbidden ground.

'Where does she live in Edinburgh?'

'Newington. Minto Street. I don't suppose you know it.'

'Oh yes, I do. I live in Solomon's Tower – at the foot of Arthur's Seat. It's just a step away.'

And with a sudden desire to be friendly and helpful I produced one of my cards. 'If you'd like to write her address on the back – I have a friend who lives close by,' I said, thinking of Alice Bolton.

Frank didn't seem very impressed. Staring at the card, he thrust it into his pocket.

I wondered if he hadn't heard me properly. 'Look,' I said. 'If you give me Mrs Breck's number, I'll call on her when I get back. Letters can take a while – I could hand a message, something you'd like to send her. Flowers perhaps?'

Turning, he stared at me as if I'd suggested something outrageous. 'What do you mean, letters can take a while? My letters get there all right.'

'Good! It was only a suggestion – you know, a package, a present or something.' I floundered hopelessly, wishing I had never raised the subject with such a difficult man, especially as he turned on his heel and walked quickly away in the direction of the dig.

Poor Frank, problems with the wife, so that was why he didn't go back to Edinburgh. I felt contrite, remembering Craig's hint that she had found someone else.

No doubt they had settled for an amicable separation and that was why he sounded so bitter, and of course, I had hit on the sore point of his existence. A chip on his shoulder about the dig and the wife who had deserted him for the bright lights of Edinburgh. And a lover.

I could sympathize although I was doubtful after this interview whether Frank could provide any information that would lead me to Thora's murderer. Our conversation hadn't been in the least enlightening. I had merely antagonized and embarrassed him and I suspected that he would avoid me in future.

A pity, but what had I been hoping for anyway? Some flash of inspirational deduction on his part?

I realized how unlikely that was as I decided to head towards the post office and ingratiate myself with Meg Flitt.

Chapter Twenty-one

Meg was standing by the window as I entered the shop: Frank and I had been under observation.

This seemed an opportune moment to quiz his landlady for any other information about him over the years.

'Frank has been telling me about the peat-bog woman,' I said. 'How exciting to have something like that on the doorstep,' I gushed, hoping to sound ingenuous and, from her dour expression, I suspected, failing miserably.

'Horrible, I'd say. Especially if it was someone we knew like Mrs Yesnaby. All those years believing she had been drowned. Dreadful it was.'

'Dreadful,' I echoed sympathetically and studied a shelf containing a selection of post-cards. I chose a couple and said casually: 'I see you also advertise board and lodgings in the window. Do you get many guests?'

'We're full. In the summer we take the lads from the dig and that's all,' she added firmly as if I might be making a request for a room.

'That must be interesting – I mean, quite different to the usual travellers who are just passing through.'

She gave me a cold look. 'You wouldn't say that if you had the archaeology team upstairs, trampling up and down through the house with their muddy boots, having damp clothes all over the kitchen drying.'

So much for respecting progress and the acquisition of knowledge about the ancient past, I thought as she went on: 'Dr Denmore is all right. Pays his rent on time and he's very polite and considerate. My Wilma thinks he's wonderful, I can hardly keep her away from the dig, and he encourages her to have big notions for her future, when she grows up,' she added with a note of disapproval in her voice.

'Doesn't that please you?'

'It does not,' she said coldly. 'It's never too soon for Wilma to know her place and that's not gadding off to college over there on the mainland somewhere.' She made the coast of Scotland sound like darkest Africa.

Then thumping the counter: 'Her place is here, on the island, with her family. Helping me in the shop and getting married and settling down with a respectable local lad in due course. Like her mother and her grandmother before her. That's what I'd like to see for her, not these grand ideas above her station.'

And handing me my change: 'And while we're on the subject, Mrs McQuinn, I don't approve of my Wilma riding a bicycle either.'

Another customer had followed me into the shop and was listening agog to this conversation.

'Good day to you, Mrs McQuinn.'

I left, feeling somewhat disconcerted at the way my first day of inquiry had begun, with two highly unfruitful encounters from which I had learned nothing of the slightest use. Unfortunately I had probably antagonized both Frank and Meg who would be writing me off as a nosy foreigner.

The next person on my list was the local constable who, by a stroke of fortune, was at that moment walking towards the church.

About to pursue him, I changed my mind. What if he did not believe this was gruesome curiosity? What if his training, unlikely as it seemed, should prompt him to ask why I wanted all these details?

No, the local constable must wait, his time might come later, for at that moment I saw two women walking into one of the handsome houses I had noticed earlier, near the church and set back from the village street.

'Dr Stern', proclaimed the brass plate on the gate. The fact that an old man with a limp was also making his way up the path indicated that this must be the surgery hour.

The limp was inspirational. Bicycling, I had pulled an imaginary tendon on my ankle. That would do splendidly as an introduction.

I trailed behind the limping man, slowly and rather painfully exhibiting that non-existent injury and making a mental list of some searching questions regarding the late Thora Yesnaby.

Shown into the waiting room, dominated by a clock with an extremely loud and aggressive tick which must have been scant comfort to patients considering their aches and pains, I took a seat near the door.

My entrance was greeted with some curiosity which I was unwilling to satisfy beyond 'Good morning.' I sat in silence awaiting my turn. It came some ten minutes later when the limping man I had followed emerged from the surgery.

Invited to enter, I found Dr Stern sitting

231

behind his desk. He was not quite as I had imagined the Yesnabys' family doctor. For one thing he was considerably younger than I had expected, a good-looking man – at least I believed his features to be handsome under the facial hair so fashionable for gentlemen, a trend set by our Royal Family which I found rather unattractive.

He wrote down my name and, regarding me across the table, said: 'You are not from these parts, Mrs McQuinn?'

I said I was from Edinburgh.

He smiled. 'A delightful place, I know it well. So what brings you to Hopescarth?'

'I am having a short holiday at Yesnaby House.'

He nodded absently, asked what was the trouble.

As I explained the pulled tendon, he came round, knelt down and in hands that were firm but gentle, rotated my ankle.

'Does that hurt?'

'Ouch,' I said obligingly and watched while he produced a roll of bandage and proceeded to wrap it rather tightly around what he presumed to be my injured limb.

'I don't think there is much damage, but try to keep off it as much a possible for a day or two. And if you have any problems, come back and see me again. Where did you say you were staying – Mrs McQuinn?' he asked, consulting his notes.

'With my sister Mrs Emily Yesnaby – one of your patients, I believe.' After a hopeful pause I added that I found Hopescarth quite charming.

'Do you not find it a little dull after Edinburgh?'

'Not at all.'

He smiled. 'I did my degree at Edinburgh University. I still miss it.'

I was the last patient and I realized that this was an advantage, that Dr Stern might have a little time to spare for gossip and, more particularly, for enlightenment about the body of Thora Yesnaby.

'What brought you back to Hopescarth?' I asked.

'My father was in poor health and I came to help him in the practice.'

'When was that?'

'Six months ago.'

'So you weren't on the scene here when the great discovery was made?'

He looked puzzled. 'What discovery was that?'

'Why, the peat-bog woman – I have heard so much about her,' I added gushingly. 'As she was my brother-in-law's first wife, I am rather curious.'

He shook his head. 'I read the account in the newspapers. My father dealt with it and was, well, rather reticent about the incident. He didn't talk much about it, but I gather he found it very upsetting, especially as he had been the Yesnaby's family doctor for many years.'

Another shake of the head. 'It is never a pleasant experience for a doctor to have to examine the corpse of someone who has been a personal friend.' He paused. 'In his case, I think the shock was very debilitating.'

'You believe that it had something to do with him giving up the practice?' I asked.

'Perhaps so.'

As he said the words, Dr Stern's manner changed abruptly. He was clearly shrugging off an unpleasant topic, and somehow managing to imply not only that the subject was distasteful but that he found a stranger's curiosity a little vulgar.

The conversation threatened to come to an end as he moved some papers on his desk.

I wasn't prepared to leave just yet. Not until I had met Dr Stern Senior.

'Now that your father is no longer active in

the practice, I trust he is happy in his retirement.'

Dr Stern shrugged. 'I believe so.'

'Does he find plenty to keep him occupied in Hopescarth? I presume he still lives here.'

A curious glance from the doctor. 'No, he decided to retire to Kirkwall. The house is small – we are rather cramped for accommodation. Three children, you know, and the surgery,' he added apologetically.

I told him my stepbrother was a doctor in Edinburgh. When I mentioned his name, Dr Stern beamed. 'Good gracious – Vince Laurie. I knew him well – we were students together. We belonged to the same golf club after we graduated.' He nodded delightedly. 'A small world,' and the next part was easy, mention of where Gran lived and my early days in Orkney.

'Father is very near there. Up beside the Bishop's Palace in Johnston House. You must know it well. We see him as often as we can.'

'He is in good health?'

Dr Stern frowned. 'As well as can be expected.' And perhaps because I was Vince Laurie's stepsister, seeing me to the door, he was suddenly confidential.

'I fear he was never quite the same man

after the discovery of the first Mrs Yesnaby. It upset him dreadfully and I noticed a remarkable change in him when I returned to take over the practice. Quite remarkable.'

Had that change something to do with signing a death certificate which he knew to be false? Had that preyed on his mind?

And I left resolving that my next visit would be to Kirkwall.

Chapter Twenty-two

On my way back through the village, I remembered that Gran had said something about salt, unimportant enough to slip my mind during my interrogation of Frank Breck.

Back to Meg's shop once more and this time I was in luck. For leaning against the counter chatting to her was Andy Green, the local policeman.

Meg was in a better mood than when I had seen her earlier and seemed eager to introduce me. 'Mrs McQuinn is Mrs Yesnaby's sister.'

The young policeman grinned. 'On holiday, I hear.'

I smiled. 'Word gets around.'

He laughed. 'Certainly does. Nothing goes past us here in Hopescarth,' he added with a touch of pride in his voice.

The bell on the door indicated another customer and, picking up the salt, I handed over the money and followed PC Green outside.

'Walking, were you?' When I said yes, he shook his head. 'That bicycle of yours has created quite a sensation, Mrs McQuinn. I expect they're quite commonplace in Edinburgh these days.' He sighed. 'We'll get them soon enough, like Dr Denmore's motor car.'

'Splendid, isn't it? I gather it is needed to transport artefacts to Stromness from the dig,' and regarding this as a suitable prelude to the information I wanted, 'I suppose there is nothing as exciting as the peat-bog woman these days though.'

'So you heard about that in Edinburgh?' he said with a grin of satisfaction.

'I believe it was in all the newspapers,' I said, avoiding a downright lie. 'It must have given the local residents of Hopescarth quite a shock.'

'Aye, it did that. Thought they had a murder on their hands,' he added with just a tinge of regret, I thought.

'What did you think?' I asked eagerly.

He laughed. 'Just what I read in the newspapers too, lass. I missed all the excitement.'

Just my luck, I thought despairingly as he went on. 'I'm a newcomer – from St Margaret's Hope.'

'I expect the constable here told you all

about it.'

He shrugged. 'Only what was written in his notes. And that wasn't very much. Jock was a bit inarticulate, even when he was sober.'

'I would like to see his notes, if they are still around.'

'I dare say they are somewhere, but...' As he shook his head, regarding me with a curious, even suspicious, expression, I hastily explained that the body in question had belonged to my sister's husband's late wife.

I felt very foolish as a look of distaste similar to Dr Stern's greeted my morbid interest.

'I expect Jock's notes are in the files somewhere at the station,' he said firmly.

He didn't add what I already knew from experience. That they would not be available for public scrutiny.

I was reluctant to confide in him and set aside his bad opinion of this nosy woman by revealing that my interest was official. That I was a professional investigator. But I bit back the words that might arouse his own suspicions. That was the last thing I wanted.

'Has the constable – Jock, you mentioned – retired now? Perhaps I could have a word with him.'

He looked at me sourly. 'Jock is dead.'

'Recently?' This was another blow I had not expected. The doctor who had issued the death certificate retired in Kirkwall in poor health, and the other witness, the local constable, dead.

Andy was saying: 'Jock died just days after Mrs Yesnaby's body was found. He had a bad heart. Perhaps the shock of it all killed him, the exertion and so forth,' he added vaguely.

Another bad heart. Another shock severe enough to disable the local doctor and kill a policeman. Too many coincidences, I thought as I asked: 'What happened exactly?'

Andy looked at me for a moment, frowned and then said: 'Well, Jock wasna convinced. He questioned the doctor's verdict. Even though folk would take more notice of the doctor than the constable who was a local lad.'

Again Andy hesitated. 'Ye ken, Jock believed it was murder. He couldna take in this preservation business and that someone could lie in the peat for ten years and look as if she had just died.'

He sighed. 'Poor old Jock. He was always arguing about it. Then he had an accident, chasing some poachers, they reckoned. He always took a drink and they reckoned he'd had a drop too much. He fell down the cliff on the Hopescarth road. Just a couple of weeks after Mrs Yesnaby was dug out.'

'Did they call in the Fiscal?'

Andy looked at me as if I'd taken leave of my senses. 'Whatever for? What good could the Fiscal do? This was natural causes.'

He was smiling, but his eyes were hard. 'We're used to looking after ourselves in Hopescarth. Making our own justice, if you like. After all, if we called in the Fiscal every time anyone died of a heart attack, or had an accident through drinking too much, he'd never be away from the island.'

Pausing, he regarded me gravely. 'Ye ken, fishing boats are always being lost, the men drowned, their bodies washed ashore and that sort of thing.'

Letting that information sink in, he said: 'Is this the way they do it in Edinburgh?'

'Usually when a dead body turns up in–' for 'suspicious' I quickly substituted 'unusual circumstances, calling in the Fiscal is a matter of course.'

He regarded me, smiling gently. 'You seem to know a lot about it, Mrs McQuinn.' And he rubbed his chin thoughtfully. 'Wait a minute. You're a Faro, aren't ye?'

When I said yes, he said triumphantly:

'Ye're the daughter of our policeman who went to the mainland and made a name for himself. Inspector Faro.' He regarded me triumphantly. 'Now I get it – that's why you're so interested in our little mystery.'

He slapped his sides delightedly. 'Well, well – runs in the family, does it?'

'As a matter of fact it does. I'm a private investigator.'

His eyes widened. 'A lady – investigating crimes?' He sounded quite shocked.

'And why not?' I asked defensively.

'Dead bodies and all that. Doesna sound quite decent – at least not for a nice lady like yourself,' he added hastily.

I laughed. 'Mostly it's quite mundane matters, like frauds and thefts, and domestic incidents, runaway wives and so forth.'

'I'm right glad of that,' he said with a sigh of relief.

I thought I'd better add a homely touch and said: 'My fiancé is a detective sergeant with the Edinburgh Police.'

'Is that so?' He smiled. 'I took you to be a widow.'

'I am. But aren't widows allowed second marriages?'

He laughed and saluted me mockingly. 'Point taken, madam.' And with a bow: 'Out of order, that remark. Beg pardon.'

'Tell me about Jock,' I said.

He regarded me thoughtfully. 'The night it happened, ye mean? Well, I dare say Jock made a routine report to the Fiscal, but a dead body turning up in a peat-bog after being missing for ten years might not have inspired a visit to Hopescarth to survey the remains.'

He shrugged. 'Fiscals don't bother much about long-dead corpses, like I said. Mrs Yesnaby had been missing for ten years and turned up in a peat-bog. There weren't any mysterious circumstances. This was what we would call an open-and-shut-case.'

There seemed nothing to add to that. But the lack of information on Thora Yesnaby's recovery from the peat-bog was adding up to a very sinister picture. I had not bargained for all the complications, the strange coincidences.

'Wasn't he curious about the unknown woman who had been buried earlier as Mrs Yesnaby?'

He frowned. 'Maybe before his time. And a bit difficult to open an inquiry on an accident, or a suicide, all that time ago.'

Why had I ever imagined it would be simple to interview the main participants involved in dealing with the legal aspects of the case? The old family doctor, first on the scene, was now feeble in health and mind. And, probably, even on his better days, fiercely loyal to the Yesnabys.

And now I had learned that the local police constable, sole representative of law and order, was dead. If he had urged an official inquiry, suspecting 'murder' and threatening to make trouble, then we were left with a very nasty conclusion.

By repute, Jock was a heavy drinker who may, or may not, have notified the Procurator Fiscal for an official inquiry and an inquest before he conveniently fell to his death off a cliff returning home drunk one dark night.

Jock's demise had been skimmed over as an accident when in fact there was a strong possibility that there had been not one but two murders in Hopescarth.

'Incidentally, Jock was Meg's husband,' was Andy's parting shot. 'Did you know that? She took it very badly.'

Any plan I might have of going to Kirkwall alone, without Emily insisting on accompanying me, would require skilful negotiation. The carriage would be put at our disposal, the suggestion seized upon as a splendid opportunity to select suitable wallpaper for the hall. I guessed that Emily's idea of a pleasant day's shopping, inter-rupted by frequent intervals for pots of tea and cake in several different cafés, would completely frustrate my own urgent reasons for a Kirkwall visit.

The only alternative was to arrange other means of transport as I did not greatly relish bicycling a round trip of thirty miles in the present spell of notoriously unsettled summer weather. Regardless of the time of year, Orkney was subject to sudden – very sudden – unpredictable downpours which I would be quite unable to deal with. There is no possibility of carrying an umbrella while riding a bicycle and a rain cape would be hopelessly inadequate.

So once again I returned to Meg's post office, as the seat of local gossip exchange and a seemingly inexhaustible source of information. My situation, however, was tricky in the extreme and I approached wondering how on earth I could angle the conversation around to Meg's late husband, PC Jock Flitt. A very delicate touch would be required, considering that Meg was by nature a somewhat prickly lady. However, on my entry to the shop I discovered any hopes on that score must be laid aside as the counter was busier than usual.

As for transport to Kirkwall, my timing had been perfect and I learned that Friday was market day and there would be plenty of carts heading in that direction and passing through Hopescarth.

Meg said that one of the farmers would gladly give me a lift, if I didn't mind a rough ride and was prepared to leave by six thirty in the morning. So leaving a message with her to warn them to expect a passenger, I returned to Hopescarth thoughtfully, considering the many gaps in my knowledge about Thora. Vital things about a woman whose life differed from Emily's portrayal of an invalid wife who, I had also been allowed to assume, had died of natural causes, leaving the way open for my sister to marry the bereaved husband.

I wasn't alone in my assumptions. The Faro family, Pappa and Vince, had also believed in this romantic fable. And it seemed that our dear Emily had deliberately – if not lied to us, then gently led us away from the truth concerning the woman she was companion to.

The visit to Hopescarth had been

enlightening in that respect. What had emerged was a very difficult, unbalanced, hysterical and even vicious woman, over-fond of whisky, who had stormed out of the house one night eleven years ago and had led Hopescarth to assume that she had either taken her own life or been drowned in a tragic accident.

I thought of Thora roaming around the huge house, devious, making secret plans. The Thora I had never known, an image built up of other people's word pictures. To it I now added another version: that of her alter ego, my client 'Mrs Smith', met briefly in Edinburgh. A greedy, vengeful black-mailer whom I had disliked almost instantly.

My thoughts continually drifted to that mysterious young lover met so fleetingly at Brightwell's Hotel. What fate had overtaken him in the drama of Thora Yesnaby? I heard again Mrs Smith saying that she had met 'someone else'. Had I been in error to believe this was the same young man who was with her in the Edinburgh hotel and who I had presumed was sharing her bed?

Had they parted before she left Edinburgh? What had happened when she sailed to Orkney? Had they some plan that she was to go alone and confront her husband and then they would meet afterwards?

If so, most important, where was that meeting to take place? And when she did not arrive to keep that appointment, was her lover not deeply concerned? Did he make any inquiries?

If he was the man in her life, the one she hoped to marry, then surely he would have been frantic and come in search of her?

If not, then why not?

The thought persisted that had he accompanied her to Orkney, then it was most unlikely that she would have been murdered. His presence would have saved her life.

Unless he had also been murdered and his body disposed of elsewhere. A tricky proposition for an amateur killer, or killers, since bodies are not all that easy to get rid of.

So what had become of him? Where was he now? The mysterious lover who refused to be dismissed from my calculations had to fit somewhere in Mrs Smith's violent end here in Hopescarth and he hovered on the edge of my mind, an enigmatic shadowy figure who alone could provide answers to the disastrous arrival of 'Mrs Smith' at Yesnaby House.

There was another missing link in this

puzzle. The Yesnaby locket, or Hopescarth jewel, which Thora allegedly was last seen wearing. One could sensibly accept a grimmer conclusion to its disappearance without trace.

That it lay somewhere in the depths of the peat-bog, a valuable historic treasure for some future generation of archaeologists.

Yet the more I sought to find answers, the more confused I became. And the possibility stared me in the face that I was on the wrong track completely.

Chapter Twenty-three

I found Emily alone that evening. Gran was at a Women's Guild meeting at the church and Erland with his monthly accounts, closeted in his study and not to be disturbed.

Our conversation began casually enough: the usual family gossip to be expected between sisters who had been long apart, for it was our first evening alone together since my arrival.

This was an opportunity I could not afford to miss. I said how shocked I had been to see Thora's memorial in the kirkyard and the manner of her death. Especially as I had presumed that she was a frail invalid.

Emily looked surprised. 'Did I give you that idea?'

'Yes, as a matter of fact, you did.' And when she frowned: 'I thought you were employed by Erland originally as Thora's companion?'

'Yes, that was true. A companion for

Thora was what Erland had in mind when we first met in Kirkwall.' She sighed happily. 'That meeting was one of those accidents which change a whole life.'

She smiled at the memory. 'It was market day and the harbour café was crowded. I was alone at a table for two and he asked if he might be permitted to join me. I said yes and I thought he had the most beautiful voice I had ever heard. He didn't look like a farmer either, too well-dressed, you know.'

Another sigh. 'As we talked, we got along famously. He was waiting to meet someone from Bergen – one of his shipping interests. As I was leaving, he said how he had enjoyed talking to me and asked if he might see me again. I never hesitated. I said yes, and gave him Gran's address. I never doubted that he would call. And he did. Gran was a bit shocked until she met him. And of course he charmed her instantly.'

She paused. 'You know the rest. I was rather taken aback when he told me that he was married. I had presumed when he wanted to see me again that he was a bachelor. Then he told me about Thora and explained that she was an invalid and needed a companion. He was often away and had to leave her in that big house on her own. And, even before he asked me if I would consider such a situation, I knew I would say yes. He was delighted. He had been thinking about me ever since we met and knew I was the right person.'

She stopped, stretched and patted her stomach in that now familiar protective gesture.

'And so I came to Hopescarth. It was beyond my wildest dreams that I would ever be Erland's wife. I honestly never gave it a second thought although I felt somehow that I had always known him and he was exactly the kind of man I had been waiting for.'

She shook her head. 'I didn't care that he could never be mine, just to be near him, to see him every day, I thought that would be enough. I felt a little like Jane Eyre with Rochester.'

I laughed. 'Yes, I do see the resemblance.' I didn't add 'mad wife and all'.

Emily looked at me sadly. 'I was never like you, Rose. You always knew you loved Danny right from being a little girl. Remember when he rescued us both from those criminals Pappa was tracking down in Edinburgh? When they kidnapped us?'

I nodded and she went on. 'How I envied

you, because I never met anyone like Danny and I didn't expect to until I met Erland.'

She paused and frowned at me. 'I sometimes think we're an odd family, born to love only once. Perhaps it's in our blood, Sibella and Hakon, Gran and Magnus, you and Danny, me and Erland...'

Feeling suddenly disloyal, I banished a quick vision of Jack Macmerry as Emily went on: 'I soon found that I had been mis-informed about Thora. She wasn't physic-ally frail, far from it. Her problems related to the whisky bottle. She was completely unbalanced. She could turn quite violent, not with me, but with Erland. On several occasions I saw her physically attack him, he had scratches on his face, once a bleeding nose.'

She shuddered. 'Any less caring husband than Erland would have had her put away.'

'As bad as that?'

'Every bit. Fortunately these bouts of violence were more usually directed at material things, ornaments and vases. Erland, who was so often away in Norway, had thought that having a companion, someone to look after her – to care for her – would help.'

She smiled at the memory. 'He said that it

was because I was so gentle and sweet, he thought I was the ideal person. And that I'd be around if she tried to do herself a mischief.'

Did he never think that Thora might do Emily a mischief, was my instant reaction to this information as Emily continued:

'The idea haunted him, that she might try to destroy herself in one of her mad rages.'

Was that why Erland had readily believed Thora had committed suicide, had walked into the sea?

'I thought it would be a good chance to save some money,' Emily said, 'and that I should regard this as a milestone in my life. I wasn't qualified for anything, like you.'

And in common with so many other women, Emily was conventional and regarded marriage as the only possible career open to a respectable well-brought-up young woman.

She sighed. 'Gran is a very dominating person, as you know. I had always seen myself tied to her, an ageing granddaughter at her beck and call for the rest of my life. But Erland had a place for her too. He seemed to understand and,' she smiled, 'Gran was transformed when she came to Hopescarth with me. A new lease of life –

she seemed to shed twenty years.'

Not quite what you implied in your letters, sister mine, I thought, remembering her description of Gran as 'frail and needing care'.

'Gran even decided to heal the breach with Sibella. I didn't know that we had a great-grandmother. But Erland was ready once more, and offered to take Sibella under his roof.'

'You were on good terms with Thora?'

She frowned. 'Yes, at first. She seemed to like me. In a way she regarded me as a novelty, a new toy to play with. Yes, I was sure she liked me. Better than Erland.'

I looked at her. 'Really?'

'Yes, really. He was her husband, he loved her and was kind to her but she despised him. She never made any secret of that. She used to tell me that he had just married her for her money – the wealthy cousin – Hopescarth needed her money.'

There was a pause before Emily continued, remembering almost reluctantly: 'Thora liked to torment him by flirting with other men whenever she got the chance – any visitors who came to the house.'

Another vision, this time of Mrs Smith and her lover. That fitted Thora Yesnaby too.

'She liked the archaeologists, they were always in the house although Erland disapproved of the dig on Hopescarth land. But Thora was always inviting Frank. She really led him on.'

'Didn't Erland object?'

She shook her head. 'He didn't care. He had lost Thora long ago and whatever marriage they once had was over. I suppose it might have been different if there had been children. Erland always wanted a family.'

Again that gesture, smoothing her stomach where the outline of Erland's baby was not yet visible, as she looked at me. 'Even if I hadn't – cared – I would have been sorry for any husband, especially such a wonderful man as Erland, being treated so badly.'

She sighed. 'There was one day I realized it was more than being sorry, I was in love with him. And I knew he loved me too. Terrible, wasn't it, Rose?'

'I don't think it was terrible. You both deserved some happiness.'

But Emily shook her head obstinately, said firmly: 'Not as long as Thora was his wife, Erland would never have suggested anything like – like that. It wouldn't have been proper for either of us.'

I let that pass. 'How about a divorce? Did he never think of that?'

'She would never divorce him. Once she knew that he loved me, she would never let him go. She told him so. That he didn't deserve to be happy.'

As she spoke, I thought, What about those ten years away from Hopescarth? What circumstances had caused her to change her mind, make her willing to exchange the Yesnaby locket for a substantial divorce settlement and that 'someone else', her love in Edinburgh?

'It must have been awful, Emily.'

'It was. I had decided I couldn't bear it any longer and I told Erland I was going to leave Hopescarth and go back to Kirkwall.' She shook her head. 'By one of those odd coincidences, I had just told him, had it all planned, the very day they had that last dreadful row. I only know that it was more violent than usual and it served to strengthen my purpose. I knew I had to leave him. I was doing the right thing, my presence was just making it worse. By staying I was giving Thora a stick to beat Erland with emotionally.

'And that–' She looked at me wide-eyed.

'That was the day she disappeared. Don't you think that was strange?'

I thought it was strange all right, but not for Emily's innocent reasons. And I didn't believe in 'odd coincidences' either.

'At first, Erland said he thought she had just gone down to the dig. To see Frank, was what he implied. She liked to cry on his shoulder, especially as Lily – his wife – had gone back to Edinburgh. Next day when Thora didn't return home, Frank was the first person Erland asked, but he denied that she had been there. He didn't know where she was.

'Erland went to Sibella after that. Thora liked Sibella, cried on her shoulder too. And Sibella was always ready with new cures and remedies for Thora's imagined ills. But Sibella hadn't seen her either.'

'Did Sibella like her?'

'I think she was sorry for her. She had only been with us a few months, since Gran and she had the great reconciliation. Erland had given her the croft and would have been very happy to have her living in the house. There are enough rooms, but good sense prevailed. Sibella and Gran under one roof...'

Her heavenward glance said it all. 'Sibella was another new toy as far as Thora was concerned. Certainly some of her cures seemed to help, or maybe it was simply because Thora believed in them. As for Erland, I think he was just relieved when Thora disappeared.

'A few days afterwards I noticed a change in him. He no longer regarded the door opening with dread. He was like a man who had just had a great burden lifted. One day he said to me: "I don't think Thora's coming back. I think she's gone for good this time."'

'Did that make a difference to your relationship?'

Emily coloured slightly. 'Yes, we became lovers – at last,' she whispered.

'Good for you, Emily. And about time.'

'You're not shocked?' She sounded amazed.

'Of course I'm not. Tell me – had Thora ever left home before?' I asked.

'Often. Full of threats that she was never coming back. But she was always home again before nightfall,' said Emily bitterly. 'I knew it was different this time, too. I could feel it all over the house. That we were rid of Thora's evil presence and now Erland and I were together – we could get married – some day.'

She paused again, regarded me thoughtfully. 'Do you know, he never shed one tear when she was – I mean,' she shuddered, 'when that poor woman's body, who he thought was Thora, was washed ashore. Thora, his wife, and him so tender and gentle, but not one single tear for her.'

I said nothing, thinking that if he knew deep down this wasn't Thora, and was eager to accept a replacement, then a certain lack of any emotion but thanksgiving was quite in order.

Again Emily seemed to read my thoughts as she said: 'Of course, I questioned him when he came back, but I don't think that he had looked too closely. I was told that bodies long in the water are fairly unrecognisable.' Another shudder, as she whispered: This particular one – arms and legs gone. Poor Erland, what an ordeal. Later, when we were married, he once said it was a good thing that Thora had drowned. That if she hadn't vanished when she did, if we had both had to suffer much longer, then he would not have been responsible for his actions.'

She closed her eyes briefly. 'A terrible thing for someone like Erland to admit, don't you think?'

Though Emily didn't understand the significance of her words they were making plenty of sense to me. And setting Erland as the prime suspect for Thora's murder.

Emily shrugged. 'I was never sure we were rid of her, really. It seemed too good to be true and I always felt the bliss I had with Erland would have to be paid for.'

Chapter Twenty-four

When I mentioned going to Kirkwall, there was some opposition, as I had expected, to my plan.

After a shocked silence, Emily said did I not know that we could go together in the carriage, that Erland would be most willing to take us both? Did I not realize how uncomfortable a farmer's cart would be for such a journey?

I side-stepped the issue by saying I really wanted an early start at the crack of dawn. About six thirty, in fact, and I wouldn't impose that upon them.

Emily, a late riser, did look somewhat downcast at that but it seemed that an argument was inescapable until Gran reminded Emily that she couldn't go with me. Had she forgotten that they were having afternoon tea with the doctor's wife?

So I decided I had best tell them that I had already met Dr Stern, in case my visit to the surgery was mentioned.

This immediately threw them into a state

of panic, which I had been hoping to avoid. Why had I gone there? Was I feeling ill, and so forth. I explained about the tendon in my ankle, blaming the bicycle for that imaginary injury.

'I might have known it. There's no place for a dangerous thing like that on these roads,' said Gran in the gloomy manner of one who hourly anticipates a fatality.

'There was no need for a doctor, Rose,' Emily cut in sharply. 'Sibella could have fixed that, she's great at treating sprains, isn't she, Gran?'

And Gran had to admit rather reluctantly that Sibella had fixed her sprained wrist in no time at all.

I listened patiently. 'I happened to be near the surgery when it happened, so I thought I'd get advice,' I said weakly. 'Dr Stern said he had taken over from his father.'

'We miss the old doctor. Such a nice man, too,' said Gran. 'As for that young lad…' She shook her head dubiously. 'His father was Erland's family doctor, you know. And very good to Emily when she had all her troubles.' 'Troubles' obviously referred to the multiple miscarriages.

'I gather he's retired to Kirkwall,' I said.

'Yes, he's in Johnston House – remember,

Rose? Up the hill from where we lived,' said Emily.

And I had a stroke of unexpected luck as she added: 'If you're quite determined to go to Kirkwall, I'm sure he'd love to meet you. He'll be very interested in you having lived in America. It was his ambition to go there as a young man.'

She paused and smiled at Gran. 'I've just thought – it's his eightieth birthday next week. I always remember, because it's the day after Erland's.'

'Would you like me to pay him a visit?' I asked eagerly.

'Oh, would you, Rose? If you have time. You could take him a plant for his room, from the garden here. He isn't very mobile any more.'

I awoke at dawn next morning and crept downstairs. On the kitchen table was a basket containing a plant, a card and some of Gran's biscuits.

I let myself out and set off briskly down the drive. I had forgotten how sharp and clear the air was, before it had been breathed by everybody, as Gran used to say.

The farmers' carts were already on the road past the post office and as I waited for a lift, Wilma looked out of the upstairs window in her nightdress.

'Hello, Missus Rose. Where's your bicycle?'

I explained that it was too far to ride to Kirkwall and back and I had lots of shopping to do.

She beamed down at me. 'Can I go and practise then – if I tell Mrs Yesnaby you said so?'

I wasn't too keen on that idea, however, I weakened and said: 'If you think you'll manage alone. I don't want you falling and hurting yourself.'

'I won't – I won't.'

'Very well. There are plenty of straight paths round the house. If you promise to stay there.'

'I will. I will.'

'Take care then and don't fall off.'

'I won't. I'll be careful.' And she gave me a warning glance as her mother appeared. I heard her asking what was Wilma doing out of bed with the window open.

The cavalcade of carts were assembled and what followed was not the most comfortable ride to Kirkwall, as Emily had warned. Alec Burray, elderly and enigmatic, had invited me to share the cart seat on his harvest load of vegetables.

Prepared to expect the worst, I was relieved when the day promised to be kind, blossoming into a warm sunny morning, almost windless, and I began to look forward to the cart ride as an interesting experience. Especially when a halt was called at Skailholm.

It was traditional that the farmers halted there, half-way to Kirkwall, for a pot of ale. They trooped into the inn where Craig Denmore was on such excellent terms with the blacksmith's wife. I followed, curious to see Maud again, whose hair was already immaculately arranged, leaving some doubt as to whether she slept sitting bolt upright.

She recognized me. 'What's yours, then?' My request for a glass of milk received a look of scorn and she said: 'You're brave to travel with that lot,' but I detected none of the hostility in her manner evident when I had been accompanied by Craig Denmore and his motor car.

Indeed she seemed quite agreeable. 'Enjoying your holiday?'

I said very much and she continued to look at me in that rather intense way, as if I was something of a curiosity myself.

'Doesn't it seem a bit dull after Edinburgh?' So she knew that too.

'It's a pleasant change – and I used to live in Kirkwall before I was married.'

She nodded. 'Your family comes from here.' As it was a statement not a question, Craig must have told her that too. Her next remark left me in no doubt of that.

'Aye, your grandfather was a policeman–'

'Maud!' It was Lenny, red-faced and busy. 'Enough of your gossiping, lass,' he said, indicating the farmers noisily clamouring at the bar.

Sipping my glass of milk, I noticed there was already one customer who wasn't with our cavalcade. Breakfasting alone, he was staring out of the window, as if anxious to dissociate himself from the noisy arrivals. Although he was sitting down, I got the impression of a tall man, heavily built, middle-aged. With a shock of straight sandy hair and a moustache he gave the impression of being a military man.

What happened afterwards was rather odd.

On her way to the bar Maud touched his shoulder and whispered something. Nodding in agreement, he turned his head sharply in my direction. Immediately leaving his table he came over to me, holding out his hand. 'Mrs McQuinn, I believe.'

I was certain we had never met before as he explained: 'Mrs Lenny told me who you were. And that you have Hopescarth connections.' He smiled. 'As a matter of fact, I am heading that way myself.'

That voice – the accent!

'You're from America?' And as I said the words my heart leapt with sudden hope. Was this stranger a contact, at last, someone come to bring me news of Danny?

He laughed. 'Folks over here often make that mistake. I'm Canadian – from Toronto. I have kin hereabouts. Jim Mainwell's the name.'

Before I could ask any more, a bell clanged.

The farmers banged down their empty pots and surged towards the door.

I stood up. 'That's for me too, I'm afraid. I'm going to Kirkwall with them.' I wanted to know more, but Alec Burray, more red-faced than ever, shouted:

'Come away, lass. We're leaving.'

As I ran to the door, the military man was standing still, watching me. He held up a hand in salute.

Farmer Burray noticed the gesture and allowed his face to fold into a grin as he helped me up on to the seat beside him.

'Nice fellow, eh? Sorry we had to tak' ye awa', lass,' he added with a knowing look.

I tried not to bristle at the implications and said rather coldly: 'He has connections in Hopescarth.'

'Oh aye. That's nice for you.' His voice was casual and disbelieving.

I knew there was no point in arguing or being outraged at any lewd suggestion. This was normal male behaviour, in Edinburgh as well as Orkney, so I prepared to enjoy the scenery, especially as the day was growing warmer, the sky cloudless.

Up hills, down hills we travelled, horizons often lost behind tall hedgerows, deep in summer's wild flowers. Our progress was marked by an escort of raucous seabirds, lured by prospects of scavenging and adding to the noise of sheep and hens carried on the carts, the lowing cattle being driven alongside.

For me, the calendar had tipped backwards and I was deposited once again into childhood memories, long before the rose-red spire of St Magnus Cathedral appeared on the skyline. Eventually a huddle of rooftops came in sight, the street where Emily and I once lived with Gran.

I laughed out loud. 'This is just great. I've

come home again.'

Father Burray seemed pleased and suddenly keen to impress me with his knowledge of past days. He and his fathers before him had travelled these roads on market day for generations past. But he found it difficult to believe that I was of Orcadian descent and had spent the first twenty years of my life here.

There was more to come and I realized I was in for yet another lesson on local lore when he said: 'Bet you didn't know the word "orc" was Celtic and that "ey" was Norse for island. Put them together and you get the Islands of the People of the Wild Boar,' he said triumphantly.

I said that my family, Faros and Scarths, had lived here for generations and they would know.

Faro, aye, he kenned the name well, but what had taken them awa' to Edinburgh? The fame of Chief Inspector Jeremy Faro hadn't reached Alec Burray.

Chapter Twenty-five

I left the cart in a noisy throng of shouting people with their bleating, mooing, clucking charges outside the cattle market and made my way up the hill past the cottage where Emily and I had spent so many years.

As I stood by the fence, a woman with a baby in her arms came out and asked me did I want something? I said no, I used to live here.

I suppose I was hoping she would ask me in, as I had been warned by Gran, in the traditional Orkney way, with the offer of tea and bere bannocks. I was really looking forward to accepting her invitation so that I could sit in a once familiar kitchen and relive some nostalgic moments of childhood memories.

Alas, the new occupant of Gran's cottage did none of these things and I suspected this was a new breed of neighbour who had not heard of the island's famed hospitality. She merely smiled politely, the baby stirred and, wishing me good day, she closed the door.

Feeling rather deflated, I walked past the cathedral, up the hill to the Earl's palace. Pausing by the railings, I watched it narrow-eyed through those peaceful sheltering trees, trying to equate the imposing ruin with Erland's story. Was this what Hope-scarth had once looked like, in Huw Scarth's days of glory when he had followed the rainbow and found his pot of gold?

On up the hill to Johnston House. A sign at the gate, 'Residential Home for Retired Gentlemen', might cover a number of possibilities, I thought, walking down the drive and up the steps.

The dark-panelled reception area, smelling of polish and something less pleasant I associated with hospitals, was inhabited by a brisk nurse wearing a white starched apron with a white starched face to match.

In answer to my question she pointed to a door. 'Dr Stern is in the garden at present. Through there.'

'This is my first visit. I come on a friend's behalf. I haven't met the doctor before.'

She regarded me doubtfully as I made this statement, somehow managing to make my request to have him identified sound rather fast and improper.

Following her directions and under her

watchful gaze, I made my way along the corridor towards a path where a nurse was pushing a wheelchair. The brisk nurse tapped on the window, indicating the shawled occupant as Dr Stern.

I mouthed a thank you and walked across the grass.

The young nurse, aged about sixteen, I guessed, turned to greet me and at my request I was introduced to the unmoving figure hunched up in the chair as: 'Mrs Erland Yesnaby's sister, Mrs McQuinn.'

She said the words very slowly and loudly, with a glance in my direction that hinted the old doctor was also hard of hearing.

'I am very pleased to meet you, Dr Stern.'

His hostile glance as I took hold of that skeletal hand did not augur well. 'My sister, Mrs Yesnaby, sends you her warmest greetings. She has asked me to give you this–' I touched the plant – 'and to wish you many happy returns of your birthday.'

Even as I heard myself saying the words, I realized how incongruous they sounded.

The doctor glared at the flower in its pot. I could have sworn that its petals shivered under his gaze and as he made no attempt to take it from me I relinquished it to the young nurse's tender keeping – I hoped!

Dr Stern meanwhile snatched the biscuits, turned then over contemptuously and thrust them down the side of the wheelchair.

He stared at me suspiciously. 'Mrs Yesnaby is dead,' he said firmly. 'And I don't know who you are.' His tone suggested that he didn't care much either as he continued: 'Erland Yesnaby would be sending me something stronger. Like a good malt whisky.' Another glare, a hint that I was here on false pretences, as he shook a fist at me. 'Mrs Yesnaby had a fine taste in whisky.'

I stammered out that the present was from my sister, Mrs Emily Yesnaby, but he grunted and deliberately turned his head away, muttering: 'Whisky – that's that I want. Not all this rubbish.'

An apologetic glance, a despairing sigh from the young nurse indicated that the lack of whisky was a constant source of aggravation and argument in her charge.

Did everyone drink in Hopescarth, I thought helplessly, remembering Thora and PC Jock Flitt's unfortunate demise, as a result no doubt of too much indulgence.

Dr Stern made an impatient gesture and banged a fist against the arm of his wheelchair. 'Let's get on with it, shall we? I'm cold. No point in standing around here.'

I fell into step alongside, wondering what to do next, how to ingratiate myself with the doctor. Then I had an idea and said to the nurse: 'I could take over from you, look after him for a while.'

Sadly she shook her head and whispered: 'You would need to ask Matron first, madam. Unauthorized visitors are not allowed to take our – residents out in wheelchairs.'

At that I surveyed the situation with deepening gloom. It looked as if my journey, from which I had had such hopes of obtaining information about Thora Yesnaby, was fast proving to be a waste of time. Indications were clear that it was going to be exceedingly difficult, not to say impossible, to bring up the subject.

Especially as Dr Stern after his outburst about the whisky had lapsed into a huffy silence, or, bored, was feigning sleep.

This lasted for a few rounds of the path through the shrubbery and around the lawn. He had dismissed my presence, if he was still aware of it, while I considered what should be my next move.

As we approached the house, the nurse gave me a sympathetic look: 'Are you on holiday, madam?'

'Yes, I'm staying at Hopescarth with my sister – she's the second Mrs Yesnaby. It was her suggestion that I should visit Dr Stern. I gather he was greatly liked by them, a close friend as well as the family doctor.'

The nurse frowned. 'His memory is quite acute – about some things. And he does hold very strong opinions.' Her tone suggested that he was a difficult patient.

Politely I said goodbye to him. He either didn't hear me or was fast asleep and I walked out of the gate and down the drive, aware that I was tired too with that early morning start and the far from comfortable journey in Alec Burray's farm cart.

A church clock struck midday. Here I was in Kirkwall with at least four hours before the return journey to Hopescarth.

If only the visit to Dr Stern hadn't been so disappointing. The day's journey was completely wasted, and all I had found was a confused, bad-tempered old man.

I went into the local hotel, which was still relatively quiet before the farmers and cattle buyers arrived for their midday meal. As I tackled soup followed by steak pie, I realized that in all my early years in Kirkwall I had hardly ever set foot in this hotel before, or eaten meals anywhere except in my own home with Emily and Gran, who would have been shocked at such an extravagance.

I decided it was quite a novel and very pleasant experience as I sat at the window table overlooking the harbour. Some of the diners were staying and collected their keys at reception.

As I watched them climbing the carpeted stairs to their bedrooms, I had a sudden impulse to do the same. Book a room, go upstairs and close the door. Spend the rest of my holiday here – pleasantly, unexcitingly drifting about Kirkwall.

Oh, the joy to leave the horrors awaiting me at Yesnaby House. Just pretend they had never happened. Dismiss them from my mind. If only I could do so. If only I could have been someone else instead of Rose McQuinn at that moment.

Someone who could thrust aside the murder of her brother-in-law's first wife.

But paying my bill, I abandoned that fantasy and decided there remained one somewhat forlorn possibility to justify my early morning visit to Kirkwall.

PC Andy Green had suggested I should visit the offices of *The Orcadian*. With directions from a waitress I made my way through the streets and entering the newspaper office requested back numbers relating to archaeological digs in the Hopescarth area.

And at last I had a piece of good fortune to make the trip to Kirkwall worthwhile. As I was making my inquiry, a man seated at a nearby desk came over.

'Are you planning to visit Hopescarth?'

When I said yes, he smiled. 'Maybe I can help you? What exactly where you interested in seeing?'

I explained that I was visiting my sister in Yesnaby House and I had heard about the peat-bog burial last year. Deciding to avoid exhibiting a morbid interest in Emily's predecessor, I took refuge in one of my many assumed roles.

I was gathering information on a travel piece on Orkney for an Edinburgh magazine which had particularly stressed archaeological finds.

The reporter smiled. 'You've come to the right person. Eric Mawson,' he said and held out his hand. 'I was on the spot.'

'Did you actually see the body exhumed?' I asked.

'Alas, no. It was removed very speedily on the doctor's orders. Apparently deterioration sets in very fast on exposure to the open air. Writing it up was my assignment and I think

I can lay hands on the articles you want.'

A few minutes later I was seated at a table with a large file of back numbers.

Chapter Twenty-six

'Peat-bog burial,' said Mr Mawson triumphantly. 'Here it is. I'll leave you to it.'

Dated 28th October 1895, the article began:

Mrs Thora Yesnaby of Yesnaby House, Hopescarth disappeared from her home ten years ago in September 1885. A woman's badly decomposed body washed ashore in a storm near Marwick Head on 30th November of that year was identified by Mr Erland Yesnaby as that of his missing wife and buried in the family grave at Hopescarth.

The November date was of particular significance as Erland and Emily were married less than a month later on Christmas Day 1885.

The newspaper account continued:

The body discovered in the peat-bog a few days ago was subsequently identified as the real Mrs Thora Yesnaby. The family doctor Joseph Stern claimed that the body had lain there since the night of her disappearance when she had stumbled into the peat-bog on leaving her home...

I scanned the rest. The preservative qualities of peat and so forth were discussed, but there was one surprising omission. No one had queried the identity of the woman buried in Thora's grave.

As I noted down the dates in my logbook, I turned back to my entry dated 2nd October 1895, describing my recovery of a locket for a client Mrs Smith, at Brightwell's Hotel, Princes Street, Edinburgh.

Since Mrs Smith was the alias of Thora Yesnaby, this indicated that her visit to Hopescarth and the discovery of her body took place within three weeks of her departure from Edinburgh.

I sighed wearily. Although I now had some actual dates for reference, I knew that recent crimes are difficult enough to solve, but dealing with those that happened a year ago suggested all the possibilities of nightmare.

But I should be grateful. All I needed to know was where the prime suspects were during the three weeks covering her probable departure from Edinburgh to the grim discovery of her body. I thought cynically: No wonder that her corpse looked so fresh, and I would have hazarded a fairly accurate guess that Thora's arrival at Yesnaby House and her departure via the peat-bog were almost simultaneous.

They had to be, otherwise too many other people would have been involved. As it was, the murderer was taking a great chance. Someone who had known her at Hopescarth might have encountered her on the journey from Stromness and realized that she had not been dead for ten years after all, and was returning home very much alive. In small communities like Hopescarth, such fascinating revelations, such sensational news would move faster than a forest fire. And that was one risk her murderer could not take.

I had to find out from Emily, by subtle means, if Erland was at home during last October. And if he was in Bergen had he an alibi? If so, who had murdered her?

What about the young lover? I must not omit him. Did he have a motive? Truth and the motive were inescapable and firmly pointed to Erland who I knew from my Edinburgh interview with 'Mrs Smith' was the reason for her visit.

The only person who knew the exact date of Thora's return, who had met her and learned her grim purpose of blackmail, had also been her killer. This was a fact I could not ignore whatever my reluctance to confront it.

But how had she travelled from Edinburgh to Stromness and on to Hopescarth without being noticed? And I was back with the mysterious question that continued to haunt me.

The picture in my mind of Mrs Smith arriving off that Leith steamer soon after I had restored the locket to her. Was she alone or was she accompanied by her young lover?

It was very irritating that I had merely caught a glimpse of him. Mrs Smith had avoided an introduction so I had no name for him, not even a false one, since he had probably registered as Mr Smith at Brightwell's Hotel.

There was so much valuable information readily available, the kind I was used to tracking down had I been conducting this inquiry in Edinburgh. Of course I could write to Jack to check the relevant details for me. But my stay would be almost over before I might hope for a response. To say nothing of lengthy explanations regarding the purpose behind my inquiries and the necessity of telling him about my interview with 'Mrs Smith' and why I hadn't mentioned those twenty guineas, my fee for recovering the locket.

Alas, there was no easy way and I had to solve this murder here in Hopescarth – alone – before my holiday ended or return home and leave the mystery for ever unsolved.

To be tormented for the rest of my life by the suspicion that my sister Emily was married to a murderer. Or, reason whispered, that my sister Emily might be accessory to such a crime.

My thoughts returned to Thora. Had she hired a carriage at Stromness to take her to Hopescarth? And I toyed with the possibility of searching out firms of carriage hirers in Stromness. But the hope of finding the same cab and the same driver – and of his remembering the fare he had taken to Hopescarth, whether or not she travelled alone – was remote indeed.

Even with such information, could I risk stirring up muddy waters which might involve Emily? She was my main concern, in need of greater protection than Erland, especially as anxiety might bring disaster to her early pregnancy.

As for Thora, if she hoped for anonymity, I did not doubt that she had taken refuge in the easiest of all disguises for any woman. Most convenient and readily at hand were widow's weeds, features hidden behind heavy veils, vague and impenetrable as her sorrow. To be revered, respected and unapproachable. And considerably to her murderer's advantage.

I considered her arriving at Hopescarth in a hired carriage, the driver showing little interest in his passenger, beyond taking her fare. There was a possibility of course that the same driver might have heard a few weeks later about the archaeologists' grim discovery at Hopescarth. But unless he was of an inquiring turn of mind, what was there to connect the corpse who had lain undiscovered in the peat-bog for ten years with the widowed lady, the fare he had driven recently from Stromness to Hopescarth?

Returning the past issues of the newspaper to Mr Mawson with expressions of gratitude, I wandered back into the streets of Kirkwall – a pleasurable experience, at least. In order to make my visit seem satisfactory, for they would want every hour accounted for, I bought some special cheeses for Erland

285

and chocolates for Gran and Emily and visited St Magnus Cathedral where Emily and I had gone to Sunday School long ago.

As I walked past our old school, the bell rang and the children came hurrying out of the gates, talking shrilly. I stood aside, guessing that many were children of my own schoolmates who had settled down in Kirkwall and married farmers, local lads.

The realization made me wish I had kept in touch with those long-lost companions.

At last it was time to join Alec Burray and the farmers on their return journey to Hopescarth and beyond. This proved to be a much quieter affair, with considerably fewer animals, and some of the farmers were very cheerful and quite inebriated. Obviously profits from their sales had been skimmed off for whisky and ale.

Once again we broke our journey at the Skailholm Inn. I wondered if the military gentleman was still there.

Maud drifted over and as if she knew what I had in mind, she said: 'That man who stayed here last night, he got a lift to Hope-scarth this morning, soon after you left.'

'I don't suppose you get many Canadians.'

She shook her head. 'First since I've been here, usually looking for their roots.'

'Did he say who he was visiting?'

'Frank Breck, I expect. Lily once said she had a brother in Toronto. Lily's husband works with Craig. Known her for years. We were very friendly when she came here in the summer. She's a city girl like myself, wanted to get away from all that mud once in a while, and she didn't care too much for Frank's lodgings come to that. Used to come over with the farmers' carts sometimes for a change of scene.'

'So this is a visit to his brother-in-law?'

She frowned. 'I suppose so. Mr Mainwell is worried about her. Hasn't heard from her in ages. Seems they never kept much in contact but he expected to see her in Edinburgh. She wasn't at that address any more, and no one seemed to know where she's gone to.'

'That's odd,' I said. 'Frank told me she lived in Minto Street.'

Maud shrugged. 'Maybe Mr Mainwell went to the wrong house. Funny thing is, though, I haven't heard from her for years either so couldn't help him. She used to keep in touch, send a card at Christmas that sort of thing. But after she stopped coming to the dig, my letters all came back marked 'gone away'. I sent them to Frank at his lodging, saying would he forward them and let me have her new address. But he never replied – and neither did she.'

I remembered Craig saying he thought she'd found someone else. Perhaps Frank's manly pride was shattered, but perhaps she would have told Maud, so I said: 'Do you think she's maybe left Frank?'

Maud gave me a hard look. 'You mean, has she got another man?' She laughed. 'I wouldn't have blamed her. But I think she'd have told me. On the other hand, maybe she didn't want Frank to find out. I was sorry we lost touch, because I liked her and I thought we were good chums.' And with a sigh: 'But there it is. Life's like that.'

She sounded disappointed and my mind drifted back to girls at school swearing eternal friendship. The classroom their bond, the grown-up world the great divider.

Friendships, firmly made, that grew apart, unable to cope with the march of time and changing circumstances, I thought sadly as the cavalcade moved homewards.

Chapter Twenty-seven

I was set down once more outside the post office by a weary Alec Burray, who had been somewhat inarticulate on the final part of the journey. That had suited me as I had a great deal to mull over concerning the information acquired in the offices of *The Orcadian,* not to mention Lily Breck and her brother.

Leaving the farm cart, I was heading down the road towards Hopescarth when the sound of a noisy engine from Stromness direction announced the imminent appearance of Craig Denmore in his motor car. He drew to a halt alongside.

'Where's the bicycle?'

The information that I had been to Kirkwall with the farm carts raised his eyebrows a little.

'I can offer you more comfortable transport, or do you intend walking back to the house?'

I accepted gratefully and told him I'd met Mrs Breck's brother at the Skailholm Inn.

Craig nodded. 'He was here earlier. Frank was off to show him the sights of Hope-scarth. They were heading to the Troll's Cave.'

'I haven't been there yet.'

Perhaps he thought I was angling for an invitation as he said very quickly: 'I'll take you – it's just round the corner, in a manner of speaking, from where Sibella lives.'

'In that case, I'll have no difficulty in finding it.'

He put a hand on my arm. 'Steer clear, Rose. There are warning notices – strictly out of bounds to strangers in the area.'

I laughed at that and he gave me a stern look. 'The Troll's Cave is a very dangerous place for the unwary. There's a funnel that goes right down to the shore. A sort of chimney.'

'A chimney?'

'Yes. The roarsts funnel up at high tide. Makes a sound like dragons roaring, according to young Wilma, who's strictly barred from going anywhere near.' He smiled. 'I presume an Orcadian lass knows all about the roaring roarsts?'

I said: 'Of course,' not confessing that I had just heard about them recently and Craig went on:

'Frank has good reason to remember the roarsts. That's how his boat was washed ashore, beaten to matchwood.'

He didn't need to complete the picture of the boat that was believed to have carried Thora Yesnaby to her death. The thought crossed my mind to wonder why it had such fascination for Lily's Canadian brother as Craig continued:

'I'll take you there sometime at low tide. It's quite spectacular from the clifftop, well worth seeing. We can take a picnic, if you have time.'

I certainly had time for a picnic with Craig Denmore, even by moonlight on a stormy night would have been acceptable.

I said, keeping calm, that I would enjoy that very much and Craig grinned: 'I'll see when we have the next low tide. I have a tide-table somewhere.'

We had reached the bridge leading across to the drive when Frank and his brother-in-law appeared from the direction of the dig.

As Frank prepared to make some reluctant introductions, I said we had met before. I thought Jim Mainwell looked angry. Whatever we had interrupted, he was clearly upset.

Frank said brusquely: 'I'm taking him to

our lodging overnight,' to which Mainwell replied unsmiling:

'I was hoping to stay for a few days.'

'There may not be room at Mrs Flitt's.' Frank's sharp response managed to indicate his hope that there wouldn't be.

'I dare say Meg will find something for you.' Craig smiled soothingly at the newcomer, earning a bitter glance from Frank. 'Incidentally, I have things to do in Kirkwall, perhaps you would care to see it?'

'Thank you, sir. I would be delighted,' Mainwell replied. 'I have only a short while to explore my surroundings.'

'An excellent idea, Craig,' said Frank gratefully, sounding relieved to have someone take his brother-in-law off his hands.

They walked on and, as I prepared to step down from the car, Craig took my arm. 'Come along, I'll deliver you to the front door. It's a tedious walk up that drive.'

Watching the two men head towards the village, I had a weird sensation of everything being out of focus, a sense of brooding disquiet as I asked: 'What do you think of him?'

Craig knew exactly who I was talking about.

'A pity he had to come all this way to see his sister. Someone should have told him in Edinburgh.'

'Frank told me she lived in Minto Street, that's very near my home. Mrs Lenny told me that she and Lily had been good friends when she used to come here in the summer, but that they'd lost touch.'

'I think the answer is rather obvious,' said Craig with a sigh. 'Lily has found another man and poor old Frank can't bear to have us know. Still keeps up this elaborate pretence that all is well in Edinburgh.'

As Craig drew up in front of the house I said: 'If Lily has found someone else, why doesn't she get a divorce, free herself from Frank?'

Craig shrugged. 'I've no idea. Divorces and marriage breakdowns are very personal things, Rose, and Frank is a very sensitive and secretive person. Doesn't talk about himself if he can avoid it. Even though I've worked with him for years now, I couldn't cal him a close friend.'

He was silent and then said reluctantly: 'Maybe Lily preferred to leave him quietly – just walk out. He does have a very violent temper on the rare occasions when he gets annoyed. Perhaps Lily wanted to avoid the big scene.'

'Surely she kept in touch with someone,' I said desperately. 'What about her family?'

'You'll need to ask Frank if she has any apart from that older brother in Canada. Probably nothing much in common.'

I couldn't imagine asking Frank such a question. Besides there was something wrong here. I could feel it.

'If they had lost touch, why this sudden decision to come all the way to Orkney? Hardly the easiest journey in the world.'

Craig shrugged. 'Who knows? An attack of conscience and maybe a desire to see his long-lost sister. Happens when families get older.'

He regarded my worried expression critically. 'Don't concern yourself about Frank and Lily. Married people split up regularly and don't advertise the fact. They often feel a little ashamed, especially when a man has to admit that his wife left him for someone else. I expect the simple truth was that Lily was bored to death, and that's why she abandoned the summer dig – and Frank.'

This confirmed what Maud had told me.

'You're a sweet person, Rose, you worry too much.' His hand on my arm was a surge of warmth that set my blood racing. My knees went quite weak at the thought of what it would be like if Craig Denmore ever crossed the boundary and kissed me.

Oblivious to his effect upon me, he was smiling, changing the subject, saying: 'You haven't told me what you were doing in Kirkwall, all alone.'

So he guessed that too and I said defensively: 'I am used to being on my own rather a lot.'

A look of compassion as he said gently: 'Poor Rose, I forgot.'

The last thing I wanted from him was sympathy for the poor young widow.

'Didn't Yesnaby offer to take you in the carriage?' he said.

'I had things of my own to do.'

And because I desperately needed to tell someone, to share my fears and perhaps even seek reassurance, I decided to confide in Craig.

I began at the beginning, the garden at Hopescarth and seeing the mermaid stone. The feeling that I had seen it somewhere else.

'Yes, I remember,' Craig interrupted. 'You asked me about it. Did I know where there was a similar stone.'

'I didn't know then that Thora Yesnaby was wearing a locket with the same design. Have you seen it – in her portrait in Yesnaby House?'

He frowned. 'Not in my time – on the rare occasions when I've been invited to cross the threshold. So?'

'So I remembered where I had seen that same locket before.' I paused dramatically. 'In Edinburgh – just last year.'

It had to come out then. I handed him one of my cards.

He read it and whistled. 'A detective – like your father. Who would have guessed it. How on earth–'

'Some day I'll tell you how I got into it, but let's keep to the facts.'

And I told him about Mrs Smith, my client who had the locket stolen from her hotel room.

Craig didn't seem all that impressed. He shrugged. 'Could have been a copy.'

'Not this time, Craig. Not when Mrs Smith was Thora Yesnaby.'

That bombshell went down like a damp firework. 'I don't get it, Rose. How could she? Thora had been dead for years–'

'So we all thought, but when Emily showed me the portrait of Thora stored away in the attics, I recognized her as the woman I had known as Mrs Smith.'

Craig was silent for a moment. 'Are you absolutely sure about this?' he demanded. 'You couldn't have made a mistake? I mean it isn't impossible for people to have doubles. And portraits aren't always accurate images.'

'I agree. I realize it could have been merely a very strong resemblance, but I wasn't wrong about the locket. Of that I am certain – you see, I held it in my hand, Craig.'

Again he whistled, said slowly: 'Are you telling me that Thora Yesnaby, after pretending to be dead for years, came back to Hopescarth and got herself murdered? That someone pushed her into the peat-bog? Who on earth would do that – and why, for heaven's sake?' he laughed shakily. 'That's too fantastic, Rose.'

I said nothing and he gave me a sharp look. The obvious and only answer as to the identity of Thora's killer had also occurred to him. He said slowly: 'Bit inconvenient for Erland, wasn't it, though? Especially when he thought he had put her in the family vault ten years previously.'

He paused, frowning. 'Wait a minute. What about that other woman? Who was she?'

Even as his words sank in, the answer was there, staring me in the face.

But I still couldn't see it.

Chapter Twenty-eight

At breakfast next morning, Emily said: 'This note was posted through the door for you, Rose.'

She looked curious as I opened it and asked: 'Who is it from?'

'Craig Denmore. He's taking me to the Troll's Cave.'

Erland looked up from his newspaper and frowned. 'Do be careful, Rose.' And then the oft-repeated warning: 'It can be very dangerous.'

I said to him: 'I promise to take care,' and with a certain unrestrained note of pride I added: 'I'm sure Craig will look after me.'

Erland said: 'You know how to get there?'

When I said I had been told it was close to Sibella's croft, he shook his head. 'It is, but you can miss it easily. The best way to approach is by the shore.'

'You will take care,' Emily said anxiously and I couldn't resist saying again: 'I'll be in very good hands, I assure you.'

When I went upstairs, I looked again at

the note. There was no heading, all it said was: 'Meet today as planned at 3 p.m. Craig.' A very brief scribble, the time altered from 5 to 3, as if the writer had been in a great hurry.

On a calm sunny day, it was too good a chance to miss, especially as access to the cave was dependent on the weather and tides.

I walked down to the shore, with the cliffs rising sheer above me. The sea looked warm and friendly, very blue, with gentle waves lazily lapping the shore and a few seals enjoying the sunshine, like human bathers after a strenuous swim.

It was hard to believe that this tranquil scene could be transformed within a few minutes to a place of death and destruction, that the sea's lace-edged calm could change suddenly from smooth sapphire into fierce white foam, ready to suck the unwary down into the needle-sharp rocks below the surface.

The entrance to the cave was a natural crevice set back against the cliff about four feet above the sand, an access to be skilfully negotiated over rocks treacherous with wet seaweed.

I made my way carefully, leaping from one

smooth rock to the next, thankful that since Craig's terse note hadn't mentioned a picnic, I had both hands free.

I was early, with half an hour to spare. The dark interior of the cave held globules of reflected light but I decided against penetrating too far into that gloomy cavern. Especially as imagination had no problem at all in conjuring up the residents with leering faces hiding in every crevice.

I felt scared, my scalp tingling as I nervously glanced over my shoulder, trying to see beyond the cave's shadowy depths.

Once I thought I heard breathing, fancied a movement where there should have been none, told myself it was only glancing sunlight.

Perhaps Craig had got here first after all.

Nervously I called: 'Craig, is that you?'

Then out of the darkness, a shadow exploded, swooped down on me. A trapped bird, I thought, and ducked to avoid a glancing blow.

I cried out as something struck out at my head.

But it was a human hand that struck me – hard.

The darkness shifted and absorbed me into its depths.

I was in the land of no-time. The centuries had turned back. In earth time, the flight of a single arrow, the shiver of a solitary leaf falling upon the ground.

I was wading through the shallows, a ship lying at anchor in the grey of a cold autumn dawn. Men came ashore in boats, in furs and rich raiments huddled against the piercing wind, the seabirds screaming above their heads.

In their midst, women wept into hooded cloaks. Ahead of them, a man solemnly bore the body of a child aloft, high above the sea.

A small exquisite girl child, the moonlight touched her face, waxed in the immortality of death. Only her hair moved, pale yellow hair, braided and entwined with pearls.

One of the younger women ran forward weeping, returned with seathrift and blue flowers, a mourning wreath to set about her mistress's brow as they made their way towards the only habitation, a crude stone building like a hermit's cell dwarfed by the bleak landscape.

The child's death had been sudden, unexpected, and had taken all by surprise. The sound of a carpenter's hammer on the shore mixed with the boom of the sea, a funeral knell, numbing the dirge of weeping women.

At last as all shivered, waiting, their work

completed, the mourners watched with folded hands, trembling against cold and sorrow as the small body wrapped in cloth of gold was reverently carried to its bier, swathed in a black velvet cloak.

I followed at a distance, conscious even then that I was an observer only and they would shrink in horror from this ghost of a time still to come.

Climbing the steep hill with no path I walked in the footsteps of the mourners.

In my dream this was a familiar place although against that dawn horizon there was nothing to break the cold barren landscape but the ruined ancient chapel I had seen from the shore.

We stumbled towards it, over boulder and rocks, as a voice called: 'Where shall we lay our young majesty to rest?'

The man who came forward staff in hand, with the important air of a priest, replied: 'Here she shall lie, facing across the sea. Towards her own beloved land.'

At his words, a keening wail from the women.

'Let it be so, as I command,' the priest went on. 'For one day, we shall return and give her proper burial with a solemn mass and all honours due to a beloved queen.'

I watched them move forward, a watcher

beyond time, when suddenly I was conscious that I was no longer alone.

There was a dog at my side. A deerhound.

Past and present became one.

'Thane,' I whispered.

But this dog was different. This dog had a human voice.

'Leave us. Go – hurry – or the sea will take you. Wake from your dream, Rose. Wake...'

But as he circled me, frantically barking, I was already in the sea, its cold spread was gripping my feet, crawling up my legs.

I had one last glimpse of the cortege of the dead. The dog was wavering, dissolving into the air, his barking growing fainter, as I called weakly: 'Stay with me. Don't leave me.'

But I was aware of danger. I was in quicksand, unable to move, the thick wetness growing higher, higher, past my waist...

My eyelids were too heavy to open, but I knew, although I dreamed, that I was in deadly peril. That I must escape from this nightmare, awaken to find myself in my warm bed at Hopescarth.

I blinked furiously, a trick I learned from Pappa long ago, to rouse myself from childhood's more grisly nightmares. But the effort of opening my eyes was like moving lead weights.

I kept on blinking furiously, squeezing my

eyelids together.
It worked. Suddenly I was awake.

Suddenly I was awake. But far from my warm bed.

Confused, I thought I had fallen asleep while taking a bath. It was dark, the lamp had gone out, the water was cold. So cold.

Then, horror-stricken, my eyes were fully open and I had stepped from one nightmare into another.

I was lying in water, the sea was rushing through what had been the mouth of the Troll's Cave.

I was trapped.

As I attempted to rise, the weight of the sea hurled me on to my back again. I coughed up salt water, tried to rise, realizing I had either been carried unconscious by the water and drifted into the depths of the cave … or I had been carried by human hands. And left to drown.

I tried to stand. But there was no light to see by. At that moment I lost all reason and panicked for there was no way I could get through that solid stream of water. No way I could reach the entrance of the cave which had vanished under the tide.

I began screaming although there were

none to hear my cries. And I ached. My head too screamed with pain, with the force of the blow I had been dealt by that unknown assailant.

It was only the brutal force of the sea that had brought me back to consciousness. Obviously I was not meant to recover my senses.

The intention was that I should be trapped in the cave.

And drowned. And this was no troll or trolls at work, no superhuman agency here. *Someone was trying to kill me.*

And I knew in that instant that I must not give in to panic. I must try to think logically against this inferno of sound, these fierce waves tearing at me. I had to use my reason – my poor ever-diminishing reason that told me I must die, that I must drown in the next few minutes, if I could not think clearly.

Think clearly. And battling to keep my head above the rising angry waters, I put out my hands like a blind woman, edged forward and was rewarded.

I touched rock, and running my hands downwards, touched a ledge. About a foot wide and a yard above the floor of the cave. I struggled to scramble on to it, while the sea tore at me, dragging me under.

At last I was on my feet, above the water. For a moment it seemed I was safe, soaked, cold. Alive. But for how long?

The water too, that raging sea, continued to rise and I remembered that this was the tide that flooded the cave, the dreaded 'roarin' roarst', and that there was a funnel Craig had told me about. A chimney-like funnel where far above my head, on the clifftop, one could watch the waters spouting out.

A spectacular show, he had called it.

And with just a glimmer of hope, I realized the presence of a spout meant more than one exit from the cave. If I could find it, if it was wide enough to take a human being.

At least I was small, and slim too. Perhaps that would save me.

I began to struggle along the rocky ledge, searching for the gleam of light that would show me where the funnel exited. And even then my heart failed me, as sense whispered: What if it is night out there, how will you see it then?

How long I had been unconscious, I could only guess. But I remembered I had left the house shortly after two o'clock, so was it still a summer afternoon outside? And even as I thought of promises, I thrust out of my mind the horror of the evil intent that had lured me here to my death.

Inch by inch, I crawled along the ledge, clinging desperately to any protruding rocks, for if I missed my footing and fell back into the foaming water I would surely drown.

Then at last I saw it. A few feet above my head, an unmoving area of light. A gleam of sky.

Which meant that I still had a chance of survival, a very slim chance and only if I could reach it.

Struggling forwards, I took my time, noting that it was not yet full tide when the trapped seas would be roaring out of that tiny space.

After what seemed like hours of careful negotiation, the spout came nearer glowing like an angel's halo above my head. And I knew that although the space was too small for a man, or an average-sized woman, I was small enough to squeeze through it.

Had I been taller I could have stood up and scrambled through, but I was too short and desperately sought footholds on sides worn slippery smooth. Sometimes I got a foot on to a protruding rock and found it too weak to support my weight as a sliver crumbled, broke off and fell back into the water, almost taking me with it.

Panting, I regained my balance and, sobbing with exhaustion, summoned up enough breath to call for help in the forlorn hope that someone walking on the clifftop would hear me.

'Help, help…' I cried at intervals, but how could a human voice compete against the roar of the waves echoing in the cave?

Then at last it seemed my shouts were heard, my prayers answered…

A face appeared, filling the round aperture above my head.

The face of my rescuer!

'Thank God – thank God,' I sobbed and reached my arms up as far as I could for that saviour to seize.

The face moved forward.

For a moment it was in focus.

'Frank!' I screamed. 'Grab hold of my arms. Quickly – help me out,' I cried, sobbing with gratitude at my deliverance.

Chapter Twenty-nine

'Frank – help me out!' I called again desperately.

But he continued to stare down at me, unseeing, bewildered.

'Help me! I'm going to drown…'

He did not move. Then his face, my last hope of surviving, disappeared.

Perhaps he was going for help – for a rope.

I could not wait for that. Again I tried to climb but my foot slipped and I plunged back, screaming. A second later and I would have been in that boiling, thrusting water. I only just regained my balance on the narrow ledge, no longer able to distinguish between the sound of the waves dashing against the funnel sides and my own heartbeat. I could not believe that Frank would leave me there to drown.

No time to reason out his odd behaviour now as the water was higher, growing more ferocious.

The ledge had saved me otherwise I would have been drowned on the floor of the cave, or in the fury of the rising tide.

As I struggled to climb those last few feet, I tried to think calmly. If Frank, as I hoped and believed, had gone for help, it was almost too late now. I had only minutes, perhaps even seconds before the waters gained full strength and funnelled up out of the spout.

Clinging with one hand, I used the other to feel yet again for any possible footholds on the slippery rock face worn by centuries of the roarst.

I knew, even as I made one last effort, that no one was coming to save me, although Frank could have done so quite easily. If he had kneeled down, his arms could have reached me, pulled me to safety.

There was a projecting lip in the rock wall near the funnel, just above my head. I eased myself along towards it, wondering if it would take my full weight when I tried to stand upright–

And then the dreaded waters were my saviour. The force of an extra strong wave propelled me forward and upwards. A moment later I was lying, half out of the chimney, clawing at the rocks, the sea rushing behind me, rising like a great spout of water.

My progress was watched by a screaming cloud of gulls, swooping over my head. Doubtless they were used to the wave washing fish and other delectables on to the rocks. Their bright eyes and cruel beaks as they swooped clearly indicated that this was an interesting new morsel.

They were just too close for comfort. I screamed as the water spout like some nightmare fountain thrust me forward. Just in time I grabbed at the rocks, for as the waters receded back into the funnel they would have taken me with them, sucked me down into the cave.

With the seabirds still wheeling above my head, I struggled to my feet on firm land, dripping water, shivering, but safe.

Safe but terrified – as the dreadful realization dawned.

Someone had tried to kill me. Someone – and logic said Craig Denmore – had sent me a note, telling me to come to the Troll's Cave – at high tide!

And he had come to make sure I was in the cave. Had hit me on the head and left me there.

As for Frank Breck – were they both in it? Was this some plot concerning the Maid of Norway's dowry?

Was I getting too close to the solution for comfort?

Squelching water at every step, my clothes weighed down with water, I staggered along the cliff path.

On the horizon, the archaeology dig appeared to be deserted. The nearest hint of civilization was Sibella's croft for I was too weak and exhausted to face the long drive up to Hopescarth.

I pushed open the gate, feebly pushed open the door.

I blinked at the darkness within, praying that Sibella would be at home.

She was sitting by the fire and at first glance I hardly recognized her. I shivered, and not with cold this time, for on each occasion we met her appearance was a shock and I realized she was starting to look – well, not quite human.

She heard me come in, turned those strange round eyes towards me. I stretched out my arms and fell sobbing against her, the water pouring from my hair and clothes.

'Rose!' she said. 'Rose, what has happened?'

I gasped out that I had been in the Troll's Cave while she seized towels and stripped the wet clothes from me. At last huddled over the fire, shuddering, inarticulate, I told her the story which was already sounding more like a nightmare than reality.

I could see that Sibella thought so too.

'Who sent you the note?' she asked calmly.

When I said Craig, she repeated, almost in a whisper: 'Craig.'

A moment later she added: 'But he would never send anyone there at high tide, Rose. No one who knows this area would do such a terrible thing. They know the consequences, there have been many drownings there…'

I could think of nothing to say to that.

'Are you absolutely sure it was Craig?' she whispered and I thought she looked worried, scared.

'Who else?' I said bitterly.

Shaking her head she nodded grimly, repeated: 'Craig.' And thrusting a bowl of soup into my hand, she said: 'Drink this. There are herbs in it which will stop you taking a chill.'

She turned her attention to drying my sodden mass of thick hair, and I winced when she touched the lump raised on the back of my skull.

'It's a miracle you managed to escape the roarst. Most folk drown. However did you get out of the funnel?' And looking at me in wonder: 'I expect the fact that you are so small you have to thank. Most grown-up folk could never get through, they'd stick half-way,' she added with a shudder. 'Even children have been caught that way and drowned.'

Regaining strength and some of my composure, I said: 'I managed to find a ledge, worked my way towards the daylight. Frank Breck was there, outside on the clifftop. He heard me shouting for help.'

'So that was it. You were lucky, lass.'

'No, Sibella, I wasn't. Frank looked down at me and then just walked away. All he had to do was lean over and grab my arms. I thought at first that he had gone for help, but there was no sign of him anywhere when I managed to get out.'

Bewildered by all this, Sibella shook her head as I continued: 'And there's more. Someone was already hiding in the cave when I got there, waiting for me.'

When I told her how I had been hit on the head, she looked even more perturbed, even a little disbelieving, as if I was making it up. She took the empty bowl and when I said it was delicious, she gave me a refill.

'Drink this, then you'd better get up to the

house and into dry clothes. We'll sort out what happened to Frank later. There must be some explanation, Rose.'

Whatever was in the soup, I stopped shivering and began to feel a little better. Anger was fast replacing my feelings of terror.

Sibella wrapped my wet clothes into a bundle and took up her cloak. 'I'll walk up with you, lass. See you safe home.'

I put out a delaying hand. 'Before we go, Sibella, there's something I want to tell you about. I'm not sure that anyone else but you might understand. They might dismiss what happened as hallucinations from that bump on my head.'

I touched it gingerly, thankful that my hair was so thick, else it might have split my skull. 'You see, when I was unconscious and the sea was coming in, slowly then, I had a dream – at least I think that's what it was.'

And I told her about seeing the Maid of Norway carried ashore by the mourners, every detail as I could remember it.

'I'm sure the place was Hopescarth – here somewhere near by. Although it was quite different then. No house of course, no garden, but there was an ancient building no larger than a tool shed where the garden is now. One of those tiny early Christian chapels you see on deserted islands, their history lost long ago.'

'Like Eynhallow, you mean.'

'Yes, but smaller than that. The kind a hermit might have built.'

She touched my arm. 'Or a saint, Rose. Or a saint.' And with a sigh. 'If the Maid is buried here, if your vision was true, I think perhaps you should keep it to yourself, for the present anyway.'

And I knew she was warning me about Craig, when she added: 'I think your vision was a blessed one, Rose. I always guessed somehow from our first meeting that you were different – one of Us,' she added in a whisper, leaving me no doubts about who 'Us' referred to.

Then she smiled. 'Someone watches over you, Rose.'

There was only one thing I had omitted from my dream. And I was reluctant to add that, for there seemed enough fantasy without a dog with a human voice.

But I did tell her, and Sibella accepted that part of the vision too.

She nodded eagerly. 'Sometimes in times of peril animals can talk to us, warn us. You realize they have an extra sense of danger, one that humans had long ago but have now lost – some of us, a very few, retain a few shreds. That's all.'

I looked at her. 'And is that what magic is all about?'

She smiled. 'That's part of the secret, Rose. Having this extra awareness is what makes witches and warlocks and animals that talk.'

'I know an animal like that, Sibella.'

And I made a sudden decision. I had never told anyone at Hopescarth, certainly not Emily or Gran, about Thane, my mysterious companion, the deerhound who had a mysterious existence on Arthur's Seat.

I watched Sibella's expression carefully. But she didn't look cynical as I had expected. As we walked towards the drive leading to Hopescarth, I saw that she was entranced by the story of Thane, asking questions, wanting to know more about him. I told her how he had saved me from the tinkers, and from a murderer.

'And no one else has ever seen him except yourself?'

'Jack – my policeman friend. He's seen him.'

She laughed. 'Ah, Jack. The one you can't make up your mind to marry.' And wagging a finger at me: 'I think you'd do well not to let this Jack go, if your deerhound approves of him.'

And there at the most interesting part, where I wanted to know more, our conversation was terminated.

We never reached the drive, for as we crossed the bridge the sound of a motor car behind us on the road said that Craig Denmore was approaching.

And there were many questions I wanted to ask him, none of which could await a more opportune moment.

Chapter Thirty

Glad of Sibella at my side, I nevertheless had a sudden desire to take to my heels, to run from the helmeted, goggled driver bearing down upon us. No longer the fascinating, handsome Craig Denmore with whom I was allowing myself to fall just a little in love, this new image was sinister, terrifying, as the motor car snorted to a halt.

'What on earth has happened?' Craig demanded. Doubtless we were a curious spectacle, the old woman and the girl wrapped in a blanket, bare-legged and carrying her boots.

It was Sibella who spoke up. 'Rose had an accident at the Troll's Cave,' she said stiffly, 'and I'll be obliged if you will drive her up to the house as quickly as you can.' And with a warm protecting arm around me: 'I'll see you later, Rose.'

'Wait, Sibella.' I wanted her to stay. I felt safe in her presence but she was already walking away, that odd walk, dragging her feet more pronouncedly than ever.

Again the startling image, that Sibella was – reverting? Was it just the normal pattern of old age? Did Erland and Emily notice?

'What on earth were you doing in the Troll's Cave?' asked Craig who looked puzzled enough to deserve a 'not guilty' verdict as he leaped down and helped me into the passenger seat. 'I warned you that it was dangerous and I told you to wait until I sent you the tide-times.'

He stared down into my face as he started the engine and shouted as it roared into life: 'You could have drowned, Rose.'

'And I almost did!' I yelled back.

'Tell me when we get you home. Can't hear a word!'

It was a short drive but a cold one sitting wrapped in Sibella's blanket.

The front door was closed and I trudged round to the back door which was always kept open. Craig followed. The kitchen was empty and I guessed that Emily would be having her afternoon nap. Gran wasn't in sight either and I had some anxious moments wondering if I'd be safe enough, after what had happened, alone with him in an empty house.

After all, was it my own fault for trusting him? For confiding in him my fears about

Thora Yesnaby and the story of that stolen locket in Edinburgh? A thought clicked into place–

'Get dressed,' he said, handing me the bundle of wet clothes. 'I'll wait.'

I shivered. 'I feel like a drowned rat.'

He grinned and said softly: 'A very pretty drowned rat.'

At any other time how my heart would have raced at that tender look, I thought as I ran upstairs, safe in the knowledge that Emily was asleep just yards away.

I hadn't time to look out dry clothes, instead I put on a robe, dragged back my hair into a ribbon.

Downstairs, Craig was still there standing by the stove. He had made a pot of tea. Pouring out two cups, adding milk and sugar, he smiled as I sat opposite him at the table.

Looking me over, he said: 'You silly girl, Rose. You know you could have drowned.'

I repeated as I had in the motor car: 'I almost did.'

And as the whole terrifying scene returned, I sobbed out: 'How do you explain this – this note you sent, telling me to meet you there?'

I threw it down between us and he took it up, stared at it.

'It is your writing, isn't it?'

He frowned. 'Yes, but I don't understand. I didn't send it.' He stopped, stretched across the table and took my cold hands, rubbed them, as if restoring life into them. 'Rose, how could I have asked you to go to the Troll's Cave – to meet me? I had to take some artefacts to the steamer, to catch the tide. I had people to see in Stromness. I left at eleven this morning.'

I shook my head. 'How do you explain your note, then? Someone was expecting me. They were waiting in the cave.'

Fighting back rising hysteria, I touched the bump on my head and banged my fist on the table. 'Don't you understand, someone tried to kill me in your Troll's Cave.'

And I gabbled out the story.

He listened patiently without interruption or denial. At the end he said: 'You were hit on the head, knocked out. And this person – whoever it was – left you there to drown.' He stared at me wide-eyed. 'That is just incredible, Rose.'

I knew it sounded like that, but I went on: 'The incoming tide, the shock of the cold water brought me back and then I realized that the cave was being flooded. I made my way to the funnel you told me about. I tried

323

to climb out. Frank came–'

'Frank?' His head jerked up.

'Yes, Frank was there, outside on the clifftop. I shouted for help and he looked down at me.'

'You were lucky that he was there to save you.'

'To save me!' I screamed at him. 'Don't you understand, he just walked away.'

'Maybe he didn't see you–'

'Oh yes he did. I was only an arm's length below him. But he just – went away...'

Craig seized the note, looked at it again, said triumphantly: 'That's it. This note, it's one I sent to him, with his name cut off. It started, I'm sure, "Dear Frank".'

Biting his lip, he gave me a bewildered look and said: 'So someone else used my note to Frank.'

'You don't believe it was him, do you? I tell you I saw him.'

Craig seemed reluctant to believe ill of Frank Breck. He looked at the note and said: 'Weren't you suspicious? I didn't sound particularly friendly in this note, somewhat curt, don't you think?'

'Yes,' I admitted reluctantly.

He smiled again, relieved this time. 'Weren't you surprised?'

'Of course I wasn't surprised, Craig. Perhaps you always write curt notes,' I said sharply but he wasn't listening any more.

'If it really was Frank who sent you this,' he said grimly, 'then he has some explaining to do.' He shook his head. 'But why on earth should he do that to you, try to – kill – you? You've never harmed him.'

'I don't know the answer to that, but I know now that I wasn't the first of his victims.'

'What do you mean – first of his victims?' he demanded sharply. 'What on earth are you talking about, Rose?'

'I wasn't the first he left to drown,' I said triumphantly.

And one of the missing pieces of the puzzle that had been bothering me for a while now, suddenly veered into focus.

Craig sighed wearily. 'I haven't any idea what you're on about, Rose. That bash on the head...'

He paused significantly. 'Frank never drowned anyone.'

'Oh yes, he did. He killed Lily.'

'Rose, you're mad!' said Craig. 'Lily's alive and well in Edinburgh.'

'She's dead. Of that I'm certain.'

He made an impatient gesture and I said:

'Your friend Mrs Lenny was telling me how she and Lily Breck were great friends.'

He nodded. 'I know that. Lily used to go across to Skailholm any chance she got to see Maud. I don't blame her for that—'

'Then, listen, will you,' I said. 'According to Maud, Lily just stopped writing to her when she went back to Edinburgh at the end of the dig eleven years ago and – according to Frank – made the decision not to come back.'

Craig sighed. 'Eleven years – that's a long time. These things happen, Rose. Even to the best of friends.'

'Please don't interrupt. The time that Lily disappeared back to Edinburgh for good – mark that well, Craig. It was just before Thora Yesnaby also disappeared. In fact, one could say they both – left – Hopescarth around the same time.'

'So? I don't see the significance of that.'

And it was at that moment I decided that Craig Denmore might be a great archaeologist but he'd never make a detective.

'Lily lodged with Meg.'

'They both did.'

'Presumably any letters from Lily would be forwarded on to Frank.'

'Perhaps they didn't write to each other.

Married people often fall short on correspondence. Feel they've said everything there is to say to each other,' he added cynically.

'Her brother told Mrs Lenny that Lily stopped writing to him and that he had completely lost touch with her.'

'That's hardly surprising – it does happen in even the best of families.'

And I remembered Emily and in particularly Pappa on his travels with Imogen as he went on: 'Besides, brother and sister with a big age gap – it's like I told you, Rose. I suspect Lily met someone else and left Edinburgh and poor old Frank.'

That was the second time I had been given that piece of speculation. It wouldn't do this time and I said: 'You make it sound very simple, all part of good old human nature and the vagaries of time. But I think there is a more permanent and less endearing explanation,' I added triumphantly.

'So you think Lily is dead.' He laughed at my solemn face. 'Come on, Rose. What on earth gives you that idea? Just because she's abandoned her husband.'

'She didn't abandon her husband willingly, Craig. He murdered her. He drowned her off Marwick Head.'

'Really, Rose! Of all the mad suggestions–'

'Mad, is it? Then listen carefully. I am certain that Lily Breck didn't find someone else and leave Edinburgh, simply because she has been dead and buried for eleven years. I think Frank killed her, put her in the sea and let his boat drift ashore to be conveniently wrecked by the roarsts. As you once said, reduced to matchwood. It was very fortunate indeed for him that Thora Yesnaby disappeared at the same time.'

Craig looked at me. 'What are you saying?' He sounded shocked.

'What I'm saying is that the woman's torso Erland identified as Thora, was in fact all that remained of Lily Breck.'

'Lily Breck.' Craig shook his head vehemently. 'No, Rose. It just isn't possible.'

'I think it is. He killed her, just as he left me to drown. He knew that I was a private investigator, a female detective. And he was scared as hell that I might find out the truth.'

'The truth! I don't see your reasoning – why should Frank be scared of you?'

'Because when I asked where Lily lived in Edinburgh, he said Newington. And by a coincidence that's just half a mile from where I live and I showed him one of my cards. Just to be friendly I suggested calling on her – taking a message from him – when I returned home. I was quite ignorant of the intricacies of Frank's domestic life – I imagined that my offer would be doing him a favour.'

I thought for a moment, recalling his expression.

'He was very sharp with me. Cautious, realizing the danger if I went to her address in Minto Street and found she hadn't been seen there for all these years. And that he had told everyone a pack of lies.'

I paused for breath. Craig hadn't said a word and I asked: 'Tell me, what did Lily look like?'

Craig thought for a moment. 'I've only seen a photograph of her taken with Maud – Mrs Lenny. She was tallish, slim, dark hair.'

I remembered Mrs Smith and said: 'From the portrait I've seen, that would describe Thora too.'

Enough resemblance for a well-decomposed torso of an unknown woman, I thought firmly and resolved to see Maud's photograph of her old friend.

Craig was staring at me in amazement.

'You don't believe me, do you?' I asked.

'I don't – want – to believe you, Rose. I can't equate my image of Frank as a trusted colleague with that of a wife-murderer who has tried to kill you too.'

He shrugged, shook his head as if to get rid of the unpleasant thought. 'In my profession, all the murders have taken place centuries ago and the killers where applicable have turned into respectable dust. Murders don't normally happen to people we know.'

We were interrupted by footsteps on the stairs. Voices.

Craig whispered: 'I'll go now, I am not a welcome sight at this particular kitchen table. You've given me plenty to think about, Rose McQuinn,' he added grimly.

Time will tell, I thought, relieved that I had been wrong about Craig and that I could still keep some of my romantic illusions intact. He passed Emily and Gran in the doorway, leaving me to explain as best I could what I was doing in the kitchen with him. At five in the afternoon – in my nightrobe.

Cheerfully ignoring their shocked expressions, I cleared two teacups off the table and said: 'Decided to have a bath. Not a good time, I'm afraid.'

It was also a very transparent lie because

the sound of a bath running was audible all over the house.

Emily gave me a hard look. 'Was the water not too cold?' she asked sternly.

I shrugged. 'It was all right.' And thought that any water would pass that test compared to the roarst in the Troll's Cave.

Gran was looking out of the window. 'Craig Denmore's motor car is just going down the drive.'

'Oh, is it?' I said. And by the way of a rapid but feeble explanation for his presence in their kitchen: 'He was leaving me a note.'

Gran wandered over to the sink and frowned sternly at the two teacups as if they might be ready with some explanation of their own. I hurriedly withdrew and left them to work it out and come to their own conclusions.

For the moment I had more important things on my mind.

Such as having a word with Frank Breck next morning.

But I was already too late.

Chapter Thirty-one

When I came down to breakfast next morning, Craig was talking to Erland.

He had brought bad news. Frank Breck was dead.

'An accident with a rifle. Early this morning. He was going out shooting, the gun misfired. I drove him in to the hospital but it was too late.'

Emily and Gran were seated at the table. Erland stood with a hand on Emily's shoulder, anxiety in his face as he watched her, as if this shock might harm their unborn child.

I had to see Craig alone. I knew that was why he was at Hopescarth and a look, a silent message passed between us.

'I need to catch the post,' I said to Emily, seizing my cape from the peg by the door.

'I'll take you,' said Craig quickly.

A moment later we were outside. A bright shining morning, with seabirds, a radiant sky, a peaceful scene about as far from sudden death as anyone could imagine.

Craig handed me into the passenger seat.

'How did it happen? This is terrible news,' I said.

Craig merely nodded, started the engine, but a little way out of sight of the house, he braked the motor car to a standstill again.

'I didn't see Frank when I got back last night and I gathered he was going to take Jim out shooting. He needed a second rifle, one he didn't often use. It had belonged to his father and he kept it in Meg's shed. He was cleaning it–' Craig stopped, drew a deep breath. 'It misfired. It was fortunate that I had the old girl here–' he patted the wheel – 'parked outside as I had some artefacts to catch the early steamer in Stromness. I drove straight to the hospital.'

He shook his head sadly. 'They couldn't do anything for him. I thought you should know that he talked to me before the end. About Lily.' Turning to me, he sighed grimly.

'You were right, clever girl. He killed Lily. It seemed there was more to it than her being fed up with weather and dullness of summer at the dig. She told him she had a new fellow in Edinburgh and was leaving him.

'They were walking on the shore, late that

night, had a terrible row. Frank went wild, hit her with a piece of driftwood. Realized she was dead, panicked and pushed her out to sea in his fishing boat. The roarsts completed the job for him – beyond his wildest expectations,' he added grimly.

'Luck was on his side, of course, since Thora had run away and everyone believed that what was washed up at Marwick Head was what was left of her.'

Craig paused. 'Poor Frank. The years passed and apart from the occasional letter forwarded to Lily from Edinburgh which he destroyed, Frank felt he was safe.'

He turned to me and smiled grimly. 'Until a young woman came to visit her sister in Yesnaby House. By the hand of coincidence she lived just half a mile away from Lily in Edinburgh.'

He looked at me. 'You know the rest. He had to get rid of you. You were a female detective, and his guilt about Lily told him that you were the nosy kind of woman who might feel it was your duty to get in touch with Lily when you got back.

'In a way it was my fault too. I told him you wanted to see the Troll's Cave and did he know where we'd put the tide-tables? The rest was easy. He took one of my notes to him, cut off the "Dear Frank" bit – and waited for you in the cave. He was certain the roarst would drown you but, to make sure, he watched at the funnel. But you hadn't drowned and were struggling to get out and you had seen him.

'He knew that was the end of the line. Better to end it now than on the gallows. The past had caught up with him. Not only a sharp young woman who was a self-made detective but Lily's brother, a policeman from Canada, who was asking a lot of questions.'

'What about Thora? Did he kill her too?'

Craig shrugged. 'I didn't ask. Jim was waiting outside. They only let me stay because Frank insisted.' He sighed. 'I tried to avoid the gory details but Jim had guessed that Lily was dead – and left it at that. He has friends in Edinburgh, so he'll visit them for a while before going back home.'

'Was he very upset?'

'Hard to tell. Said the truth might as well go to the grave with Frank. How could anyone prove it now – after all this time. And a scandal like that, the newspapers and so forth. I think he wisely decided that they should both rest in peace.'

He smiled wryly and turned to me. 'Well

done, Rose, that's your mystery solved.'

'One down and one to go,' I said. 'Did he kill Thora?'

Craig shrugged. 'That we'll never know, but I doubt it,' he said, starting up the engine and cutting short the possibility of answers to the many questions I wanted to ask.

Before the engine's roar put an end to any further conversation, he grinned. 'Now you can go ahead and enjoy the rest of your holiday. We'll maybe manage some of those picnics yet.'

We had reached the bridge. 'I'll walk down to the post office now. I expect you have loads to do.'

He made a grimace. 'None of it very pleasant, I'm afraid. I'm more used to dealing with long-dead bodies not those of friends and colleagues. Andy Green will notify the Fiscal. I imagine it'll be an open and shut case as far as the law is concerned, accidents with rifles aren't all that unusual.

'As Frank had no family surviving, after the inquest I'll have to arrange the funeral. I doubt whether Jim will want to stay for that. Then I'll have to look for another archaeologist for next year's dig – someone who is enthusiastic enough to take on an Orkney dig, weather regardless.'

He looked sad. 'Poor old Frank. He'll be hard to replace, he was good at his job, I'll say that for him. Quite dedicated.'

He looked down at me. 'Let me know when you want to go into Stromness or Kirkwall. We can make a day of it. You came a long way to be with your sister,' he said solemnly. 'Try and put all this behind you and enjoy your holiday.'

I watched him drive down the road. So I was to go back to Hopescarth and enjoy the rest of my holiday.

Everything neatly put away, a killer found who had murdered his wife, had tried to kill me and, tormented by an evil conscience, had very obligingly committed suicide, surviving long enough however to confess to Craig.

Simple, wasn't it?

Unfortunately, I didn't believe it.

Oh yes, I did believe the part about Frank having murdered Lily and his reasons for feeling he had to dispose of me. The arrival of Jim Mainwell must have seemed like the last cruel twist of fate.

But had Frank also killed Thora Yesnaby? He hadn't confessed to that for the simple reason that he had loved Thora. And he didn't do it.

Someone else killed her. There was still the unknown young man, Mrs Smith's lover in Brightwell's Hotel, unaccounted for. And I still had at least one more murder to solve.

At the post office I found Meg in a state of shock, surrounded by a crowd of locals to whom she was breaking the news. The men were shaking their heads, full of deadly warnings about old rifles, and the women sighing like a Greek chorus, recalling other violent deaths on the island.

It was all quite dreadful. I managed to squeeze in and put my postcards on the counter.

Meg saw me and said: 'Mr Mainwell wanted a word with you – asked where you lived.' She gave me a curious look. 'You might save him the journey. He's upstairs in Frank's room, sorting things out.'

I went upstairs unsure what condolences to offer. I was spared the embarrassment when he put aside a sheaf of papers, stood up and shook hands.

'Please take a seat, Mrs McQuinn.'

'I'm sorry about Frank,' I began. He nodded absently and picked up the address card I had given Frank when I asked where

Lily lived.

'Mrs Rose McQuinn. Lady Investigator, Discretion Guaranteed.' He looked grave. 'Was Frank wanting you to look into Lily's disappearance by any chance?'

'No. I discovered quite by accident that Mrs Breck lived near me in Edinburgh.'

'Not any longer, Mrs McQuinn. And not for a very long time, I'm afraid.' He handed me some letters addressed to Mrs Lily Breck. 'These were returned to me. But Lily had indeed "gone away". And that is what I came over to investigate.'

Pausing, he smiled at me. 'Yes, Mrs McQuinn, I'm in the Canadian Mounted Police, a Mountie, maybe you've heard of us – the ones who always get their man – or woman, as the case may be.'

Leaning back he regarded me critically. 'So we are in the same line of business. I'm a lot older than Lily and we lost touch after she married Frank. I remembered she always adored children and, I gather, never had any of her own. I wrote to tell her about the birth of my twin daughters and asked her to be godmother, but she ignored the letter completely.

'I made allowances, perhaps she couldn't bear the thought of her brother having children when she had none, but early last year my dear wife died. Again I wrote to Lily, I expected acknowledgement. Some sympathy for a widowed brother, perhaps the possibility that she might want to see her little nieces, but again there was nothing, not a word.

'I was hurt but there was more to it than that. I was alone, my little girls were being taken care of by relatives, so I decided that I must see Lily again, get in touch, put a bridge over those lost years.'

This was so much my own story about Emily, I thought, losing touch, except that I had found my sister alive and well – and, reason whispered, perhaps married to a murderer.

Jim went on: 'Then something occurred that made it imperative that she be found, her whereabouts traced, alive or dead,' he added grimly. 'An old man on our mother's side who struck it rich gold-mining in '49 died childless in California. We were the only family – remote cousins, it is true, but his money was to be shared between us. A few thousand dollars, not a vast fortune but enough to keep us comfortably off with a few careful investments.

'I thought of my little girls' future and

what it would mean to them and to Lily. I guessed that an archaeologist's wife would be glad of some extra cash. Hence this trip to Scotland, but the only information I could get from her last Edinburgh address was that they believed she had gone to live in Orkney.

'I tracked down the friend who had helped her run the lodging-house and learned that although they had been close friends Lily hadn't been in touch with her since she left Edinburgh eleven years ago, to spend the summer with her husband in Orkney. Neither she nor Frank had returned that autumn and it seemed odd because all Lily's possessions were uncollected.'

He paused and said grimly: 'I was beginning to be alarmed, and decided to talk it over with a detective in Edinburgh, a pal from the old days. His advice was to come to Hopescarth. Well, as soon as Frank saw me, he made up a stack of lies, that Lily had gone off with some other man years ago.'

He sighed. 'And there it was. If Lily had lived, Frank would have been a rich man too.'

He looked at me. 'I'll be straight with you, Mrs McQuinn. Frank killed Lily and got away with it, another woman's body washed up by the sea, I gather from Dr Denmore. Lucky for him that there wasn't an active police force, or much crime in this remote area.'

And confirming what Craig had told me, he added: 'There's no way to prove it. Frank has killed himself and they're both gone now. So I'm agreeable to let the matter rest there.'

I'd already decided not to mention that Frank had tried to kill me in the Troll's Cave when footsteps on the stairs and a tap on the door announced Meg.

Meg was never very good at concealing her feelings or her curiosity. She was dying to know what Mr Mainwell had wanted to discuss with me so urgently.

'There's food downstairs, if you want it,' she said to him, squinting at the papers and books he'd spread on Frank's desk. 'How's the sorting out going? Take anything you want.'

Jim shook his head. 'There isn't anything really.'

'What am I to do with all his possessions then?'

'From the contents of his wardrobe, Mrs Flitt, you won't have much trouble there.

Just a few well-worn clothes and boots. And his old books. What I was really hoping for were photographs of my sister to show to the family back home.'

As he spoke he opened a desk drawer. 'Ah, this is more like.' He took out photographs, mostly of artefacts taken before they went across to the mainland and the waiting museums.

'Nothing of Lily, I'm afraid.'

'I'll see what I have downstairs,' said Meg.

We followed her down and she took from the sideboard cupboard a box of photographs and began to search through them.

'Nothing of your sister, I'm afraid, Mr Mainwell.' And handing a group photograph to Jim, she said: 'This was taken a couple of years ago. Frank thought I might like a copy. It's the only one I have of him. Take it, if you like.'

A good photograph with the shadow of Yesnaby House in the background. A group of students. In the middle Frank scowling as usual. A young bearded man at his side.

A man I recognized…

Chapter Thirty-two

A face I recognized, knew – and loved.

My heart was pounding. I could hardly speak.

'The man with Frank – who is that?'

'Which one?'

'With a beard, standing next to him,' I pointed.

And before she said the words, I already knew the answer.

'Why, that's Dr Denmore, before he shaved off his beard.' Meg laughed. 'Mind you, I have to say it is a great improvement. He said he never liked it much but it saved shaving every day–'

I was no longer listening.

The photograph trembling in my hands was of Mrs Smith's young lover!

I set it down on the desk, murmured that I had to go, my sister was expecting me for lunch.

I left them staring after me and outside my legs began to shake.

The puzzle was complete. The photograph

had given me the answer to the second murder.

The very last answer I wanted to the question of whether or not Mrs Smith had abandoned her young lover in Edinburgh. How he had apparently disappeared from the scene and she had come back to Orkney on the steamer, travelling unobserved to Hopescarth as Thora Yesnaby.

I had the answer now, clear and positive. She had not been alone.

Craig Denmore was her escort, the anonymous young man from the hotel who had never drawn anyone's attention.

He was no stranger in Hopescarth, they knew him well. In their midst, a familiar sight every day, Dr Craig Denmore, the archaeologist.

And if I needed further proof, he had lied to me about the beard. Even if I hadn't recognized him, he had known right from the beginning who I was.

And dear God, I had confided all my suspicions about the double murder in him.

I couldn't face Emily and Gran yet. So I went into the kirkyard and sat among the tombs of the dead, trying to work out what exactly had happened when Thora arrived at Yesnaby House.

I did not doubt that she had confronted Erland alone. I hoped that she had met him without Emily's knowledge.

Meanwhile Craig would have stayed discreetly out of sight, in his lodgings. The more I considered that, another grim possibility came to mind.

That Thora had never met Erland at all. Craig had decided to get rid of her, and steal the Yesnaby locket.

Was I secretly hoping that was the solution, that it was nothing to do with Erland and Emily?

I told myself that Craig knew the archaeological world and how unscrupulous collectors of antiques were not too fussy about the origins of pieces they wanted. If that was the reason then the locket had indeed disappeared for ever. The disposal of Thora in the peat-bog would not have been difficult for a strong man like Craig.

I had another picture now. Of Craig going on that lecture tour taking the locket with a ready buyer from abroad, praying that in his absence one of the team would make the discovery of Thora's body.

But as I brought to mind again what I knew of Craig Denmore and his aristocratic background, I wasn't sure any longer that he would risk killing her for the locket alone. He wasn't desperate for money. There was that rich father Sir Miles Denmore with the whisky distillery – his inheritance. As for the locket itself, it was certainly too modern for his personal taste.

The cold-blooded murder of Thora didn't fit the pattern at all. I didn't see him as the passionate jealous lover who would kill his mistress for taking another lover. I had already marked Craig down as a man who would have his choice of women and, from what I guessed of Thora, finding a new lover had never been one of her problems.

Craig might have been disappointed but there is a long way between disappointment and murder, especially for a clever young man with good looks and a family fortune. An ill-assorted pair they seemed in memory, the older Thora and Craig, the discarded lover, who would bow out calmly, saying: Thank you and goodbye.

And now another chilling doubt struck my heart. Had he lied about Frank too? Had Frank really made that confession?

My dismal theories had a new accompaniment. It began to rain and huge drops as large as coins spattered down, turning the gravestones black.

I didn't feel like a second soaking in twenty-four hours so I hurried back along the road leading to the drive. Absorbed as I was by the complexity of my tortured reasoning, Craig's motor car was almost upon me before I heard it.

Dear God, was he trying to run me down? I leaped aside and landed in the wet hedgerow.

The motor car wheezed to an angry halt a few feet down the hill. Craig left it, shouted: 'You idiot, Rose, didn't you hear my horn blasting away?'

'You nearly killed me.'

'I didn't see you until I was at the top of the hill. You know I can't stop quickly on a steep slope.'

Close to me now, he said: 'What's wrong with you, Rose? You look dreadful. That white face doesn't become you.' And taking my arm: 'Are you ill?'

I looked up at him. 'I have just had a terrible shock.'

He nodded sadly. 'Frank? I know. It was awful.'

'Not Frank this time, Craig. This time I've just solved Thora's murder.'

His grip on my arm tightened. 'Get into the motor car.'

'No!' I struggled to free myself.

'Rose, get aboard – we're both getting soaked standing here arguing.'

'I can walk–'

'No you can't. And I want to talk to you. There are things we have to discuss – now that Frank has gone.'

Weakly I followed him. I wanted to talk to him but as he handed me into the passenger seat, it did occur to me that maybe he meant to kill me too. And I had no defence.

We couldn't talk above the engine's roar but as we reached the bridge, I said: 'Put me down here.' He ignored that, so I added: 'I'll walk up the drive.'

'I'm taking the old girl home. She doesn't like getting wet, it isn't good for her.'

As I knew, the motor car's 'home' was the old barn beside Sibella's croft, convenient for the dig.

And I thought of the cliff path, how easy to drive past the croft then push me out – down – down – and into the sea.

But Craig merely drove very neatly through the barn doors and, switching off the engine, turned to me and said: 'Well now, we always seem to be meeting in the rain.'

'And parting too,' I said.

He gave me a sharp look. I took a deep

breath and said: 'We have met before, you know. You must remember, Craig. It was Brightwell's Hotel in Edinburgh.' I managed a mocking smile. 'And yet when we talked yesterday and I confided my fears in you, you never said a word about that.'

He turned his head away. 'I don't know what you're talking about.'

'Oh, I think you do. We met very briefly at an afternoon tea in Brightwell's Hotel on Princes Street, last October. You had a beard then.' In a guilty gesture, his hand went to his chin as I continued: 'You were there with Thora Yesnaby. She was posing as Mrs Smith and you were her lover.'

He laughed harshly. 'Don't be ridiculous, Rose.' And then with a weary sigh: 'I'd never met Thora. I remember Mrs Smith though. I was staying at the hotel testing it out as a possible venue for one of our conferences. Mr Brightwell said he had a guest staying who was also going to Orkney. We were introduced and had lunch together.

'She told me she'd been living in France since she left Orkney years ago and would be grateful for a travelling companion. She didn't care for the idea of a lady travelling alone. Naturally I agreed to escort her.' He paused and looked at me:

'Whatever made you think we were lovers?' Without giving me a chance to reply to that, he went on: 'She had a French count who wanted to marry her and she was hoping for a divorce. It never occurred to me there was any connection with Erland Yesnaby, whose wife had drowned in tragic circumstances.'

I wanted to believe him. Having seen him in Mrs Smith's company, I had presumed the rest.

Craig was staring at my grim expression. 'Marry her – for heaven's sake, Rose. Your imagination let you down there. Didn't you think she was bit old for me? My father would have had a fit. Besides I have a young lady back in Inverness: right age, good family, excellent breeding prospects.'

I was just a little disappointed by that news. He shrugged. 'Necessary for dynastic purposes. We've known each other all our lives. However...' He paused and his look was both tender and searching as he put an arm around my shoulders.

'A pretty young widow would give Father a heart attack. Apart from the fact that you are a high-ranking policeman's daughter, your profession might not meet with the family's approval. And I doubt whether the bicycle would find a warm welcome in their hearts–'

'Don't try to get round me by changing the subject, please,' I said, pulling free from his embrace. 'I want to know why you killed Thora.'

'The answer is that I didn't. I never knew she was Thora in the first place. I believed like everyone else that she had been dead and buried in the Yesnaby grave years before I set foot in Hopescarth. I'm telling you, I only knew her as Mrs Smith, a woman I met in Edinburgh. I'd never seen that portrait of Thora you told me about.'

His frown said he was very exasperated. 'As I was saying, Rose, if you'd only listen. We reached Stromness, a boring voyage and she stayed in her cabin most of the time, nursing the whisky bottle, I'm afraid. We hired a carriage to Hopescarth and stopped at Meg's. When Mrs Smith said her destination was Yesnaby House, I told her she should have kept the carriage as it was a long way up the drive in the dark. She said she knew that, but wanted to surprise them.

'I felt obliged to see her as far as the bridge.' He stopped suddenly. 'That's all, Rose. I'm sorry. There's nothing more to tell.'

I stared at him in amazement. 'I don't

believe it. You killed her. You're making this up!'

'No, Rose. He isn't.'

A voice behind us – someone had been listening to our conversation.

Chapter Thirty-three

Someone moved out of the shadows by the door.

It was Sibella.

'He's telling the truth, Rose. Now, both of you, enough of this nonsense. You'll catch your death sitting out here. Come indoors where it's warm. At once!'

We followed her across the yard, meek as two naughty children, and sat down by the fire.

She smiled at Craig. 'If there are any important pieces I miss out, you'll need to remind me, because my memory's not as good as it was.'

Turning to me she said: 'Before she went up to the house, Thora told Craig she wanted to see me first. When she walked in, I thought I'd seen a ghost, a very un-welcome ghost. For me, she had been dead for the past ten years. I had grieved for the poor distressed lass who we all believed had drowned in the sea down yonder.'

She sighed. 'I saw immediately that this

Thora was different. I asked her where she had been all these years. She said she'd been living abroad. And I asked her why then had she come back.'

She looked across at Craig: 'You were going to leave at that point, but she said he was to stay, that she'd maybe need a witness for her business up at the house. I asked her what that was and she laughed and said: "To return the locket and in return get a large divorce settlement. My lover is a penniless French count, we can only marry if I can provide him with a dowry. In return I won't make it public that his marriage is bigamous and any children are illegitimate."'

Sibella sighed. 'She turned to me and said: "I presume that he married his precious Emily and that there are children?" And I could have bitten my tongue for I spoke too soon, I told her that Emily was going to have a baby after all these years. If I had hoped for her compassion I soon found out how wrong I was. She screamed with mirth, clapped her hands. "That's even better for my purposes," and I knew then that she had no pity or goodness in her heart and that she meant to destroy them both.'

She stopped, shook her head and said slowly: 'And I couldn't let her harm a hair of my precious Emily's head.' Turning to Craig, she said: 'You remember how agitated she was? She behaved like someone demented.'

Craig nodded in agreement and Sibella said: 'She was already drunk but she kept shouting that she needed a drink. I hadn't any whisky and that infuriated her. She dived among my jars scattering them. "You're lying, you're lying. Everyone here has whisky."'

Sibella sat back in her chair, her face stricken, and Craig said: 'We tried to calm her down, so she demanded some of Sibella's herbs, the ones she used to get in the old days–'

Sibella took over again. 'She said there was a special one. I knew which she meant. She held a jar up, screamed: "This is the one!" It was a drug and not to be taken lightly. "Just a few drops then," I said but she tried to snatch it from me. And at that moment I knew exactly what I had to do.'

Sibella stopped, shivered. 'It was like a revelation, like a voice whispering in my ear. A plan. And I thought, whatever happens this night, Erland and Emily need never know. They will be safe. For them Thora had been dead for years. So unless their lives were to be ruined for ever and my Emily lose her precious baby, then Thora – must – remain – dead.

'So I took the bottle and gave her enough for a fatal dose.' She stopped regarding me with those strange round luminous eyes.

'I killed her, Rose. Poisoned her. The only thing I didn't know was how long it would take to work on top of all the whisky she'd had before she came. And would it work quickly enough to stop her going up to the house. I watched her gulp it down. But amazingly, she said: "I feel wonderful now, ready to make my way up the drive and shatter the happy family."

'She swayed a bit and Craig took her arm.'

Sibella stopped and looked at him. 'He didn't know what I had done, poor lad.'

'I was still shocked at finding my travelling companion was the resurrected Thora Yesnaby,' said Craig. 'I hadn't any idea what Sibella had given her, but she screamed that she wanted more of that precious tonic. Sibella held it away from her, and she grabbed a knife off the table and said; "Give me that!" She lunged at us wildly with the knife, I grabbed her and she dragged Sibella on to the floor.'

He paused and I visualized the dreadful scene as Sibella continued: 'The drug had

357

given her tremendous strength and we could hardly hold her. The next thing I knew, I had her head and was banging it on the floor.'

'She lay still,' said Craig. 'Everything was so quiet and we both knew she was dead. Between us we had killed her,' he added quietly.

'No, lad. My drug and my striking her head like that. We didn't know what to do. We had a dead body on our hands. We looked at each other and panicked "The sea?" I asked him.'

'Not again, I said. We can't hope for another roarst and a second burial. I had a better idea. The peat-bog,' said Craig. 'It was just a short distance to carry her. You know the rest.'

He paused and they looked at each other, silently, reliving the horror of those last hours.

'I went off next day and it was our secret,' said Craig.

'Always has been, lad. No one ever knew of Thora's second arrival at Yesnaby.'

Or of Erland and Emily's lucky escape, I thought as I asked: 'What happened to the locket?'

In answer Sibella unlocked a drawer, took

it out. 'That's where it's been for the past year.' And for the second time I held it in my hand.

'I think it's time it was resurrected from the peat-bog, Craig,' she said. 'And returned to Erland. He'll be delighted.'

There isn't much more to tell. I went back to the house and slept soundly. I still had more than a week to enjoy my holiday with Emily with nothing more nerve-wracking to anticipate than those promised bicycling lessons with Wilma.

Jim Mainwell returned to Edinburgh. I didn't expect to see much of Craig and we wouldn't go to Frank's funeral. Ladies stay at home and make the sandwiches, is the general rule.

Early that week, however, one of Craig's students made a surprising discovery.

A piece of jewellery shining in the thick green moss of the peat-bog, identified as the Yesnaby locket. Craig had been good to his word and the young man received a handsome reward from a very grateful and surprised Erland.

That was the most exciting thing to happen. But I still had one more discovery to make. On a warm sunny afternoon I went down the steps into Erland's garden and wandered past the Ghost orchid to the ivy-covered embrasure with the stone carving of the mermaid.

For me, this was where it all began. The long-awaited holiday with my sister which had changed into nightmare and murder. Not one murder, but two.

The stone seat, so tranquil in sunshine, aroused terrifying memories of those hallucinations when I was knocked unconscious by Frank in the Troll's Cave. They do say your former life flashes before your eyes at the point of drowning, but mine was even more extraordinary, for I had been transported to another era.

The funeral procession of the Maid of Norway.

It would always remain vividly in my mind, despite all that happened afterwards. And now as I looked around I knew for certain that it was Hopescarth I had seen before Earl Patrick had built his palace. The landscape and the sea were unaltered, this fragment of an ancient wall once part of the hermit's cell where the mourners had halted with their little queen.

To dig a grave.

Looking closer I saw that this had not been

intended as a seat. And although the search for the Maid's dowry would continue, I had solved another mystery.

I looked up at the house and Erland was standing at his study window watching me. He waved, I waved back. And stayed where I was, certain he would come into the garden.

And he did. He made preliminary remarks about being glad I was enjoying the sunshine on his little sheltered seat.

I shook my head, said quietly, 'It isn't a seat, Erland, it's a stone coffin.'

'Now what makes you think that, Rose?' he asked cautiously so I told him about the dream.

'This is where they laid her to rest. This is her grave.'

Erland had listened silently. Now he smiled. 'My grandfather found her grave when he was working on the garden. Here deep in the earth and he told no one. The information was to be a family secret, passed from father to son. If we have a boy, then I'll tell him, and he must swear to keep it secret in his turn.'

'Does Emily know?'

'No one, only the eldest son. Otherwise we will have folk clamouring to dig up the poor lass's bones to put in a museum.'

He shook his head. 'There was something strange though. Her grave clothes had rotted but, after all those hundreds of years, her golden hair was long and beautiful, as it had been in life.

'Grandfather Scarth replaced her reverently, exactly as he had found her. He took only one thing to keep and preserve in the family for ever.' His smile was a question.

'The Yesnaby locket? That can't be, Erland. It's mid-Victorian.'

He smiled. 'I know that. Grandfather had it specially made. But it has a secret. Inside is the one memento of the Maid, a lock of her hair.'

When he looked at me, there were tears in his eyes. 'Will you keep our secret, Rose McQuinn? You who have, I suspect, to keep so many people's secrets in your life.'

'Yes, Erland, I'll keep it.'

He took my hands, kissed them, his eyes closed for a moment, then we walked back towards the house.

Conscious of being watched, I looked up at the window.

There was someone there.

I was having one of my hallucinations again, I thought. Don't be daft, Rose, it couldn't be – if wishes were horses – beggars would ride.

In the kitchen, Emily and Gran had a faintly conspiratorial air. The door opened and–

'*Jack!*'

I rushed forward, threw myself into his arms. We hugged and kissed regardless of the rather embarrassed audience who quietly withdrew...

As he released me, I drew a deep breath.

'Jack Macmerry, what on earth are you doing here?'

He looked at me solemnly. 'I know you don't believe in coincidences, but this one was very strange. I've been working on a fraud case. The man was last reported in Stromness and looking through the old newspapers the headline "Hopescarth peat-bog burial!" caught my eye. I was sure you'd be interested.

'Later that day, I went to Solomon's Tower to see everything was all right and Thane was sitting at the back door.'

He seemed reluctant to continue and I panicked.

'He was all right, wasn't he?'

At that Jack smiled wryly. 'I don't know how to put this, to describe it, but I got the impression that he was – well, imploring me to do something. He started running round me in circles.

'Well, I thought he was just missing you, hungry – but when I offered him some scraps, he looked at them disdainfully.'

Jack stopped, bewildered. 'There was more than that, Rose. If that dog could speak, the words he would have used were that – you – were in danger.'

Pausing to let that sink in, he added: 'It has happened to me before. Remember when that madman tried to kill you and when you were in deadly danger in a fire. I hate to admit to things I can't begin to understand, Rose, but Thane has a link with you somehow–'

'Can you tell me when this happened?' I interrupted.

'Oh yes. 30th August. About four in the afternoon.'

And that was when I had been in the Troll's Cave, unconscious, with my dream about the Maid of Norway and Thane urging me to wake up – that I'd drown.

Jack was saying: 'Anyway, I decided I'd come to Stromness with the lads, my excuse to apprehend our fraudster. So here I am.'

'Thane – how is he?' I had a sudden

longing for my deerhound as Jack said gently:

'Whatever forces move Thane, he'll know that I'm with you and that you are all right.' And he took my hands. 'I've got a few days' holiday, don't need to rush back. I'd love to see Orkney.'

'First, I have someone else you have to meet,' I said.

'Another member of the family?'

'Yes, my great-grandmother. She's a seal woman and she's 101. Her name is Sibella.'

As we walked to the door, he said: 'Seal women, they are sort of witches, aren't they?'

'Something of the sort.'

He groaned good-humouredly. 'I don't think I'm strong enough for two witches in the family.'

'You'll like this one. She's fond of animals.'

Jack kissed me and said: 'You are looking well, Rose. Obviously a good restful holiday away from crime has done you a power of good.'

And we walked down the road to meet Sibella.

The publishers hope that this book has given you enjoyable reading. Large Print Books are especially designed to be as easy to see and hold as possible. If you wish a complete list of our books please ask at your local library or write directly to:

Magna Large Print Books
Magna House, Long Preston,
Skipton, North Yorkshire.
BD23 4ND

This Large Print Book, for people
who cannot read normal print,
is published under the auspices of

THE ULVERSCROFT FOUNDATION